A NOVEL BY

SEAN MICHAEL DEVER

SO OTHERS MAY LIVE

SO OTHERS MAY LIVE
Copyright 1994, 1998,1999
Sean Michael Dever

ISBN 0-9658180-2-0

Published by, and copies may be obtained from:
Fox Books, Inc
An imprint of Duchess Publications
PO Box 150053
Cape Coral, Florida 33915-0053
1.888.274.5371

Distributed through Ingram Books and Baker & Taylor Books

See order form at the back of this book for additional copies. SO OTHERS MAY LIVE may be obtained by retail outlets at special rates.

This book is a work of fiction. The characters, names, incidents, dialogue, and plot are the products of the author's imagination or are used fictitiously. Any resemblance to actual persons or events is purely coincidental.

123456789
First Edition June 1999
Cover Art and Design by April Pederson & S.M. Dever

Fox Books Inc

For **Gunnery Sergeant Jones, USMC**, NACCS Instructor,
a hard and fair man who taught me, during my weeks at Pensacola, that with a lot of determination I could accomplish anything.

And for all those who risk their life every day, sometimes bending the rules if they need to, so that others may live.

Acknowledgments

Thanks to the following people for their help and support:
Dr. Erica Kobylinski, **Paul J. Nedley**, Master Chief, Royal Navy, Ret.;**William Dever; Ammie Frantz; Misty Wright**; **Angela Ammirati**; **Steve Lawrenz**; **Larry Mallek** and **Bridget Gillaspie; Laura Ann Martin**;

Special thanks to **April Pederson**, a fellow author, and my best friend and someone who has made me both a better writer and better person;

My family, who's support of my writing has never wavered;

And to **Tom Reilly**; my mentor and my friend. Thank you for the advice, wisdom, and encouragement over the last few years. I owe you big time for helping my writing career; (but really all I want to do is direct)!

ACCM Tom Pruett, US Navy, Ret., for the help I needed on a hot June evening when my memory failed me; and to **Steve Samanan**, for the countless hours he gave helping me realize a script (that would become this book) when we both were working on the film Just Cause in the summer of 1994. Go Seminoles!

A NOVEL BY

SEAN MICHAEL DEVER

SO OTHERS MAY LIVE

Prologue

***

The loud crack from a log splitting under the heat of the bonfire boomed through the humid night air. Rick Cox instinctively turned toward the sound, but all that was visible through the mangroves was the red glow reflecting on their branches. This deep in the Everglades of South Florida, a person could only see a few yards in any direction. That was why Rick and the other Naples High School seniors had their parties out here. No one could hear the noise from the forty or so teenagers, and even if they did no one could find them.

Rick had wandered away an hour earlier, and sat on an old fallen pine tree. He stared up into the clear night sky. He could see a million stars out here, or so it seemed. The lights of civilization did not invade the blackness of the Everglade's horizon any more than the bonfire did the mangroves. He was alone with his fears. He was alone with his dreams. Sometimes the two were the same. Rick did not need to be by himself. His older brother was back at the party, as was Karen, Rick's girlfriend.

His brother was the favorite son of their high school and of Naples. A record-setting quarterback and runner, Tim was now winning the hearts of Florida State University and Tallahassee as well. He had just finished his sophomore year at FSU, and in the fall would no doubt be their starting quarterback. The pro scouts were already watching. This was in part due to the Sports Illustrated story that ran after their mother had died last year.

Their father had left when the two were just babies, and their mother had raised them the best she could. No one outside their home knew about her cancer; she would never have stood for it. It was this pride that drove the siblings on the football field. And it was her memory that motivated them now that she was gone. The two brothers now had only each other. They both had hoped that their father would initiate contact after the magazine interview came out, but it was not to be.

Rick waited his turn to go to FSU and be on the gridiron with his brother. He still lived in their old house in Naples, but it was for sale. Another month and he would graduate from high school and move up with his brother. This was their going away party. The two were so talented that their friends knew neither one would return. They would make the pros. It was a sure thing. The Cox boys were too competitive not to. Always the first at practice and last to leave, neither one could stand to be anything but first. It was a blessing that Tim played offense and Rick defense, so that they would not be on the field competing against each other. But even this did not always work. In the weight room, as on the practice field, the two would always try to outlast everyone else, including each other. Rick had gone so far as to tear tendons in his shoulder once while trying to outdo his brother. Pain meant nothing, winning meant everything.

Rick gazed up in the sky and thought of his mom, and of being a Seminole and playing in front of thousands of people. Of his future. Of the past. Of why he was so talented on the playing field. Of what did he do to deserve having his parents leave him and his brother alone.

Closer to the party, Tim had also wondered away. He was sitting in the middle of a dirt access road and removing his pants to add to the pile of clothes beside him.

"C'mon in. The water's fine," his girlfriend giggled. He told her to hold on and removed the last of his clothes before running down the embankment into the water. He felt his foot sink into the soft, slimy, black mud. "How can you stand this?" he said. She laughed. He stepped carefully, waiting for snakes or sticks or anything else his feet may discover in the darkness. His girlfriend was barely visible as she stood in the neck high water.

"There might be gators," Tim said feeling a very real concern. Another giggle told him he was the only one who cared about the danger. Tim was in slightly deeper now and crouched down in the waist deep water. He did not like this, but a bet's a bet.

The Jeep came flying through the underbrush and out onto the road. Its seventeen-year-old driver and his female passenger were not drunk, just enjoying her first time four-wheeling. He occasionally turned the lights off to get a reaction from her, which were usually screams of terror and delight. She grabbed the spotlight that sat between the seats and turned it on. She stood up and held on to the roll-bar with one hand, while shining the spotlight through the mangroves with the other. The driver turned off the headlights again and she turned the light to shine down the road.

"Come on slow poke," she said.

"I'm getting there," Tim replied, not liking this one bit. "Keep your pants on."

"I'm not wearing any!"

The light was only showing the ground right at the jeep's front bumper. The driver grabbed it from the girl and was showing her where to place the beam so that he could see. He was still looking at her when she suddenly started screaming. He spun his head around to see what was in front of them, but it was too late. He quickly turned the wheel to avoid hitting what looked like a body in the road, but the jeep was too unstable to make such a sharp turn. Losing control, it was all he could do to steer away from the other cars and toward the water. In a split second the jeep was airborne and spinning, throwing both driver and passenger out of the vehicle and into the shallow swimming hole.

Rick heard the screams pierce the night air. Figuring the party was out of control or a fight had broken out, he decided it was time to get Karen and head back to the house. He headed back through the thick brush to the bonfire. When he came to the clearing, he saw no one around. Hearing voices down the road, he followed the sound down the dirt road that led back to Naples. It wasn't long before he saw everyone standing along the side of the road. There were some cars parked with their lights on, pointing off the road into a pond.

Rick walked up and through the crowd. He came out on the other side and slipped down a steep embankment, splashing down onto the plant and slime covered water. Above him, headlights pierced the darkness over his head and onto the surface of the tea colored water. Rick tried to see what everyone was looking at when he felt two sets of hands grab his arms. He felt himself being pulled back up the embankment by two of Tim's friends.

"It was an accident," a bystander said.

"What was?" Rick asked. That was when he noticed the lights. At first it seemed to be a reflection, but as he looked close, it became clear. Under the murky water, a single headlight shined. And then he saw where one of the tires of the flipped over jeep broke the surface.

"Holy shit!" he said, starting to laugh in disbelief at the half submerged vehicle. "What dumb ass did that!"

"It was an accident," the kid repeated to him.

"No shit," Rick said. "No one drives their car in like that on purpose. Is he okay?"

"The people in the jeep are, but not the other guy...," someone said.

"What other guy?" Rick asked. He saw Karen approach and walked over to her before getting an answer. She was crying and wet. "Are you okay," Rick said wiping mud from her face. "What happened? Did you see this?"

She nodded, and the tears streamed down her cheeks. "It's Tim!"

"Where is he?" Rick asked, and looked into the crowd. "Let's get him and Heather and get out of here before cops come."It was then that he saw Heather on the ground surrounded by a group of their friends. Rick was confused. He went over to her; she looked up at him, crying hysterically. She jumped up and hugged Rick so tight he couldn't breathe.

"I'm sorry! I'm sorry!" she cried. "I should never had made him do it!"

"Where's Tim?"

No one answered, they just stood there shaking their heads and looking over the water. As he looked around in the crowd, he realized why Karen had come running.

"Trapped in the mud," Heather told him through her tears. "Under the car."

"Oh God!" Rick screamed as he felt his strength leave his body. He turned to run toward his brother, but Heather would not let go.

"It's been too long! He's been under too long!" He pulled away toward the water again, breaking free of his brother's girlfriend, only to be grabbed by the others. Some of them were wet and mud soaked. "We tried to pull him out!"

The EMS helicopter arrived a few minutes later, as did the Collier County Sheriff. Within an hour other emergency crews were on the scene, along with a crane, two tow-trucks and local television news crews. The cameras recorded the arrival of worried parents and grief stricken friends, and the end of both Rick and Tim's dreams.

*

It was six weeks later, a few days before graduation, and still the guilt and questions had not left Rick's mind. Karen could not handle him, and the two split shortly after his brother's funeral. Everyone had come, including the press. Sports Illustrated did a second story on his brother, but Rick would not be interviewed, and had not bothered to read it when it came out on news stands.

Rick was alone again, sitting in front of the television on a Monday night. The clock on the wall read eleven o'clock. It was dark outside. Quiet except for the crickets and frogs. He grabbed the remote control and flipped on . He had rarely ever watched the news before, but he couldn't stand the pain of watching Monday Night Football or any of the other sports shows. He had turned down all the football scholarships; they just reminded him of his brother.

On the screen Rick watched the various news stories of other people's tragedies unfold. They were important, they were horrible, they were there for one minute and forty five seconds and then gone. Rick thought back to the night of the party and wondered if there had been someone else in a dark room at midnight, just as he was, who watched the news of his brother's death, but forgot it just as quickly because they too had lost someone. He watched as a news crew interviewed the mother who had just lost her two small children in a fire. She escaped the flames, they had not. Then the story of the six car pileup due to fog somewhere on a Georgia or Texas interstate. Cars had continued ramming each other for almost thirty minutes before help arrived, no one even realizing that the cars ahead were blocking the road. Then he saw a story that would change his life.

It had happened in Sunrise, Florida, a suburb of Miami. A car had gone off the road earlier that day. Not only had it slid off the interstate in the rain, but had flipped over and into a drainage pond alongside the road. The news reporter was interviewing the mother who had been driving the car. She had not been injured, but her child had been in the back seat when the car went over. Yet, the tears that ran down her cheeks were not from pain or guilt. They were tears of joy.

The person standing beside her, with whom she would not let go, was not her husband, or a policeman, or fireman. He was barely a man at all, just an eighteen-year-old kid like Rick. His shaved head was not stylish for someone that young, nor was the confidence in his voice fitting his age. This was not some punk who was skipping school; he was a rescue swimmer in the United States Navy.

As the interviewer asked question after question, Rick became more intrigued. The sailor was a helicopter rescue swimmer, he had told the reporter. This was exactly what he had been trained for; in fact, he had just finished training a few weeks ago. It was just luck that he had been driving north back to his base in Jacksonville when he witnessed the accident. But the woman did not say it was luck.

"He was there for a reason," she said and gave the guy a kiss right there on national television. And at that moment, Rick knew there was a reason he was watching too.

1

***

Good Friday

Through the open door of the helicopter, Petty Officer First Class Rick Cox stared down at the churning emerald sea as it rushed past a few hundred feet below. The wind howled, and the salty spray lashed against his bare cheeks, stinging his skin; but he sat oblivious to it all, as his mind raced back to that night so many years before. Though he had rescued hundreds of people since, he still felt the guilt and helplessness of standing on that sandy bank while his brother drowned.

Behind Rick, inside the helo's cabin, Adam Giles ripped open the velcroed black bags they had thrown inside just moments before takeoff. He poured the contents onto the steel deck, and swiftly began the well choreographed routine of separating the gear. Just as he finished, and right on cue, Rick pulled his feet inside and turned to Giles. Without a sound he double checked the gear, then began to dress. First his wetsuit, then survival vest and rescue harness. The hood came next, then gloves, fins, mask, and snorkel.

Giles checked Rick's gear, then checked it again tugging at the harness making sure it was tight. When he was satisfied he tapped his friend's shoulder and gave him a thumbs up, which was returned. They had repeated this so often it had become second nature, but Search and Rescue was a deadly serious business, and both men knew better than to become complacent.

Rick scooted back over to the door, as Giles keyed the microphone attached to his flight helmet. It was Good Friday, and Rick had volunteered to take duty for the Easter weekend so that another instructor could spend time with his family.

"Flight, swimmer is ready."

"Swimmer ready," the pilot repeated back. "Be aware I don't

want the swimmer in the water until I call for it."

"Your call, flight. Standing by."

"Four minutes till intercept," the co-pilot called over the headset.

Fifteen miles away, and three thousand feet above the helicopter, the two crippled aircraft flew in loose formation toward the white sands of the beach and safety. Their gloss white and red paint was now covered with scrapes, the aluminum panels torn and sliced, leaving jagged metal teeth around a gaping hole in the forward fuselage of Eagle One. Eagle Two had fared a little better, losing only two feet of the left wing when the two Navy jets had collided.

Though severely damaged, both planes were still airworthy. The main problem now was not mechanical, but human. Eagle Two's plexiglass canopy was gone. Shattered by a bird strike. Eagle Two had observed that the student pilot in the front seat was unconscious or dead. His head had been rolling from side to side, and he had not responded since the collision with the bird. The condition of the instructor behind him was not much better. He had been showered with glass and debris during the impact, and the surprise had caused him to momentarily loose control of the trainer during the close formation practice. A chain reaction combined with Murphy's law. It was by sheer luck that he had survived the birdstrike, and an act of God that both aircraft were still flying after the subsequent collision. Eagle Two reported that they had heard some sounds over the radio, but had not seen any movement. Yet someone had to be flying the plane.

It was Rick who spotted the smoke trails low over the horizon. He slapped the back of Giles leg to get his attention.

"I see 'em," Giles said. He notified the pilot, who adjusted his course so that they would be flying parallel to the crippled aircraft who would soon catch up with the helicopter; for even a damaged jet flew faster than the SH-3 could on a good day.

"Fifteen miles to feet dry," the pilot called over the radio. "Eagle flight, we have a visual. We are at your two o'clock low. SAR SH-3."

"Roger SAR. This is Eagle Two, we can't see you, copy. That's a negative on the visual."

"Copy Eagle Two. How about you Eagle One? Can you see

us?"

There was silence, then what sounded like a couple grunts.

"Say again, was that you Eagle One?" The radio was silent. "Eagle Two, this is SAR. We are now at your two o'clock low."

"Still a negative on the visual, SAR. Please don't lose us." There was desperation in the Eagle Two's voice. If only he would hold control for just a few more minutes. They were so close. They could almost glide to the beach.

"Keep it up, Eagle Two. You're almost home. You too, Eagle One." Only a few more seconds and they'd be feet dry over the beach.

"Giles, this is flight," the pilot said. "Tell the swimmer he can relax."

"Roger, flight." Giles tapped Rick on the shoulder then gave him the cut off sign. Rick nodded and scooted back from the door.

"Oh shit!"

"What's going on, flight?" Giles called over the radio. But before the pilot could answer, both Rick and Giles saw the problem with their own eyes. Out the door they watched as Eagle One pulled straight up, then banked onto its side and headed down towards the water.

"Eject! Eject!" The crews of both Eagle Two and the helo screamed in unison over the radio. They saw a pair of flame bursts as both of Eagle One's ejection seats burst out of the cockpit. Within seconds, the chutes had automatically deployed and seats had separated. The SAR helo banked and followed the chutes down toward the sea. The aircraft had hit almost a mile away from where the chutes came down. Unbelievably, the crew landed only a few hundred feet apart in the Gulf.

"Did you see movement?" Giles screamed over the noise of the engine. Rick shook his head--no.

"That sea state's too rough," the pilot said. "Wait till we see movement before the swimmer goes in. Get the basket ready."

"Getting the basket," Giles said. He pulled a five foot metal mesh basket out from the back of the helo as the pilot maneuvered near the first parachute in the water. The waves were ten to twelve feet high, and Rick could feel the rotor wash on his skin. He leaned out the door and watched as the water pounded the parachute. He caught a glimpse of a flight helmet, but it disappeared below the surface of the water.

"Swimmer in the water!" Giles called as he watched Rick step out of the helicopter as soon as they were low and slow enough.

"Dammit, Giles!"The pilot called. "I told you to wait for me to call it!"

"He went out on his own," Giles told him.

Rick had pushed out and fell ten feet into the waves. He popped up to the surface and fought hard to get to the downed pilot, swallowing salt water with every breath. He made it over to the first chute, cutting and spreading the shroud lines until he reached the pilot. It was the instructor. Rick released the parachute harness, and tore off the helmet but the lifeless eyes that met his told him he was too late. He looked up at the helo, and gave Giles the thumbs down. The dry crewman pointed off to Rick's left . The rescue swimmer let go of the instructor and started toward the second chute. The sea was getting rougher and he could not see over the swells, but he continued to kick and pull his way through the water until he saw the green sea dye surround him. He knew he was close when he felt the shroud lines surround and tangle his legs.

Rick felt nauseated by the water he had swallowed as he cut through the lines. But even as the bile crawled up the inside of his throat, he continued on. The helicopter stayed off to the right, but the rotor wash caused a heavy mist to swirl above the surface, cutting Rick's sight to a few feet. The bright green sea dye marker that had automatically released from the student pilot's survival vest had almost completely dissipated when Rick found him. The floatation bladders in the man's SV2 survival vest had malfunctioned. Following the shroud lines, Rick finally found the student's body floating a few feet under the surface of the water, entangled in his own parachute. Rick cut the body loose and towed out to where the helicopter was hovering. He signaled Giles who replaced the basket with what was unaffectionately called "the meat hook." The hook slowly lowered into the water. After rigging the student pilot to the hook, Rick retrieved the instructor's body and repeated the process.

Finally it was Rick's turn. He had been in the water close to an hour when he finally was pulled inside the door by Giles. Once inside, Giles started to help Rick take off his gear, but Rick pushed him aside.

"I'll do it."

Giles backed off. He had seen his friend like this before and knew it was better to just give Rick his space. Giles went over and covered the bodies with some blankets while Rick stowed his gear. When he was done, Giles handed the swimmer a flight helmet and the two went and sat down.

"Eagle Two just made a safe touchdown," the pilot said. "I

thought you guys might like to know."

"We'll be sure to inform their two friends back here," Cox replied. Giles just shook his head, but said nothing.

*

"Feeling better?"

"I don't feel anything," Rick replied.

"Here. Drink this," Giles said and handed his friend some coffee. They were sitting in the gedunk, the small snack bar located in a shack along the flight line. They were still on duty, still standing by in case another plane is heading down, or a ship sinks, or any one of a thousand other possible emergencies that would require a helicopter and swimmer.

They had not spoken of the two dead men they had pulled out of the Gulf of Mexico six hours previously. Nor would they probably ever bring it up. The only rescues that swimmers ever talk about were successful ones. Rescues made reputations in this business. There were no heroics in pulling a dead body from the sea.

Two hours later, their relief showed up. The crew consisted of two other Rescue Swimmer School instructors and two officers: a pilot and co-pilot. Rick and Giles gave them the rundown on sea states, weather, and other important information. They had just signed the logbook, officially turning over the watch, and walked outside to the parking lot when Lt. Jackson, Rescue Swimmer School's Officer-in-Charge, drove up.

"Giles, Cox, Come over here. I want to talk with you." The OIC said. The two men put down their gear and walked over to the Lieutenant's car.

"Yes, sir?"

"I thought you might like to know. The base hospital just called. They said that instructor pilot was dead before he hit the water, probably killed during the ejection. Who knows?"

"What about the student?"

"They said his injuries were so bad, he would not have lived even if he made it back."

"When did they think he bought it?" Cox asked.

"It doesn't matter. Anyway, his squadron C.O. wants to put you in for a decoration. He feels you deserve it, and so do I. Those seas were rough and you didn't have to recover the bodies."

"Sir, when do they think the student bought it?"

"It doesn't matter," Jackson said. "He's dead, but at least his family will be able to say goodbye."

"Sir, was he dead before he hit the water?"

"No, but there was nothing you could have done for him."

"So I screwed up!"

"It's not your fault," Jackson told him. "Knock it off. His survival vest malfunctioned. How the hell would you know?"

"It was a command ejection, I should have known," Cox said. "Shit! The student was in control."

"Unless you followed the chutes into the water, there is no way you would know that- now knock it off!"

"I did follow the chutes down."

"Look, I don't give a shit!" Jackson said. "This ain't personal. Don't beat yourself up. You did the best you could, better than most men would do. Dammit, you shouldn't even have gone in the water, Cox."

"I thought..."

"I'm not bustin' your ass for that," Jackson said. "Although I should. But if you had followed orders, those medics wouldn't have any bodies to find that shit out!"

"I ain't taken the medal," Cox said, "I don't want it."

"You will accept that decoration, Sailor," Jackson said. "And you will do it with a smile on your face because that man's family is going to be there. You will not disgrace his memory! And I don't want to hear any more about it, do I make myself clear?"

"Yes, sir." Giles said.

"Cox!?"

"Yeah...Sir," Cox said. "I'll accept it because his family is there, but I will never wear it, sir!"

"That's your choice. Goodnight, Gentlemen." Jackson said, then drove off. Rick picked up his bag and quick-stepped toward the parking lot. He threw the black canvas bag into the rusted-out bed of his twelve-year-old pick-up truck as Giles pulled around in his car.

"You want to go get a beer or something?"

"No," Rick answered.

"You sure?" Giles said smiling. "You did good, Buddy. I wouldn't have gone in with those waves. You'd have had to jump in and rescue me if I had."

Rick nodded and climbed into his truck as Giles threw his own gear into the trunk of his car. Soon all that was left of them were two sets of taillights disappearing into the twilight.

2

***

The ceremony had gone just as Lt. Jackson had said. Almost. Reluctantly, Rick was awarded a Navy Commendation Medal for his actions. But he had not hidden his displeasure when Commander Harding, Rick's Commanding Officer, had pinned the medal to his uniform. He had made the shortest speech that anyone could remember, saying only that he was doing his job, and for that he did not deserve any recognition.

After the formalities were concluded, Rick was introduced to the instructor pilot's wife and children, and to the student's parents. Again he uncomfortably accepted their thanks, and was relieved when Harding came over and stole him away.

Rick's Commanding Officer put his hand on his shoulders as they walked away from the others. "Lt. Jackson tells me you had thought of applying to the Warrant Officer Program."

"Yes, sir, I had spoken with Mr. Jackson about it," Rick replied. "I had asked him to keep it between him and I, sir."

"I went through OCS," Harding said. "Why don't you come see me next week, and we'll talk about it."

"I haven't decided if I want to be an officer yet, sir," Rick said.

"Well, come anyway. We'll talk about it."

"Yes, sir," Rick replied as they walked over to the refreshment table, where they both grabbed something to drink. They stood there in an uncomfortable silence. The fatherly talk by Harding had caught the ten-year enlisted man by surprise.

"I understand you were a hell of a football player, Cox," Harding said putting down his drink. This really caught Rick by surprise. He had never mentioned football to anyone in his entire naval career.

"Yes, sir. Was."

"Miss it?"

"No," Rick said swallowing what was left in his glass. "I don't play or watch it."

"Oh?" Harding said. He paused a moment before adding, "I played."

Rick could have cared less.

"Florida State University," Harding added, gaining the instructor's interest. "Of course that was before your brother was there."

"How do you know about my brother," Rick said. "If you don't mind me asking, sir."

"I keep in touch through the alumni and boosters," Harding said. "I remember reading about you, too. But you never brought it up so I didn't either."

"Sir," Rick said. "I ask that you never bring it up again, if you don't mind." He placed his glass down as Giles and Jackson waved him over. "If you'll excuse me, Skipper. I need to talk to Lt. Jackson."

"Certainly," Harding said. "But I am very sorry about your brother. I wanted you to know that."

Rick ignored the apology and quickly walked over to Jackson and Giles who were standing among the other attendees of the ceremony.

"So what did the big man have to say?" Giles asked.

"He asked me about officer programs," he replied. "Now where would he get the idea that I was even thinking about that, Lieutenant?" Rick looked at his division officer accusingly. It was obvious that Rick had thought Jackson had broken some kind of trust.

"I thought it would be a good time to try and push it through," Jackson said, defending himself. "I was only trying to help."

"Sir, the next time I tell you something in confidence, please let me know if you can't keep it to yourself." Jackson thought of reprimanding Rick for his obvious insubordination, but he also realized that the instructor had asked him to keep it between themselves. The officer was wrong, and deserved the criticism.

"I can't wait to have you back in school," Jackson said as they headed towards the door. "I miss your diplomatic way of speaking."

"I bet," Giles said.

"But first thing's first," Jackson said. "Your class only has a few weeks left, then you would be rotated to duty status anyway-so you won't be training anyone for at least a month and a half. Use it to take some leave."

"I don't see any point in taking leave, sir."

"It's convalescence leave," Jackson replied. "Don't worry, Cox, you can abuse us all when you get back."

"I'm serious, Lieutenant," Rick said. "I just don't want to lose the edge."

"The edge?"Jackson said.

"Training, sir," Rick said. "Right now I'm in a zone when I'm with the class. I'm working at the highest level I can! I'm right on the edge. If I stop training, then I lose it."

Jackson looked long and hard at him. Cox rarely asked for anything, and the instructor's eyes were pleading, his voice strained. He was on the edge all right. That was exactly the reason he wanted Rick to stand down and take a break.

"I know how you feel, Cox." Jackson said. "But it's not a request. It comes straight from the skipper and I agree with him."

"Sir, you just pinned a medal on me for going above and beyond the call of duty," Rick said. "I could not have done what I did unless I had that edge! It was what allowed me to recover those men!"

"It almost allowed you to die in the open sea! Or did you forget that?" Jackson waited for his words to sink in, then continued. "There is a fine line between bravery and stupidity. You got lucky."

"But..."

"You've got until sixteen hundred hours to get off this base," Jackson said. "I don't want to see you for thirty days." With that, the Lieutenant turned and walked away.

Rick looked down at the medal on his chest,"The hell with this!" With his right hand he ripped it from his uniform and threw it across the hanger floor towards some officers from the dead men's squadron. When they looked up, Rick asked them what they were looking at. Luckily, Giles grabbed him and pulled him away before they realized what had happened..

"Shit, Rick," Giles said as he lead him outside, "Calm down! What are you trying to do, get sent to the brig?"

"The hell with their medals, the hell with everyone--no one understands what we're doing!" Cox said. "Christ-- a medal-- for letting some kid die! Time off for fucking up? Where the hell are the priorities of these people?"

"Chill out, Rick. Just go to Panama City," Giles said, trying to get Rick's emotions under control. "It's a nice place to relax. Make 'em happy. It's not like you have a choice, Buddy. " Rick took some deep breaths, and tried to clear his anger. Giles was right.

"I guess I have no choice."

Giles put his arm around his friend's shoulders. "C'mon, I'll call and make the reservations."

"Panama City--that's about a four hour drive."

"Yeah," Giles said. "It will take away the temptation to come back early."

*

It was dark by the time Rick pulled into the circular drive of the Beaches Hotel and Golf Resort. The nine-story white stucco hotel was lit up like a beacon. Bright white lights splashed on the walls, while hidden colored lamps washed out the Spanish moss and palm fronds overhanging the entrance. The valets were spotless, yet showed no displeasure when they climbed into Rick's old pick-up. They would not let him carry his own bags to the room, even when he insisted. They checked him in and headed toward the bungalow that Giles had reserved. It was not in the main building, but in a small compound on the side of the hotel.

He followed the young man from the concierge desk along the pathway that led to his suite. Over the tree frogs croaking and warm humid air, Rick could hear music playing. It was soft and rhythmic, yet with a Cuban-Miami beat. Beyond that, the surf could be heard lapping at the sugar sand just beyond the pathway. It reminded him of Naples, of home, if there was such a thing anymore.

Rick resigned himself to this penance. He was glad Giles had the foresight to rent the bungalow. He needed the solitude. They were more expensive; more than he should have been able to afford.

But Rick was a blue water sailor, and had been most of his life. He was a loner, not by choice but by circumstance, and he accepted it.

There had once been a woman in his life, one that he had trusted and loved. But she had ended it quietly, slipping away one night after two years of what he thought was a prelude to marriage. She left a letter, but it said simply she was not happy, and he was not the man she wanted to spend her life with. No arguments, no other explanation. Like everyone else in his life, not even a goodbye.

So he had lived a solitary life since. Not celibate, but he knew he would never let anyone get close to his heart again. It had hurt and haunted him. So he sank himself into his work and saved his money. At sea, there is little reason to spend a dime if you don't have anyone waiting, and he had a small fortune put away for a rainy day. Or better yet, a sunny day, he thought. It seemed to rain his whole life. But now it seemed as if that day was coming. Not as bright a day as he hoped, for he had given up the thought of being happy with someone else. But he had enough to buy a sailboat he could live on, and maybe a dog to keep him company. He was halfway to retirement and not even thirty yet. At twenty years he would take his savings and go sail the world.

Maybe this vacation was a blessing after all. Or maybe he was slowly losing it as his expectations grew higher and higher of himself and those around him.

His bags were already in the room when he opened the door to the bungalow. He had a headache from driving and the events of the day, so he took a quick shower, popped some Advil, and went to bed.

He awoke the next day to a knock on the door. "Room service," the woman said through the door. "Would you like fresh linen for the bed, sir."

"No, thank you," he replied then looked for his watch. It said 11:30 a.m. He shook off the remainder of sleep and quickly jumped into the shower. He never slept this late. After showering he put on his shirt and black leather flight boots and went for a run down the beach. He knew the currents here, and ran along with them for close to three miles. He stopped, then walked into the water until it was waist deep. He started to swim back towards the hotel, fighting the current all the way. It was his punishment for oversleeping.

When he was finally in front of the hotel's beach, his muscles burning with each stroke, he gave in to the temptation and body surfed in, allowing the water to propel him the last fifteen yards to the white sugar sand. He stood up uneasily and looked at his watch. One-fifteen in the afternoon. His time was better the last visit. He went inside to shower his salt encrusted body, and thought about what his class was doing at that moment.

3

***

Thursday, June 11

The waves gently lapped at the seawall and the sun was high over Pensacola Bay as the Navy helicopter hovered above the water. Only one hundred yards from the old seaplane ramps that led to the warm water, the spray from the helo's rotor washed down on the converted hanger that now housed a gymnasium and recreation center.

Men dressed in black wetsuits and fins jumped out of the open side of the helo into the water, then waited as a small boat came by to pick them up. The scene was repeated over and over as the Rescue Swimmer School students practiced the helicopter operations phase of the course. Near the seawall stood a smaller, non-descriptive, well maintained, brick building. Above the double white doors that lead into the building, a large blue sign with gold block letters read:

UNITED STATES NAVY RESCUE SWIMMER SCHOOL
SO OTHERS MAY LIVE
*
Bldg. 656

It had been four weeks since Rick had been in Panama City, and the heat and humidity of the summer had taken hold of the Florida Panhandle. The instructor was back. For his new class, there was absolutely no doubt about it. Petty Officer Cox was back.

Inside building 656, Airman Johnny Lorner stood sweating and at attention, facing the cinder-block walls below the row of large picture windows that surrounded the pool. By tilting his head slightly, he could see the reflection of his twenty classmates. He could also see Petty Officer Watson, one of the instructors, standing by *The Tower*. *The Tower* was a tall steel structure, about thirteen feet high, that the students use as a platform to drop into the water. It was at about the same height as a helicopter would be above the water. But the ladder to the top was not being used today. Today was differant, and every student knew it.

The class of young men, most new to the Navy, now stood around the Olympic-sized pool. Evenly spaced, each man stood at attention, and except for the singing, none dared make a sound, nor look into the pool.

They all knew what was coming. Officially it was listed on the schedule as Final Multi practice; but to students it was known as Sharks and Daisies. It started with them singing the National Anthem. The idea of the singing, they were told, was to relax the men; but it had just the opposite effect. As Lorner looked up into the reflection of the window in front of him, he could see by the faces of the others that he was not the only one who was afraid.

The idea was relatively simple: to place a student rescue swimmer in a situation he would face in an actual rescue with more than one victim. The student was grabbed at random from behind and pulled into the pool to simulate the disorientation of jumping from a helicopter. Once he hit the water, the clock would start and he would have thirty minutes to "rescue" the three instructors in the pool by hooking them up to a helo winch.

If the student did not complete the task in the allowable time, then he would be dropped back to the next class and go through it again or be dropped from the program and sent to the fleet, all his training and sacrifice for naught. It was basically one shot that could erase twelve weeks of aircrew school and four weeks of Search and Rescue (SAR) training. The requirements had not changed since the schools inception in the early 1980's.

The problem had been the competitiveness of the instructors. Like the Special Forces, or Navy SEALs, it takes a unique personality to finish a school based on physical and mental toughness. Self doubt or giving anything but one hundred percent was the difference between life and death, and the stronger one's will, the better a person became in his field.

This had a snowball effect over the years at Rescue Swimmer School or RSS. The instructors coming from the fleet were progressively tougher, which in turn produced stronger students. But at some point, the ratio had crested and now it seemed, at least to the students, that their goal was not to learn as much as survive. These thoughts were clearly in

Lorner's mind as he waited for his trial by fire.

He and the others could hear the instructors swimming around the pool, they felt their heart skip a beat as the water was splashed on their legs as the "sharks" decided on a victim. As they started singing the second stanza, they heard a muffled scream, then a large splash as a classmate was selected. But no one dared turn around. They knew what was happening. The instructors would be holding the "daisy" under water, ripping off his mask and fins, holding his arms hoping to cause panic and fear to set in. Of course, the instruction manual stated that they were helping him react in a trained and efficient manor in the rescue of three hysterical shipwreck or plane crash victims.

But this was eerie. There was no screaming, just water splashing. Occasionally Lorner could hear someone hit the surface and gasp for air, but he would not turn to see-that was the easiest ticket to becoming the next target. He was trying not to think about his classmate being held under by three instructors. They would take turns going up for air while two of the instructors held the student under. Lorner started to shake from fear, and his eyes welled up, the tears started streaking down. He did not want to do this, but he couldn't Drop On Request, better known as D-O-R. He had made it this far, overcoming his greatest fear, that of failure.

"I wonder who it is?" Lorner heard the question, but ignored it. "Who'd they get?"

"Shut up, Lee!" Lorner ordered under his breath. Damn him, he thought. Robert Lee was his friend and roommate, but he had a knack of getting himself in trouble and this was not the time.

"I hope it was Willy."

"Be quiet!" Lorner said. Just then they heard a loud splash and a scream. It was just bad timing that Lee had turned around to look as all four of the men in the water broke the surface. Lee was staring like a deer caught in headlights as the head instructor turned and looked right at him. He held the stare just long enough for Lee to know he was caught, then the instructor placed his attention back to the daisy in the water.

"He saw me!" Lee said after quickly turning around.

"Who?"

"Cox! I'm dead!"

"Are you sure?"

"Yeah. Shit, I shouldn't have looked!"

"I told you," Lorner said. "Who was in the water?"

"Daley."

"Be thankful for that."

"And he had Giles and Watson under each arm."

Better him than me, Lorner thought. *They probably took him first to break everyone's spirit.* Daley was six-foot-four, two hundred and fifty pounds of pure muscle. He had been a wrestler and star football player in high school, making the USA Today first team as a linebacker. He had standing offers from all the top colleges. But he had gone to a high school that cared more about sports than academics and when he couldn't muster the SAT scores to satisfy the NCAA he set his sights on the Navy's SEAL program. But Daley was not known for his patience, and when told he would need to wait six months to apply, he asked for RSS and aircrew. He'd been a handful for the instructors at every turn of the course.

Only eight minutes had elapsed when Daley's voice boomed out, "That's one!" He was making a game of it, thought Lorner, and making sure that everyone knew it. He could see the reflection of Petty Officer Watson standing at the side of the pool, he was holding his head.

Back in the water Daley was having a harder time with Giles and Rick. By a twist of fate and Navy paperwork, the two instructors had served together for over six years. They knew each other's reactions. They also had a healthy respect for natural talent like Daley, something that Watson did not have.

Rick was holding Daley under from behind as Giles went to the surface for a breath. Daley struggled, but the two men were almost the same size and for the moment, Rick had the advantage. But Giles was only five foot four and no match for Daley, so the student waited. He could feel Rick trying to get to the surface, and Daley looked for something to hold him under. He struggled to get deeper until they were rolling along the bottom. It had only been seconds, but it seemed like hours to the two men. They struggled on the bottom until Daley found what he wanted--the drain. He gripped hold of the mesh opening and hung on. He knew that Rick was exerting more force, burning more oxygen, so he waited.

It was not long before Rick let go and shot to the surface. At the moment he was released, Daley spun around and looked toward the light from above. He saw Giles coming back towards him. Placing his feet on the bottom of the pool, Daley pushed as hard as he could, propelling himself past Giles and up to Rick. Catching him by surprise, he placed him in a choke hold and before he knew it, the instructor was hooked up to the winch.

"That's two!" Daley screamed then dove back under. He had two instructors in less than ten minutes, a record pace. As soon as he was under, Giles lunged at him. But the instructor missed and the student took the advantage and soon had Giles hooked onto the hoist.

"Are you coming?" Giles asked sarcastically to his student.

"I think I'll go for a swim," Daley replied and started doing the backstroke.

"Get out of the pool!" Rick yelled. "This isn't a damn joke!"

"Calm down, Rick," Giles said. "Give the kid a victory lap, he just beat the record."

Daley had "saved" all three instructors in just over eleven minutes. The fastest time recorded for the exercise was thirteen minutes, and that was by Rick Cox over ten years earlier.

"In here, that's *Petty Officer Cox*, Petty Officer Giles! This isn't the Olympics, this is training." Rick addressed the room. "Do you all understand that- This is not a fucking game! Daley, get out of the water and give me thirty stock market sit-ups! Watson- you count!"

Daley quickly exited the pool, and laid on the tile. "Up a third," Watson instructed, "Down an eighth..." As they continued, Giles and Cox slid back into the water. The room was quiet.

"Where's the singing?!" Rick's voice boomed. The class instantly started the National Anthem again. Lorner heard the swishing of the instructors come from behind and his heart began to race. They stopped right behind him, and he could hear the water drip onto the tile. He waited anxiously and took a breath, holding it so he would have some oxygen when he was pulled in.

Then he heard Rick whisper, "Thought I'd forgotten you?" Suddenly Lee disappeared from his side.

Lorner heard the scream of his friend end with a splash. He continued to sing, while wondering if his friend had been able to take a breath before being pulled under. Lorner hoped the instructors were tired from Daley. There was not as much splashing, there didn't seem to be much movement at all in the pool. Lorner glanced up at his reflection in the window and began to believe he might just make it. He silently thanked Daley.

In the pool, a pair of hands rose up out of the water, followed by the rest of Lee. As he gagged on the water he swallowed, he attempted to swim to the side of the pool. Frantically grabbing into the air, his frightened eyes searched around the pool looking for help, but no one was watching. His fingertips were inches from the wall when Rick suddenly appeared from the water in front of him. Seizing his shoulders he began pushing the young airman out to the center of the pool.

"I D-O-R! I D-O-R!" he screamed out, but Rick was already below the surface and pulling him down. Giles rose up out of the water and pulled off Lee's mask. The two disappeared, leaving only bubbles of air rising to the surface. The scream of D-O-R had raised the curiosity of the students, but any movement had been quickly quelled by Watson.

At first Watson had threatened them by asking if they wanted to be next, but now he seemed as concerned as those under him. The bubbles had stopped, yet there was movement under the water. It was only when Giles broke the surface gasping and signaling to Watson for help that they all realized something was wrong. Within seconds, Rick was also gasping as he towed Lee's body to the side. Watson dove in and over to Rick and began mouth to mouth resuscitation.

"Call an ambulance," Giles said spitting water. But no one moved, they just stood there, in shock, watching what was happening. "Dammit, someone call an ambulance! Daley!"

Daley looked over at Giles, then to Lee, then back to Giles. He took off running into an adjoining office. He picked up the phone and dialed 9-1-1 and waited for someone to answer. It wasn't long before he realized he was on base. 911 did not work on base! He cursed himself as he searched for the emergency phone list, finally spotting an old, yellowed paper taped to the desk that had base security's number on it.

"I'm a student at the SAR school, we need an ambulance," he told the dispatcher. She told him to stay on the line until help arrived.

*

The white navy ambulance was parked in front of the school, surrounded by Lorner, Daley, and the rest of class 733. The double white doors to the building were held open as the stretcher holding Lee's body was hurriedly brought out and placed in the vehicle. Rick and Giles climbed inside as the driver hit the siren and pulled away. Nearby, out on the obstacle course class 732 stopped training to watch the commotion, much to the dismay of their instructor.

"Class 733, fall in!" Watson called out. He waited for the men to get into the two abreast formation. "Petty Officer Daley, front and center."

Daley came out to the front of the formation and stood at attention face to face with Watson. "Petty Officer Daley, reporting as ordered."

"Daley, march the class back to the BEQ," Watson said quietly. "No one is to leave the base, or even the barracks. Any problems, call the duty officer. Training is finished for today obviously, but I'm sure that somebody is going to want to talk to everyone."

"Some of the guys want to go see...."

"No, I'm heading there now. I'll call when you can see him."

"What if...I mean he didn't look good," Daley said. The instructor turned and faced the class.

The concern was evident on every man there.

"I'm sure that Airman Lee is going to be fine, but we can't have twenty people over there getting in the way. Lorner, you're his roommate aren't you?"

"Yes, sir."

"Fine, you come with me," he said to the young airman. Then Watson turned to face the class. "Listen up! I'll send Airman Lorner back with any news, and a schedule for visits. Daley is taking you all back to the barracks. C'mon, Lorner." Watson headed towards the parking lot as Daley marched the class back to their rooms.

*

The ambulance ride was just a few minutes, and both RSS instructors assisted the paramedics as best they could. They had been able to eject some water from Lee's lungs with CPR but now it was all up to the young sailor's will to live. They could not get his heart started again, regardless of what was tried.

They arrived at the hospital and both Rick and Giles were pushed out of the way by the rush of nurses and hospital staff. In less than an hour, the young sailor had gone from a healthy young man to something that resembled a lab experiment. There were tubes in his throat and in his arms. He was stripped of his wet clothes and placed on a gurney for the run into the emergency room. Rick tried to follow them into the ER, but was blocked by a corpsman.

"Let us handle it from here," he told the two rescue swimmers. Both men tried to look through the windows in the door, but realized it was futile. After watching the exhausted paramedics come out from the emergency room and head outside, Rick and Giles went to the waiting area and sat down. Both men were still dripping in their wetsuits.

Watson and Lorner walked in a few minutes later, and handed them some shorts and shirts to change into.

"How's he doing?" Watson asked.

"I don't know," Giles replied. "No word yet."

They nodded to each other, but said nothing else about it. They would just have to wait.

"I'm gonna use the head and dry off," Giles said. "I'll be right back. Anyone need anything?" The others shook their heads, no. "Kid, you want a coke or something?"

"No. Thanks," Lorner replied. After Giles disappeared down the hall, Rick looked at Watson who was leaning back in his chair, eyes closed.

"Jim, why don't you go back to the school and start writing this up," Rick said.

"You sure?"

"Yeah. I know you've been on duty all night, and we all don't need to be here," Rick looked at Lorner. "And take him with you."

"I'd like to stay," Lorner replied.

"There's nothing you can do here."

"Respectfully, he was my roommate and friend. Besides, the class is depending on me to tell them how he's doing."

Rick didn't feel like arguing. "Fine, stay. I don't care. Just stay out of the way." Watson stood up, patted Lorner on the shoulder, then walked down toward the door.

*

Laura Wilson adjusted her pillow as she lay curled up on the couch in front of the television. She had already checked her E-mail and returned the few messages that had been sent. She had also finished running, showered, and had studied for the Bar Exam which she would be taking soon. She had graduated from Mercer University a scant six months earlier, and was realizing just how little law school had prepared her for the exam.

She had a bowl of ice cream in front of her, chocolate, smothered with chocolate sauce, and she slowly stirred the two together while she settled down with the John Grisham novel her father had sent her. She could have been out on a date, but between work and studying, she did not have the time to start a relationship. Besides, she had convinced herself that she would need to put off men until her career took off, or at least until she passed the Bar and became a full-fledged lawyer.

Her empty social life wasn't for lack of interest, she was disappointing a great many men who did ask her out. She was one of those women who looked beautiful with or without make-up. Her long brown hair, hazel eyes, and firm 115 pound, athletic body did attract a lot of attention in college and even more at work, but most potential suitors had been law students or in the legal profession, and though they seemed to impress themselves quite a bit, it did not do much for her. Instead she preferred the gym or home, alone with a good book or movie. And Grisham was her all time favorite. So she wasn't very happy when her pager went off, just as she started chapter two.

*

Rick, Giles, and Lorner had been sitting for over two hours before a nurse had come and brought them into another room. She asked that they wait, the doctor would be there momentarily. They sat down in a leather, overstuffed couch. The room was bare, except for the couch and various medical instruments hanging in the locked glass-door cabinets on the wall. There was the sterile stench found in most hospitals. It made Lorner long for the chlorine smell of the RSS building.

"Attention on deck," Lorner yelled as the door opened. Commander Anthony Craft, USN, MC, walked in.

"At ease," he said as he sat down opposite the sailors.

"Which of you is Petty Officer Cox?"

"I am, sir." The doctor looked down at the floor, then back at Rick. He hesitated for a moment before speaking.

"Cox, this is never easy," Craft said, his voice breaking up. "We haven't even contacted his family yet..."

"What?" Rick asked. Craft looked over in Giles direction. Rick took the cue. "Giles, take Lorner back to the barracks."

"I'm not..." Lorner was cut short by and turned away from Rick's icy stare. Nothing more was said until Giles closed the door as he stepped out.

"Airman Lee was pronounced dead about fifteen minutes ago,"Craft said. "There was little we could do."

"Shit," Cox said and fell back into the couch. "It's not supposed to happen this way! We were training!"

"There was nothing you could have done. We tried to resuscitate him for over close to 90 minutes."

"But the kid was so young?"

"Age had nothing to do with it, Petty Officer Cox. No one could have saved him. There was just too much damage."

"Dammit!" Rick said. "I should have been able to do something!"

Craft stood up and placed his hand on Rick's shoulders. "I know how you feel, but sometimes the body can't take anymore. I don't want you to feel responsible, you couldn't have known. It's not your fault."

"Look, Doc-- Don't tell me how to feel! I was the person who held him under! I.." Rick was cut short when there was a knock at the door. Craft opened it. Standing at the door was a nurse. Short and plump, she was at least forty years old with freshly dyed red hair. Lt. Spring was written across her name tag.

"Yes?"

"I'm sorry, Commander. That student's command is on the phone asking about him."

"Fine, tell them I'll be right there.'

"Yes, Sir." She closed the door.

"Petty Officer Cox, listen to me!"

"Yes, sir."

"Cox, Lee didn't drown. His heart gave out"

"Sir, I felt him go limp, I saw the water and blood leave his mouth during CPR," Rick said. "He is dead. He died in my arms."

"You're right," the doctor said. "He is dead. Maybe this isn't the best time for you to be thinking about this stuff."He took out a small pad and wrote a prescription on it, then handed it to Rick, who handed it right back. "I don't want it. It will take me off flight status."

"I'm grounding you anyway, Petty Officer Cox."

"Why?"

"Because I don't believe you are in any shape to be flying right now. You are stressed out, and this event hasn't even hit you yet," Craft said. "I just want you to relax a few days, make sure that this doesn't cause any emotional problems for you."

"I'm fine, Doc." Rick said. "I can handle this. It isn't the first time."

"What you are going through is not a part of everyday life."

"Well, it seems to be happening a lot lately."

"I know all you guys in that school think that events like this don't take a toll on you, but they do," Craft said. "Look, it's just a few days, maybe a week. Then I want you to come see me and we'll talk about what happened."

"If I come back," Rick asked, "once you see that I am fine, will you give me an up chit?"

"I'll give you a medical clearence on the spot," the doctor replied. "And Petty Officer Cox, do me a favor?"

"What?"

"Remember, this was a training accident," Craft said. "This wasn't your fault."

"But sir..."

"No buts, Cox. Now I need to go speak with your Commanding Officer," The doctor said as he opened the door. "Take care, and if you need to talk to someone, call me. I'll arrange for you and your class to get some counseling."

*

"What's up?" Laura asked.

"We had a kid die in training over at that Rescue Swimmer School," her boss told her. "I think it's time you put your hands in the fire, Laura."

A real case. Hot damn, it was about time! "What do you want me to do?"

"Just meet me in the morning," Litton said. "We're going to interview the instructors and some students who were there."

"Who was the student?"

"I don't know yet, a messenger is bringing me some reports now," Agent Jack Litton said. "Welcome to the real world. Now get some sleep."

Litton hung up, and Laura felt the butterflies in her stomach start to churn. It was about time. The last few months she had started to regret not accepting the appointment offered to her by the FBI. In fact, the offer was still good and she was going to look into a transfer if she hadn't been assigned a real case soon. She had done nothing but investigate minor traffic incidents and two sailors caught with a joint.

She had wondered to herself lately why she chose the NIS. She knew how overqualified she was, that unlike the FBI, most of the people she worked with weren't law school grads. Yet, she remembered her dad's stories of his time spent in the service, traveling around the world, dealing with various governments when sailors were in trouble. The NIS recruiter had convinced her she would be working on important cases: counter-espionage, homicides, blackmail. Meaty stuff. But reality had crept in after six months and the closest she got to a foreign government was watching a dumpster to help the Secret Service when Air Force One parked overnight at the base on its way to Africa. But she knew deep inside that she didn't go to law school for this. But she also wasn't sure she wanted to go to a courtroom everyday, either. She had been a tomboy most of her life, and enjoyed being out in the world. The investigation side of the NIS appealed to her.

And here was a real case. She felt some guilt at being happy about getting the assignment since a young sailor had died. But, she was actually working for the victim. That's what the Naval Investigative Service did: investigations of criminal acts that concerned the U.S. Navy. She forgot all about Grisham and immediately started to plan what questions she would ask. Then she would call her parents. Her father would be so proud of her. The downside was she would be working with Litton.

She didn't like him. No one actually liked him. But he had been doing this longer than anyone else and she had to respect that. There was just something about him that was wrong. But who cared anyway--at least she would be on a case!

*

The sun had not even come up when Lt. Jackson arrived at Harding's office. The young OIC of Rescue Swimmer School was standing at attention in front of his Commanding Officer's oversized government issue wooden desk. The junior officer had been called into the C.O.'s office fifteen minutes earlier, just as the Commander's phone rang.

This time it was the aide to Admiral Tract. Tract commanded all the Navy's aviation schools of which Rescue Swimmer School was a small, but as of late, highly visible part. The Admiral's aid, Lieutenant Commander Hunt, was informing Cdr. Harding of the Admiral's strong desire to find out what happened, and find out "pretty damn fast!"

"Tell the Admiral that I understand the concern," Harding said loud enough for Jackson to hear. "But I can't do a goddamn thing if every person with gold on their shoulders keeps calling me!"

"I'm sure the Admiral is sorry that we are taking up your precious time, Commander. But I think he has a right to know what the hell is going on in his command. Don't you?"

Harding did not like taking abuse from an officer that was subordinate in rank. But regardless of what he thought of Hunt, the little weasel had Tract's ear. The Commander looked up at Jackson and shook his head in disgust as Hunt continued to recite for the hundredth time the obvious: that this investigation should be completed before the press caught wind of it.

"Look, Hunt," Harding interrupted. " I have Lt. Jackson here in front of me. I would like to speak to him before he retires. I will call you as soon as I know anything!" He slammed the phone down before Hunt could respond. He then sat there a few minutes and silently gathered his thoughts before looking up at the man standing before him.

"Jesus H. Christ, Jackson. What the hell did your overzealous sea apes get me into this time?"

"I'm not sure yet, sir." Jackson said. It was the worst possible answer for an officer to give a superior, and the Lieutenant knew it.

"Mr. Jackson, I've got every officer on the goddamn base calling me wanting to know why a man drowned in Rescue Swimmer School, do you realize that?"

"Yes, sir..."

"Shut up! Who the hell asked you to talk, Lieutenant?" Harding stretched out the last words. "You do want to stay a lieutenant in this man's Navy, don't you."

Jackson said nothing, but stood rigidly at attention.

"I asked you a question, Mister!"

"Yes, sir!" Jackson said. Harding stood and walked around from his desk, and scratched his head. He walked behind Jackson and stood facing a mural of two Man-O-Wars firing at each other, in some forgotten battle a hundred years ago.

"Mr. Jackson, you do realize that the entire reason for being of that little school of yours is to train men in rescue techniques. Water rescue techniques. Is that correct?"

"Yes, sir."

"You also realize, I'm sure, that every naval aviator in the fleet depends on the men trained under your command to save them from danger if ever their aircraft should go down. Isn't that correct?"

"Yes, sir," Jackson said.

"How many men, instructors and students, were in the immediate area when the event occurred."

"I'm not sure, sir."

"Guess."

"Twenty or so students, three instructors, sir."

"And how deep was the water?" Harding said turning around behind the lieutenant.

"Twelve feet, sir," Jackson answered. "The pool is twelve feet deep."

"I see," Harding replied, walking back into Lt. Jackson's view. The senior officer walked slowly up to his subordinate, stopping only when he was sure his breath could be felt on the young officer's cheek. "So what do you think the fleet thinks of the men in RSS now?" Harding asked, "After hearing that your men can't even save one of there own. In a swimming pool. With twenty men trained in rescue techniques standing around?" Harding paused and walked around to his desk and sat. "Take your time, Lieutenant. I know this one is hard."

Jackson stood quietly for a moment, before looking down at his C.O. "Sir, do you want me to answer the question?"

"What do you think?" Harding replied as he placed his feet up on his desk and crossed his arms on his chest.

"Sir, I understand what you are saying."

"You do," Harding said surprised. "Good, glad to hear it. But I want to make sure we are both on the same page." Harding stood and leaned across the desk until he was nose to nose with Jackson. "You understand that I, not you, not the Admiral, but I now have to call a family and tell them that their son, who they entrusted to me, is dead but I don't know why or how. You understand that because of your men's overactive adrenaline glands, and your school's macho pseudo-bullshit that my career is probably over. Mine and yours and any other sad-assed dick that had anything what so ever to do with this boy's death. That was what you meant when you understood what I was getting at."

Jackson stood quietly, waiting. He felt beads of sweat forming on his forehead and upper lip. Harding relaxed and sat back down. "Sir, I...what am I... What do you want me to do, sir?"

"Simple, Lieutenant. I want you to find out what and how something like this could happen." Harding said, "Do I need to paint you a fucking portrait?"

"I was trying to do that, sir." Jackson said. "You said yourself it's hard to get started if everyone keeps asking me to explain what happened. I'm waiting..."

"Waiting for what, Mister? Waiting for my career to end? Waiting until your court-martial comes through? What?"

"Sir, I wanted to.."

Harding jumped up and back in his face. "You know, I really don't care what you want. All that matters is what I want." Harding said slamming the desk with his palms. "This is what I want. I want you to bring me the names of the instructors that were there. I want you to bring me the names of the students that were there. And I want you to bring me the ass of whoever was responsible for this kid's death. Do I make myself clear!?"

"Yes, sir." Jackson answered.

"Also," Harding continued, "I am issuing a direct order that this is not to be discussed. Period. By anyone. Understood?!"

"But sir," Jackson asked, "How can I stop them from talking among themselves. It's impossible."

"Wrong answer, Lieutenant," Harding said. "When I say understood, you say, 'Aye, aye, sir.' Understood?!"

"Aye, aye, Sir."

"Wonderful. You're learning," Harding said. "Oh, and if you are wondering if the powers-that-be think this is serious, I've already been asked if RSS is really necessary. I just thought you might like to know that. Dismissed, Lieutenant."

Jackson performed an about-face and walked out of the office. He decided that he was going to find out exactly what happened regardless of how many careers it destroyed. He was not going to watch his reputation or that of the RSS go down without a fight.

4

***

Friday, June 12

"The Senator is not in right now, can I help you?"

The aide had his ear to the phone and wrote down the information. He hung up and sprinted down the hall to the Senator's office. He did not knock, and almost crushed a campaign volunteer as the heavy oak door crashed into the wall as it flew open. The aide stormed into the Senator's office, and grabbed the phone from the Senator from North Carolina's ear and quickly hung it up.

"What the hell are you doing!"

"Senator," the aide replied. "I already have someone making arrangements."

*

"Agent Wilson, come in."

"It's Laura," she said and walked into the office. Special Agent Jack Litton scurried around from his desk to greet her.

"Have a seat," he said and brushed by her when he went over to close the door. She sat down in the overstuffed leather chair that faced his desk. He came up behind her and placed both hands on her shoulders, bent down and whispered in her ear. "Welcome to the big time."

She shifted her body quickly; he let go and walked around in front of the desk so that his short, plump little frame was only a few inches from her.

"I asked for you specifically," Litton said. "I wanted you to learn the ropes."

She pushed herself as far back into the chair as she could. He just stood there looking at her, and she felt his eyes go up and down her body. She didn't like it, but at least she had heard the warnings from the other female investigators in the office. She tried not to react, but she was sure the disgust showed on her face because Litton soon lost interest and moved around to sit behind his desk.

"You have a lot to learn," Litton said. "You've been here almost six months and I think its time."

"Thank you, I'm looking forward to working with you," she replied. But Laura was already having second thoughts. He was a pig, but he was also her boss. Litton had been the senior NIS agent here for as long as anyone could remember. She couldn't afford to piss him off, but she had already decided how much she was willing to take. He pushed over a file containing the military police report.

"This is some preliminary work from yesterday." She took the file as Litton continued "I'm sorry, but I will need you to work all weekend. Welcome to the big leagues."

"That's okay, I was only going to go home to my parents," she said. "I can cancel. Not a problem."

"I want you to find out who was there in that class, who else might have witnessed the event, everyone who was involved," he said. "This seems like a typical training accident. But who knows?"

"No problem."

"I'll handle meeting with the brass myself," Litton said. "Tomorrow, we'll meet here at ten. No sense waking at the crack of dawn, the kid's already dead. Is that okay?"

"Ten? Sure," she said. "Mind if I work on this at home?'

"No, just use copies of any documents and leave the originals here," Litton said. "I'm sure that I don't need to remind you that anything classified stays on base."

"Of course," she said. "Do you think there will be?"

"I doubt it, but who the hell knows what they do at that school over there," Litton said. "Oh, if anyone gives you a hard time, just give me their name. Also, if the media contacts you, refer them to me."

"Okay,"she said and stood. He scrambled around and opened the door for her. He slapped her on the ass as she passed by. "Go get them."

*

Lorner and Daley were sitting on the couch in the small common area of their barracks watching MTV and packing. The black canvas gear bags were still new enough for the stenciled names to be read. The two were checking the gear they would need for the class exercise that evening.

The barracks common area was small, but comfortable. It had brown industrial grade carpeting, a television set with VCR, a wall unit, two small desks and a kitchen table with four wooden chairs. The furniture was vinyl covered motel quality, designed more for durability than comfort. The room was surrounded on three sides by bedroom suites. Each suite contained two to three beds and a bathroom, or head. In this case, two of the suites were assigned to two students each, while Daley as class leader, had his own. The suites also had footlockers and small desks as well as more personal items such as photographs and posters displayed. But it was in the common area that the seven men assigned to the trio of rooms spent the majority of their time.

The common rooms also had a refrigerator, microwave and small sink. A large picture window along one wall faced out into the courtyard, and through it Daley saw two of the other inhabitants walk by. On a normal day, Daley may have hidden behind the door and playfully attacked his two classmates as they came in the door. But not today. Nick and Rolo walked in and headed straight back to their suite. They soon emerged with their fins, masks, snorkel, and wetsuits. There was little of the playful chit-chat that normally took place between them.

"Shit!" Rolo said holding up a fin. The strap had a tear in it, rendering it useless since it could not be tightened on his foot. "Where is Lee's stuff, Lorner."

"Why?"

"I need to use one of his fins. This is busted and if I lose it in the bay, I'll never find it."

"Yeah, well you'll have to use your own stuff."

"Daley, tell Lorner to let me use Lee's fin," Rolo said. Daley reached over and took the swim fin from Rolo and examined it. The strap was torn, and there was no way to replace it this late in the day.

"Lorner, Cmon," Daley said. "Let him use it."

"No." Lorner said without looking up. Rolo huffed, stood up and walked into Lorner's room. Rolo went over to the footlocker at the base of their dead classmate's bed. He was quickly followed by Lorner. "What the hell are you doing, Rolo!?" he said and pushed him out of the way, placing himself between the footlocker and his classmate.

"I'm getting the fin, myself," Rolo said. "Lee's not going to use it anymore."

Rolo reached down to open the locker when Lorner pushed him back. Though Rolo was much larger, he had been caught by surprise and fell back against the wall.

"Listen, little man," Rolo said when he got back to his feet. "I realize you two were friends, hell we all were. But I need that tonight."

"No!" Lorner said, holding his ground. Daley was in the room now, as was Nick. Daley knew that Lorner and Lee had become best friends, and that Lee's death was going to hit their young classmate harder than the others. Lee and Lorner were both only eighteen years old, both came from prominent households, and had each lost a parent who they had been close to.

Now Lorner had also lost his best friend. Daley was the oldest of the group, and was a Petty Officer Third Class, the highest ranking. He felt a responsibility toward Lorner and the rest of them. He looked out for them, and they knew it and respected it.

"I don't know why they didn't cancel class tonight," Daley said. "But they didn't and Rolo needs a new fin. We all know that if Lee was here, he would lend it to him, just as Rolo would lend his to Lee."

Lorner looked over at Rolo, who was standing quietly holding out the broken swim gear. Without a word, Lorner took it from his hand, crouched down and unlocked his roommate's footlocker. He switched fins, handing the good one to Daley and silently walked back out to the couch. The others followed.

"Thanks, Lorn," Rolo said. His classmate just nodded. The four continued packing the gear, then changed into their wetsuits as the time came closer for them to leave. There came a knock on the door and Nick opened it. It was Willy Simms, and he was standing there with a beer in one hand and his car keys in the other. His four classmates just stared as he stammered into the room, and plopped himself down in the chair.

"What the hell are you doing, Willy?" Daley asked, dumbfounded that even he would be stupid enough to be drinking on duty, let alone before night ops.

Willy took a moment to focus his eyes to where the question came from. "Fellas," he said with a smile as his head rolled back and forth, "Hey D. Want to go down to Seville Quarter? It's nickel beer night!" He turned to Nick and started to laugh for no apparent reason.

Nick waved his hand in front of his face.

"Dude," Nick said leaning away. "I could get drunk off your breath!"

Willy ignored him. "C'mon. Plenty of babes there," he said then chugged what was left in the brown bottle. "Hell, Lorn, even you could get laid there."

Lorner looked over at him with disgust. Willy sneered at him, then threw the empty bottle toward Lorner, who ducked as the glass shattered against the wall.

"Faggot," Willy said.

"Will, we got ops in, like, fifteen minutes," Nick said. "What the fuck are you thinking?'

"Not me!" Willy said as he tried to stand up. He finally was upright and he pulled a white piece of paper from his pocket. "I got this." He tried to unfold it, but after three unsuccessful attempts he just threw it at Daley. The class leader opened it up as Willy went over and searched the refrigerator for more beer. Daley read it and handed it over to Nick.

"How the hell did you get a light duty chit?" Daley asked.

"Easy," Willy replied. "I told the flight surgeon, Commander whatever-the-fuck-his-name-is that I had watched my friend die today, and that it really upset me and shit. So he gave me this."

"You didn't even like Lee," Lorner said. "You weren't his friend! You weren't anything!"

Willy turned around. "I'm sorry, faggot. Did you say something?"

Daley gave the paper back to Willy. "That ain't right, Will. What if we all did that?"

"Then I guess we all could go to nickel beer night together, D." he replied. "Fuck it, and fuck you guys. Have a good swim, I'm going to go find me a waitress that will feel pity for a poor ole boy like me who lost his best friend." Willy headed towards the door, when Daley grabbed his arm. It took a few moments for Willy to figure out what was holding him back.

"I don't think that's a good idea, Will." Daley said.

"Why not?"

"Because," Nick said, "Master Chief Russo said that if anyone talks about it, the C.O. will take us to Captain's Mast."

"Fuck him!"

"You say that now, but when they restrict you to base and take three months pay, you'll be crying a different tune." Willy gave them a drunken smile and slowly raised his hand up to Nick's face, extending his middle finger when it was in front of him. "This is what I say to the old man. He can't take my money."

"Yeah, Willy," Daley said. "He can. He can put you on bread and water if he wants to."

"Yeah right. They don't do that shit, anymore." Willy said, trying to stand up straight, but slowly failing. "They just bust you, and I'm an E-1 so I'm as low as I can go already."

"They can throw you out of school," Lorner said.

"Hey, fuck you, faggot. You're just mad 'cause Lee is fish food." Willy said. Lorner jumped up and stood directly across the room.

"You want a piece of me, faggot!?"

Lorner did not even answer. Before anyone could respond, he had sprinted across the room, lowered his shoulder and caught Willy square in the chest. His anger providing the momentum, Lorner had hit Willy hard enough that it knocked the drunken sailor out cold. His three roommates stood in astonishment at what their small young friend had done. Daley checked Willy's pulse, and pupils to make sure he was not injured. Then he and Nick laid him on the couch.

"Problem solved," said Rolo.

"Yeah," agreed Nick. "Nice work, Lorn. Remind me never to piss you off."

Lorner smiled. Strangely, he felt a little better knowing that Lee would have approved.

"Maybe we should flip him over on his stomach, in case he gets sick and pukes," Rolo said, "He could choke."

"And maybe we should put him on the floor, in case he wets himself," Nick joked. They all laughed, but then looked at each other and realized it wasn't that bad an idea.

"What about the carpet?"

After placing Willy face down on Daley's bathroom floor, the four headed over to the RSS building to meet up with the rest of the class.

*

The silhouette of the helicopter was barely visible through the rain. Floodlights tried to cut through the torrential downpour that had started just after dark. The turning rotors did not help any, and the six men tilted their heads down towards the concrete tarmac as they ran out to the helo.

Once inside, Daley, Rolo, Nick, and Lorner struggled to find a seat harness and strap in. Giles, who was much more familiar, helped his students get ready for flight. Meanwhile, Cox, who had noticed the date on his down chit was mistakenly listed as tomorrow, began checking the students gear.

As he felt the SH-3 lift off, Lorner turned to Daley who was seated beside him. "Willy is such an asshole."

"What do you want?" Daley replied over the mind-numbing noise of the engine. "The kid was a gangbanger in Miami. His attitude is ten times better now than when we went through boot camp."

"It's still no excuse," Lorner said. Daley shrugged his shoulders, then leaned back. The helo was bouncing all over and Daley's stomach was reminding him of it constantly.

Giles wasn't enjoying the ride either. He hated night ops, and hated operations in the rain. And the fight he had with his girlfriend hadn't helped. He was going to ditch her. They'd been together five years, yet she still did not understand why he had to go when and where the navy told him. Giles then looked over at Cox. Rick was sitting there, eyes closed. Giles had seen this before. Rick's intensity bothered him. He compartmentalized everything. It was that intensity, that focus on winning, on beating the elements that Giles admired.

But now he wondered if Rick's intensity wasn't what killed Lee. Sometimes Rick's concentration was so narrowed that he would ignore everything else. Had he heard the kid's plea to D.O.R? Giles had, but in the middle of the exercise, it gets so crazy sometimes..or was Rick so upset that Daley had beat him that he felt the need to prove something. Giles had no answers, but his mind raced until he felt the helicopter begin to slow down.

Cox stood up and leaned over toward the pilot and nodded. He then returned to the cabin and held up his hands, fingers spread apart. "Five minutes. Are you SAR dogs ready?"

The students all made loud barking sounds and gave the instructor the thumbs up. Rick visually looked over each student as a final check. When he came to Nick, he noticed a strap that was twisted. He rushed over to him and grabbed the strap, pulling a surprised Nick to the floor.

"Who checked this man?! Who checked you?!" Nick and the

others were speechless as they watched the outburst from their instructor. Rick lifted Nick up by the strap.

"What else did you forget?! Are trying to kill all of us? If you're not taking this seriously, then D.O.R. Just D.O.R. I already had one of you die on me!" Cox pushed Nick back on the bench seat of the helicopter cabin. He looked into the eyes of each of the others, including Giles. "Which of us won't be able to do our job because we have to rescue you? Think about it. Think about what happened in the pool . Use your fucking head for more than a hat rack!"

Rick stepped over to the open cabin door and looked out over the dark water. The others sat silently realizing that they could have died just as easily. The helicopter pilot slowed, then hovered low over the water.

"Let's go, ladies," Cox said. "We don't have all night." The five students and two instructors stood in line. Giles placed his hand over his mask and stepped out the door. The rest followed, single file, dropping into the darkness below.

5

***

Saturday, June 13

Laura woke up around eight o'clock Saturday morning and drove over to her office to meet with Litton. When she arrived, the phones were already ringing. The one problem with bases that housed training commands was that the sailors were young and many of them were experiencing life on their own for the first time. It was somewhat like living in a college town, except that the students here had a lot more rules to go by. Along with Rescue Swimmer School, the Navy's Aviation Officer Candidate School was at Pensacola, as well as various technical training units. This meant that every Friday, a class of young sailors or newly commissioned officers graduated and celebrated in town. The results of those who went too far the night before could be seen by the ringing phones.

Litton arrived a few minutes after ten, and walked right back to his office, where Laura was waiting. She told him that she had received a list of names from the training command's administration officer, and that she had an appointment with Lt. Jackson, the Rescue Swimmer School's Officer-in-Charge, at noon.

"Sounds like everything is going okay then?"

"Yeah," Laura replied.

"I have a meeting in a few minutes as well," Litton said. "So I won't hold you up. Maybe we could have dinner tonight."

"I don't think so," Laura said.

"A working dinner," Litton replied. "To discuss what you find out."

"Why don't I just call you tomorrow morning instead?"

"Fine," he replied with a huff. "Call me at home around nine."

"Okay," she said and walked out quickly, glad to have escaped that one.

*

It was not a long drive out to the Jackson residence. It was a small home, rented probably. There were some toys in the yard, and Laura noticed a child seat in the Lieutenant's mini van when she walked up to the door. She was greeted by his wife, a young woman, very pretty, who invited her in. Once inside, Jackson came out from the back hallway and offered her something to drink. He was still wearing his jogging shorts and shirt.

"I'll bet you don't mind seeing trees for a while?" Laura said.

"No," he replied. He talked about how he sometimes missed living on an aircraft carrier, of flying, and even jogging along the flight deck. But since the baby, he was more than happy to come home every night to the small house.

"You don't sound like a career man," she said.

He laughed and told her quite the contrary, that he loved the Navy and planned on retiring--after he made admiral, of course.

"Of course," she agreed.

"So what can I help you with?" he asked.

"I wanted to get some information on the events of the other day," Laura said. "I wanted to ask about some of your staff and some of the students."

"Shoot..."

*

Litton walked into the Officer's Club a little after eleven. He was met by a tall, trim naval officer who did not seem all that pleased to be there. The two men took a table in the back of the club, closer to the bar than the windows.

"So what is this about?" Litton said.

"I wanted to give you our take on things," the officer replied. "I'm glad that you are handling this yourself."

"It's not completely by myself," Litton told him and started to explain about bringing Laura into the investigation, but was interrupted by a waiter. They gave their lunch orders, Litton wanted a beer, but the officer's look made him change his mind. "What's the big deal. It's probably just a training accident anyway."

"The deal is that the Admiral has ordered training suspended," the officer said. "I could give a shit about some fucking kid dying. But the last thing we need is one more media circus blaming the Navy for some screw up."

"That isn't going to happen."

"It better not."

"I'm trying to find out what happened as we speak," The NIS agent said. "Who the hell knows who's at fault here. It's only been a day. There may not be anyone to blame. Sometimes it's just an accident."

"The kids father is gonna want to blame someone."

"Screw the kid's family," Litton said. "I don't answer to them. I find out whatever I find out. That's the way it works."

"This case may work a little different."

"Why?" Litton asked.

*

"Any known problems?" Laura asked.

"No," Jackson replied. "Some of the instructors are a little more gung-ho than the others, but no problems. If they were problems, they'd be gone from this school."

"What about this guy Cox," Laura asked. "He was the one holding the victim."

"What about him?"

"Is he gung-ho?"

"He's a tough instructor, but Cox is Cox. " Jackson said. "Have you read his record?"

"Not yet."

"You should," Jackson said. "That guy is straight as an arrow, he doesn't mess around. In fact, if something like this had to happen- and I wish to God it never did or never does again- I'm glad that he was the instructor there."

"Why do you say that?"

"Because Cox is the kind of guy that would do anything to save someone."

"Does he have a hero complex or something?"

"Not hardly," Jackson said. "Do you remember hearing about those training jets that went down about a month ago?"

"Faintly, I remember reading something about it."

"Cox was the guy that pulled the pilots out of the drink,"

Jackson said.

"But I thought both pilots died."

"Yeah, they did. But Rick didn't know they were dead," Jackson said. "In fact, he disobeyed a direct order not to go in, but he jumped anyway."

"He disobeyed a direct order?" Laura asked. "Then why wasn't he disciplined"

"You don't get it," the Lieutenant said. "We tried to give him a medal. The order for him to stay in the helo was from the pilot. But as it turned out, the pilot and the Commanding Officer of the training squadron who lost the jet put him in for a decoration."

"So he does this for the medals?"

"No, he recovered the bodies for the families. So they could have a decent burial, and so their loved ones could say goodbye. We had to force him to take it. He doesn't wear 'em," Jackson said. "You should talk to him."

"Can we make that happen?" Laura said. "I'd like to meet this guy."

"Sure, when?"

"As soon as possible, today if I can."

"I don't know where he is today," Jackson said. "How about we set it up for Monday morning?"

"Monday morning's fine," Laura said after checking her small leather daily planner. "If he's half the god you make him sound like, it should be interesting. Have you spoken to him since the accident?'

"Briefly," Jackson said. "I think it's better to leave the guys alone for a day or so when these things happen."

"Where can I get a copy of his records?"

"The instructor on duty can get them for you, over at the RSS building," Jackson said. "If they have any questions, tell them to call me. I'll be home all day."

"Thanks, Lieutenant."she said. "Monday morning?"

"Monday morning."

*

Rick Cox was cooking breakfast when Giles walked into the apartment. The smell of bacon and eggs drew him right into the kitchen, as it did most every Saturday morning. His friend was prepared, and had cooked enough for both of them. Neither instructor had duty for the weekend and when they were done eating, the fish were waiting. Outside in the parking lot, Giles had his bass boat's coolers full of bait and beer, and it would not be long before they were out on the water. He grabbed a plate and sat down on the stool facing the kitchen.

"Good grub," he said between bites. "I haven't eaten in two days."

Rick stood near the sink and ate his. "That's kinda stupid."

"I haven't been real hungry. I keep thinking about what happened," Giles said. "I mean, he wasn't under that long."

"Forget about it," Rick told him.

"Are you telling me you haven't thought about that kid?"

"That's exactly what I'm telling you."

"Your full of shit."

"It's not worth it," Rick said. "The shit happens. He's dead. What can I do about it? Do I feel bad about it? Hell yes! Is there anything I can do about it? No. Can I let it bother me? No. Neither can you. We need to just get out on that water and relax today."

"Bull," Giles said as he placed his dish in the sink. "You might get away with this crap telling some of those kids it doesn't bother you, but I know you- What did you do last night?"

"Why?"

"I'll bet you just came home and sat and thought about what went wrong."

"No, I didn't," Rick said. "In fact I came home, worked on my truck, then went to sleep."

"Yeah right," Giles replied. "I just feel bad for the kid, that's all."

"You know what, I'm sick of worrying about this shit," Rick said. "You know it. I know it. That's why I don't try to be friends with students. You know better. Let's just drop it and go fishing."

"I'm not gonna apologize for feeling human."

"No one's asking you to," Rick said. "I just think you're wrong trying to get close to them. You need to just walk away."

"Yeah, whatever." Giles looked at his friend and walked out into the kitchen shaking his head. Of course both of them were right, and both were wrong. But either way, the fact remained that one of their students was dead. "You ready to go?"

*

"If Jackson said you can have them, who am I to argue?" Petty Officer Watson said. He took the list of names from Laura and placed them on the desk. "This will take me a few minutes, there are a lot of files."

"No problem," she replied. She walked around the instructors office, reading the training schedules and other notices, and watched him search the drawers. "Did you know the sailor who died?"

"Yes, ma'am."

"It's a shame," she said out loud to herself as she read the list of classes and instructors assigned. "He was so young."

"Yes. Ma'am."

Laura looked closer at the schedule. "It says here that you were one of the instructors assigned to the class." Watson turned to her, holding a handful of personnel files. "Yes ma'am. I was there."

"I didn't know that," she said. "What happened?"

"Typical Multi Exercise."

"What is that?"

"Lee was just doing a standard multi-victim scenario," Watson said. "One student, three instructors."

"Did you see what happened?"

"He was under water. Rick grabbed him, and next thing I know him and Adam..."

"Who's Adam?"

"Petty Officer Giles, the other instructor there," Watson said. "They pull the kid up to the surface, and start screaming for an ambulance and give him CPR."

"So you didn't actually see what took place?"

"As I said- they were under water."

"Had either Petty Officer Cox or the other instructor had any confrontations with Airman Lee prior to this?"

"No, not really."

"Are you sure?"

"Well, I mean the standard stuff," Watson said. "Rick made an example of him a few times because he couldn't keep up with the class."

"When was the last time?"

"A few days ago," Watson said. "Tuesday, I think."

"Tuesday?"

"Yeah, it was in the morning, we just came back from the cross country run," Watson said. "We had the class doing cracks out in front of the Aircrew building, and the kid tried to DOR."

"What is DOR?"

"Drop on Request- basically quit," Watson explained as he looked through the gray metal file cabinets, pulling out records of the students and instructors who were at the pool.

"What are Cracks?"

"Cracks is when we have each student stand on a slab of sidewalk," Watson said. "Each has one crack between them. And then we make each student do a different exercise, one does push ups, another sit ups, jumping jacks, squat thrusts whatever."

"So they just exercise?"

"No," Watson said. "They all must do it to the exact same cadence, exact same count."

"But if they're doing different exercises," Laura asked. "Then how can they do the same count. That's impossible?"

"Exactly," the instructor said. "They do it until the instructor says to stop. It builds stamina."

"And the victim said he wanted to DOR?"

"Right," Watson answered. "So the policy is they say it three times, then they are done. They go to the fleet to be reassigned."

"And Cox had a problem with that?"

"No," Watson said. "Rick had a problem because after he DOR'd , Lee was allowed back into training."

"And that's a problem?"

"Yeah," the instructor said. "It doesn't work that way. If you are out- then you are out!"

"Then why was Lee allowed back?"

"I don't know. Ask the Master Chief," Watson said.

"So this made Petty Officer Cox mad?"

"Ma'am," Watson said. "It made everyone mad. Instructors and the SAR dogs going through training."

"Mad enough for Cox to do something about it?"

"If you are asking me if I think this was done on purpose, I would say never," Watson replied. "We are professionals. But do I think that Lee should have been in that pool? No, he should not have been there. He died because he should not have been there. Is there anything else you need, ma'am?"

She signed out the records in a log book Watson handed her, and took the records from the counter. "No. Thank you for your time.

Where can I make photocopies?"

"There's a copy machine over in that room."

It took Laura a little over an hour to copy the files she wanted, and after returning them to Watson, she asked if she could go into the pool. He escorted her there without offering a word. He waited by the door as she walked into the chamber. Her steps echoed as her heels hit the concrete and tile deck. She leaned down at the edge and placed her hand in the water. The sounds of the splashing bounced off the wall and around the room. The smell of chlorine reminded her of the pool at her parents house. Everything was spotless and in perfect order. The swim fins along the wall, the helmets lined up on the wire racks. It was hard to imagine someone had died there just a few days before. She turned and said "thank you" to Watson as they headed back out to the office.

She picked up the files, the instructor had given her a box for the copies, and went out to her car. It wasn't long before she was crossing the bridge outside the main gate that led away from the Naval Air Station. Once home, she stuck a Paul McCartney CD in the stereo and began reading.

*

Litton sat at his desk, reviewing the application packet for the job in Washington. He had everything they were looking for: twenty years experience, a good record of convictions based on his investigations, some awards--though most came early in his career. But he had no recommendations from anyone who counted. His immediate boss wrote him a letter, but that was standard for all the applicants.

What he needed was something that would stand out. But he had burned too many bridges over the years. His tactics and methods were not approved of by those who knew about them. "This is bullshit," he said to himself and tossed the application across his desk as the phone rang.

"Litton," he answered.

"Yes sir," the receptionist replied. "There's a Commander Hunt on the phone for you."

Hunt? Hunt? Litton's mind raced through his memory. The name was familiar. *Oh, yeah! Hunt!* "Put him through," Litton told her.

*

Rick unlocked the door to his apartment as Giles pulled away, honking his horn. He slapped the four catfish down onto the counter and checked his messages. There were two. One from a Laura Wilson, whoever she was. The second was from Jackson. He said that the NIS would be meeting with them Monday in the Commanding Officer's office. Rick made a mental note of it, and started cleaning his dinner.

6

***

Sunday, June 14

"Jack?"

"Who's this?" Litton asked into the receiver as he rolled over in bed. As he did, the twisted cord pulled the phone off the night table causing a loud thud and ringing sound as it hit the floor . He changed hands and started to untangle the phone. He looked at the clock. Five minutes after nine.

"Laura Wilson," she answered. "I'm sorry, did I wake you?"

"No. Yeah, kinda," he said lifting the phone off the floor by pulling on the cord. "What do you want?"

"You asked me to call at nine, remember?"

"Oh yeah," he said. It was too early for him to remember. He had been out late last night working on some personal business. His camera bag and spent rolls of film sat on the chair across from the bed attested to last night's work. "So what's up?"

Laura sat out on her porch swing and gave her boss the play by play of the previous afternoon. She told Litton about Rick and Giles, and what Watson had said regarding Lee's DOR's. She said that after reviewing the instructor's files, she figured it was worth speaking to them again, even though they had all told the initial military police what had happened. He agreed.

"I already spoke with the OIC- a Lieutenant named Jackson, he said he would arrange a meeting in the morning."

"Great. Let me know what time."

"I also checked on the victim," Laura said. "I didn't see anything out of the ordinary. He was ordinary, nothing outstanding in boot camp.

I'm going to get his medical files in the morning."

"Wait until after we talk with this Cox guy," Litton said. "Is there anything I should know before we go in?"

She told him about his disregard for orders in the rescue the month before, and of the citation he received. She told of the family that praised his efforts of retrieving their son. But she had found he also had a temper. "But, given the guy's job, that's understandable."

"Do me a favor," Litton said. "Write me up a quick report on this guy and on some of the other people you think are noteworthy, and drop it off the office by, say, noon."

"Today?"

"Yeah, I'll stop by and pick it up after lunch," Litton said. "Thanks."

"Oh, one other thing," Laura said. "The instructor at the school today hinted that the victim was receiving preferential treatment by the command's top enlisted man, a Master Chief Joseph Russo."

"Okay," Litton said. "Let me check into that, you concentrate on the report."

"See you in the morning, Jack."

*

Rear Admiral Donald Tract crouched down and concentrated. He stood up and moved fifteen feet to his left and studied the angle again. Though in his late forties, he had climbed up the ladder of command very quickly, even for someone who was number one of his class at Canoe U, as non-graduates called the Naval Academy. He was known for his hands-off approach to command. Let the talented men in his charge do their jobs. That was Tract's style in everything.

Everything except his two passions. Flying had been the first, but he rarely found himself in the cockpit anymore. He was currently enjoying his second love.

"Let's go Donald," retired Admiral Alan Steinmen remarked. The former Commander of the Atlantic Fleet shook his head with disgust.

Tract just grunted in response and moved back to his original position. "I was an ensign when we started this hole," Steinmen said.

"Okay, okay," Tract replied. He lined up the shot and tapped the ball with the putter. It rolled across the green as if on tracks, and dropped straight into the hole. "Gotcha, Baby!"

"Don't rub it in or anything."

"You owe me a hundred and eighty bucks Alan!" Tract said, holding out his hand. "Twenty bucks a hole. You want to try the back nine?"

The Admiral declined and fished out the cash from his wallet. He promised his friend that one of these days Tract would be paying him. They loaded up the cart and headed back to the club house. The NAS Pensacola course was booked solid on weekends, but rank had its privileges on these greens. When the two flag officers came into the clubhouse, the attendant gave Tract a message. He excused himself, and told his friend he'd meet him inside for lunch. The Rear Admiral then walked around to the lounge where his aide was waiting.

"It's Sunday, Hunt," the Admiral said. "This couldn't wait?'

"I just spoke with Litton," the naval officer replied. "He told me that this was probably an accident, pure and simple. The instructor involved is a little brazen, but he's not a wildcard or anything."

"I don't care what his record was," the Admiral told him point blank. "I want someone's ass for this. I want a name, Hunt. I thought I made that clear?"

"Yes sir, but..."

"No buts on this," Tract continued. "You do what you have to do to make this go away quickly, This is not gonna stain my record."

"Yes sir," Hunt said. "I know what this means to you."

"Did you contact the Senator?"

"Yes, sir. He said he'd contact you either today or tomorrow."

"Fine," Tract said. He sighed and ran his fingers through his full head of hair. "Christ, I knew this would bite me in the ass." He thought for a moment, Hunt waited. "You take care of it Do what you have to do! This command isn't gonna be blamed, and I sure as hell am not gonna be the fall guy for this. You get Harding, and you tell him I want a name of whoever is responsible for this. You understand me?"

"I already have, sir. He knows."

"I want that name!" Tract said. "I want it now, I want to be able to give that boy's father a name. And no one in that school does a goddamn thing before I get it."

"Litton said he'd like to put all his effort into this, but he needed something from us first?'

"What's that weasel looking for now?" Tract said.

"He is going for some job in D.C. and needs a letter of recommendation from someone," Hunt said. "I thought this might speed things up if you wrote him one."

"What are you- fucking insane?" Tract said. "I will not write anything good about that thug. I've had to deal with him for years--If I could prove half of what I think that slimy bastard has pulled since I was here he'd be in jail somewhere."

"Everyone knows he's a snake, Admiral, but.."

"No buts, Commander," tract replied. "You tell Litton to get off his ass and do his job! Or I will write a Gaddamn letter to his boss!" With that he turned and headed to the restroom to wipe a cold towel over his face. By the time he arrived at the table for lunch, the Admiral was totally relaxed. He trusted Hunt. He had never failed him before.

*

Lt. Jackson was outside getting ready to grill dinner for his small family, and trying to enjoy the calm before the storm that was sure to start. But it was hard for him to keep his mind off the dead sailor. It was the first casualty that had ever came under the twenty-seven-year-old officer's command. Every time he looked at his own child, he thought of what Lee's parent's were going through.

He had laid the chicken on a plate when he heard the phone ringing in the house. He saw his wife watching their baby, and went inside and answered it. "Jackson residence."

"Lieutenant, Commander Harding."

"Hey, Skipper."

"Mr. Jackson, I just got the call, Classes are canceled until further notice." Harding told him. "I already contacted the duty office, so don't worry about that. They'll give notice to the instructors, but I doubt the students will all find out so just handle it.":

"Aye, aye, Skipper."

"You'll need to keep those kids busy," Harding continued. "I don't want them just hanging around. I'm sure you can think of something for them to do."

"Yes, sir."

"Enjoy the rest of the weekend, and I'll see you first thing in my office with Cox, right?"

"Yes, sir." Jackson said and hung up. He went back outside and explained to his wife that he would have to pass on going to the movies that night. He had to figure out how to keep a few hundred people busy. He threw some chicken on the grill and opened a coke before sitting down at the picnic table to watch his son play in the sandbox.

*

Laura's eyes hurt from reading all day. She looked at the clock. It was only six o'clock. She put the files away, and placed the notes she would need for the meeting on top of the table. She changed into her jogging clothes and grabbed the walkman from her gym bag.

It was a short drive back to the base. She parked in the RSS parking lot and took off down along the water toward the health trail. Running on base was more of a hassle than near her apartment; but it made her feel safe, and since she ran alone, convenience took second place to safety. She had not found anyone to workout with yet. Just one more thing she missed about college.

*

"Well?" Litton asked.

"The Admiral said he'd be happy to write a letter," Hunt told him.

Litton relaxed and sat back. He looked over at the other patrons of the oyster bar. He watched a young family eating a few tables away. A child, she couldn't have been more than four-years-old, was throwing pieces of her dinner over the side of the wooden peir where the restaurant was located. A pelican walked over to her and she threw the rest of the food at it and ran back to her dad, giggling. The rest of the family laughed, too, as they watched the bird eat. *What a bunch of fucking loser's,* Litton thought. *Don't they know what is important in life?*

"So tell me what's going on with the investigation so far?"

*

7

***

Monday, June 15

Rick sat outside Commander Harding's Office. It was close to nine o'clock in the morning, and he and Lt. Jackson had been sitting in the outer office for almost an hour. They were both in dress uniform, as ordered. They were both nervous, but no one would know that by looking at them. The door opened and both men rose to their feet. The Command Master Chief and senior enlisted man of the command stepped out. Master Chief Russo was also in dress uniform.

"Lieutenant, the C.O. is ready, sir, " Russo said. Jackson nodded then walked past him and through the doorway into Harding's office. Russo then looked at Rick. "Let's go, Cox."

Inside, Harding was sitting behind his desk. Across from him sat a scruffy, squat man who was smoking a cigar, and, by the odor, not a very good one.

The chair beside him was occupied by a very attractive woman who Rick guessed was in her early twenties. She was busy writing in a legal pad, and did not look up as he walked in. There were two empty chairs next to her.

Master Chief Russo followed in behind Rick and closed the door. He did not take a seat, but stood near the door along the wall behind them. Rick walked up in front of the desk. Lt. Jackson was also standing.

"Petty Officer First Class Cox reporting as ordered, sir."

"Have a seat, gentlemen," Harding said and gestured to the empty chairs. The two men sat down with Rick taking the chair near the young woman.

"Petty Officer Cox, Lt. Jackson," Harding said, "This is Agent

Jack Litton and Agent Laura Wilson of the Naval Investigative Service. You both know Master Chief Russo. The NIS is investigating the death of Airman Lee and would like to ask you some questions."

"Sir, I need to go.." Jackson interrupted. Litton looked over at Harding, obviously disappointed.

"Very well, Lieutenant," Harding said to Jackson, then turned to the agents. "Mr. Jackson notified me yesterday that he would only be available until eight o'clock. We are in the process of shutting the school down temporarily, and as you can imagine, his schedule is quite busy today."

Litton's left eyebrow lifted. "Too busy to answer a few questions, Lieutenant? I'm sure you realize that the sooner we conclude our investigation, the sooner we can all get back on schedule."

"If you can give me a number to contact you," Jackson said. "I'd be more than happy to sit down after lunch and answer any questions that you may have, sir." Litton reached into his pocket and handed over a card. Jackson took it and excused himself. Russo closed the door behind him.

"I suppose we can continue now, uninterrupted," Litton said. Harding nodded. "Thank you Commander. Petty Officer Cox before we get started, I need to read you your rights."

"Why do I need my rights read?"Rick asked. "What the hell is this about?"

Litton spoke up. "It's to protect you."

Rick looked around at Harding and Russo, who both looked away. There was no help in their faces. Obviously Litton was running the show. "Protect me?" Rick said. "What kind of questions are you asking that I need protection from?"

Laura Wilson turned her attention away from her notepad and to Rick."It's not the questions, it's to protect you from anything you say,"she replied. "Some people feel more comfortable with representation. If you want a lawyer present, we can do this another time."

It was easy for Rick to believe her. Sitting this close, he could smell the fragrance of her hair, and noticed she did not wear perfume. It had been a long time since he had been so close to a woman, and he momentarily lost his focus. "It's up to you," she said.

"I don't like lawyers," Rick said. "But I also don't like being asked questions as if I did something wrong, ma'am."

"You don't need a lawyer," Litton added. "You're not under arrest, we're just trying to protect everyone's rights in this investigation."

"This is an accident, not a criminal, investigation," Laura said. It was obvious to her that the instructor did not know the impact that an investigation like this could have. But he was a grown man, and she wasn't a defense lawyer.

"Damn right this was an accident," Rick said.

"Cox," Litton said. "We are not saying it wasn't, not yet. As far as we know- you did nothing wrong.."

"If you don't know an answer or feel uncomfortable with a question, let us know." She said cutting off Litton for the second time. "You are not required to answer anything you feel would incriminate you."

"Excuse us for a moment, gentlemen." Litton said. He reached over and practically pulled Laura to her feet. "Agent Wilson, may we have a word in private?" They walked out into the outer office, closing the door behind themselves.

"This is not a good first impression you're making," Litton said. "I expected better from a law school graduate."

"What do you mean?"

"I mean I don't know what the hell are you doing," Litton said. "I was hoping that you would follow my lead here, being this is your first major investigation." Laura could see the tips of his ears turning red, a sign she learned meant that her boss was on the warpath. He still had her arm, and was squeezing it tighter until she pulled away. She composed herself before answering. "What are you talking about?"

"I mean you're telling that man not to answer my questions."

"I was not, I was telling him his rights," Laura replied. He let her go and turned away and faced the wall for a moment. After gathering his thoughts, he turned around, frustrated.

"You were telling him how to fuck up and slow down my investigation."

"I was telling him what he is legally allowed to do," Laura said defending herself.

"Well now I'm telling you, as the senior agent assigned," Litton warned. "You keep those pretty little lips closed."

"What did I do wrong?" She was confused. This was not at all like she pictured it last night. He headed to the door, but before turning the handle he turned again to her.

"We run this thing the way I say we do, or you go wait in the car," Litton said. "When you are a senior agent, you can run investigations the way you see fit. Got it?"

The door opened and the two agents walked back inside Harding's office and sat down. Cox noticed that Laura did not even look at Litton, and that she seemed upset.

"I'm sorry," Litton said. "We just needed to review some things before we started." That brought a mean glance from Laura, which was ignored. "So, Petty Officer Cox, did you want legal representation, or may we begin?"

"I guess it's fine," Rick said. "I just never had to be read my rights before."

"Yeah, well it is standard procedure," Litton said. "Honest, we are all friends here. It's just a simple deposition to find out what happened."

"Fine," Rick said, resigning himself. "Let's just get it over with."

"Great! Agent Wilson, will you read Petty Officer Cox his rights, then we'll get started." Litton was eager to get this going. "Do you mind if we tape this?" he asked taking out a small cassette recorder.

"No, I don't care." Rick answered.

*

"I need his name, social, and a copy of his record, Mister Jackson."

"May I ask why, sir" Jackson asked.

"No, you may not," the officer said. Jackson had never met Lieutenant Commander Hunt, but now he knew why Harding disliked the Admiral's aide so much. The guy was cocky as a fifteen-year-old school yard bully, and had the social skills of a hand grenade.

"On who's authority is this request coming from, sir?"

"Admiral Tract's on behalf of Senator Lee," Hunt said. "If you care to call the Admiral, be my guest." Jackson was not about to jeopardize his career over this, but was amused at Hunt's expression when he picked up the phone.

"This is Lt. Jackson," he said. "I have Commander Hunt from Admiral Tract's office here requesting copies of Petty Officer Cox's records....Yes, I'll hold."

Jackson knew that Hunt was thinking he had called the Admiral, and was amused by the evil stare he received when RSS's Administration Chief picked up the line. "Hey Chief...yeah..can we send them over right away? Thanks."

"No sweat, sir," Jackson said. "You'll have them within the hour." Hunt stormed out of the office, not enjoying being one-upped. Jackson felt the urge to disinfect his office.

*

"...and that was when you felt the victim stop resisting you." Litton recounted.

"Yes, sir," Rick said, "It was during the Sharks and Daisies exercise." He was tired. It was almost noon and it seemed as if he had told everything that happened at least ten times. He just wanted to be out of there, but Litton just kept asking him over and over the same questions.

"And you let him go" Litton said, referring to a yellow legal pad that he kept scribbling notes on.

"No, not at first."

"Why not?"

"I told you," Rick said. "I thought he was trying to fool me into letting him go."

"You didn't know he had stopped breathing?" Laura asked.

"I wasn't sure. I mean the whole reason that we do the exercise is for the students to escape." He paused as he heard the tape recorder click.

"Hold that thought," Laura said quickly changed cassettes.

"I don't know," Rick said once the recorder was back on. "Maybe he was resting or something."

"So now you say he was resting?" Litton asked.

"No, that's not what I said," Rick replied, annoyed at the way Litton had constantly tried to twist his words. "I said I thought he *might* have been. We teach these kids to think about what they are doing when they're in the water. I figured he was trying to remember an escape move or something. How would I know that he smurfed?"

"Smurfed?" Laura asked.

"Stopped breathing," Rick replied. "Turned blue, like the cartoon character. We call it smurfing when someone stops breathing during an exercise."

Litton nodded. He leaned over and placed his hands together, as if in deep thought. There was silence in the room as they waited for whatever was coming."So when someone stops breathing you all treat it like a joke?" Litton asked.

"No. It's not a joke," Rick said. "It's a way to deal with it. It helps calm the fear."

"Having my breathing stop sounds scary to me," Litton said.

"Yeah, to you I can understand it." Rick said. He was sick of Litton's attitude. "I want to get something straight right here, Mr. Litton."

The NIS agent sat back in his chair and let out an exaggerated breath. "Go ahead."

"To anyone who hasn't gone through this training it might seem overwhelming or cruel," Rick explained. "But it is nothing like an actual rescue. Smurfing happens in our training. But it happens a whole lot more out in the world. The only time anyone questions us is here in training, not when you have a sea state of four, with waves trying to drown you, and a plane in the drink. Then everyone wants us to just get out there and be heroes."

"Cox!" Harding said, but the instructor ignored his Commanding Officer and continued. "But if we made this training so that any limp dick kid who watched Top Gun could get through it," the instructor said, "we'd not only lose swimmers in the ocean, but you can kiss goodbye many of the people we pull out as well." His voice was getting louder. "We made this course so that people would only pass who would have the skills and the balls to jump into the water, and sacrifice themselves *So That Others May Live*. That's not just a patch or some motto. It's what we do. I very much doubt that you would understand that."

"I get your point," Litton said.

"I don't think you do, sir." Rick interrupted. "I smurfed when I was in this school. If it hasn't happened to at least one person in the class, we aren't training hard enough. Yeah, people die here, but better here when they are only depending on themselves, than when others need them."

"Wasn't Lee depending on you to be there for him?' Litton said.

"Yeah, he was!" Rick said. "Don't you think I know that?"

"Enough!" Harding said. This was turning into a shouting match. "Cox, be quiet for a moment. We all realize the importance of

SAR swimmers."

"Commander, are you aware of this practice?" Litton asked.

"What practice?"

"Smurfing."

"I've heard of it," Harding lied. "But even so, I think we could move on to something else. Personalities are conflicting a little too much." Rick shook his head and sat back in his chair. The frustration in his face was evident. No one wanted to hear about how things were, just how they wanted things to be. "It doesn't matter anyway," Rick said out loud to no one.

"What doesn't?" Laura asked.

"I said it didn't matter whether he smurfed or not," Rick replied. Litton looked over at the instructor and then to Harding.

"I would think it would matter a great deal," Harding said.

"Lee did not die from drowning," Rick said.

"Excuse me," Litton asked. "But the medical examiner hasn't filed a report yet."

"The doctor told me. In the emergency room."

"He just blurted it out to you?" Litton said.

"He told me that Lee had died of heart failure," Rick replied.

"That is a side effect of drowning," Litton said. "Most deaths are caused by a person's heart stopping. In fact, I would say all of them."

"All I know," Cox said. "Is what the doctor said."

"Let's wait for the autopsy, okay?"

"Mr. Litton, if you don't believe me," Rick said. "Ask him yourself." He pulled the unfilled prescription from his wallet and handed it over to Litton. "That's his name." Litton handed it to Laura who wrote down the information.

Harding looked at his watch. "Let's try to wrap this up soon, Gentlemen and Miss Wilson. I didn't realize this was going to take so long."

"Fine." Litton agreed. "I have just a few more questions." He flipped the legal pad, scanning his notes. "Where were we?"

"Petty Officer Cox and the boy were under water." Laura read from her notes.

"So at this point, you said you had intentionally drowned the victim?" Litton asked.

"Bullshit," Rick said nearly jumping from his chair. "I never said that!"

"Sit down, please," Litton said. "You just said, on the record, that you felt you had killed the kid. You said that was what you told the doctor."

"What I said was..."

"I can rewind the tape if you prefer," Litton said.

"You know what I meant," Rick said, then turned to his C.O., "Skipper, he knows what I meant. That son of a bitch is putting words in my mouth, sir."

"Okay," Harding said, hitting the desk and pushing his chair back. "Meeting's over."

"I'm not done yet," Litton said. Harding looked down at the man.

"Everyone is tired, and tempers are flaring," Harding said.

"So I don't get to defend myself?!" Rick asked.

"Cox," Harding replied, "No one is saying that the death was intentional."

"Not yet, anyway," Litton interjected.

His sarcasm drew Harding's attention. "Enough! Mr. Litton, I am not saying the NIS cannot question this instructor at another time."

"I hope not," Litton said, drawing Harding's wrath..

"Dammit- that's enough! It's little comments like that," Harding told him. "That makes everyone defensive and uncooperative in these things. Respectfully, Mr. Litton, just shut the hell up!" Harding did not like losing his temper in front of men in his command, but enough was enough.

"You're right, Commander," Litton said, without any apology in his voice. "We have been here a long time, and we should get back." Litton stood up and stepped over to Rick. He stuck out his hand. "Petty Officer Cox, you have been helpful. Thanks for putting up with me." Cox refused, turned away and crossed his arms.

"If I have any more questions," Litton said. "I'll contact Commander Harding, all right?"

"Yes, sir. You do that," Rick said.

"Commander, may I speak with you a moment." Litton asked. The two men walked out into the other office leaving Laura and Rick alone. Laura packed the cassette recorder and notebooks in a black leather attaché and stood up beside Rick.

"It was nice to meet you, Petty Officer Cox," she said.

"Yes, ma'am," Rick said still angry.

"I'm a little to young to be a ma'am, Petty Officer Cox." she reached into her purse and handed him her card. "It's Laura. And I agree with a lot of what you said about training."

"Thanks, Miss Wilson," he replied reading her card. "I'm Rick."

"I know." she said smiling. "If you think of anything, or have any questions, don't hesitate to call me. I promise not to be so hard on you."

"Thanks."

Harding and Litton were standing by the door, waiting for Laura. She shook hands with Rick and walked out. "I'll meet you in the car," Litton said. When she was gone, the NIS agent turned back toward Rick. "I have a question, if you don't mind."

"I thought this was over," Rick said. "And the recorder is with Agent Wilson."

"This is strictly off the record," Litton said. Rick looked over at Harding, who nodded.

"What?" Rick replied.

"If Lee was yelling that he wanted to Drop On Request before, why didn't you stop right then?"

"I was under water."

"So you didn't hear him?"

"I did not say that."

"Then why?"

"Because," Rick answered. "He had tried to D.O.R. before, but then came back to class. He was using it as a way of ending the exercises faster."

"Even though the policy is once D.O.R. is called, training should stop immediately?"

"Yes."

"I see," Litton said nodding. "May I ask one more."

"One," Rick said. He was tired of these games.

"I understand you have a brother?"

"Yeah. I had a brother," Rick said trying to figure out what his brother had to do with anything. "What does that have to do with anything?"

"I understand he drowned as well?"

"I think you should go, sir."

"I'm sorry about him," Litton said. Rick bet he was.

"Why?"Rick asked. "You weren't there."

"I was just reading through your file, that's all." Litton turned to leave, but then spun around again. "Do you know Senator Robert Lanford Lee, Petty Officer Cox?"

"No, sir," Rick said. "Should I?"

"I don't know, you tell me," Litton said. He turned and thanked Harding for his time and finally left the room. It was not a moment too soon for Rick. Harding came back to his office and sat down at the desk. He dismissed Rick, but told him to find Master Chief Russo and send him in. Russo was in his office when Rick found him. It was right down the hall from Harding's.

"Have a seat, Master Chief," Harding said as Russo walked into the C.O.'s office. "Joey, you're going to sit here and tell me all about Sharks and Daisies, Smurfing and anything else I should know. I don't appreciate looking like an idiot."

Litton saw Laura standing next to the white, government issue sedan when he walked out of the Schools Command Building. It was a typical summer day in Pensacola, and the heat hit like a wall as Litton stepped outside. The puddles from the previous evening's storms were long gone, but the humidity was still there. The NIS agent took his sunglasses from the breast pocket of his sportcoat and stood a moment.

Although he was already soaked in sweat, he knew Laura could see him. It probably aggravated the new agent that her boss was making her wait, but Litton wanted her to know where her place was. He wanted her to know that he still made the rules. NAS Pensacola had been his stomping ground for a long time, longer than anyone else on the base as far as he knew. Of course longevity brought him respect. And fear. People with something to hide always had fear, and when you've been around as long as he has you find out things. Nobody can keep a secret forever.

Litton walked down the steps deciding that Laura had waited long enough when he spotted a young naval officer heading his way. The officer was too busy reading from a manila file to see Litton standing there. Litton waited until just the right moment before sidestepping into his path.

"Ensign Davis, how are you today?" Litton said. The startled officer stopped just short of colliding into the NIS agent. Davis looked up into the familiar face.

"Um, fine," he answered, and tried to step around Litton. The agent grabbed his arm, and Davis stopped in his tracks. He did not pull away, but stood there. He also would not turn to look at Litton.

"Please let go," Davis said politely. "I have a meeting, I'm already late."

Litton leaned up and spoke into the Ensign's ear. "Why don't you just get on your fairy wings and fly there?"

Davis immediately yanked his arm, breaking Litton's hold and rushed inside the building. He could hear the agent laughing as he walked down the hall.

Litton was still amused with himself when he walked up to the car. Laura was leaning on the drivers side door, the attache was on the roof. The car engine was running, letting the air-conditioner cool down the interior.

"Who was that?" Laura asked.

"A friend."

"He didn't seem happy to see you."

"Who? Davis?" Litton said. "He's happy to see any man." He opened his door and sat inside. The interior was still over one-hundred degrees. Why he couldn't let the air-conditioner do its job, Laura could not understand.

"What are you waiting for?" she heard Litton ask. Laura opened the car and sat down behind the wheel. She pulled out of the parking lot and turned left, away from the office.

"Where are you going?" Litton asked.

"I assumed we were going over to the base hospital," she replied. "To talk to that Doctor. Craft, right?"

"Why?" Litton said.

"Because it would make sense, right?" Laura said. "I mean we are this close."

"What makes you think that I haven't already spoken to him?" Litton said. Laura looked at him with astonishment, then suspicion.

"Then why didn't you say something?"

"Why should I?" Litton asked as he took out a cigar. "Cox doesn't need to know everything I do." He bit the end off, rolled down the window and spit it out.

"I meant why didn't you tell me?" Laura replied.

"I don't have to tell you everything, either," he said, and lit a match up to the cigar. Laura pulled over to the side, rolled down her window and grabbed the cigar from Litton's mouth. She threw it outside. "I asked you before not to smoke in this car!"

Litton took another cigar from his pocket and put it up to his lip. Before he had time to bite the end, Laura had grabbed and discarded it. "Those are real Cuban cigars, I hope you know."

"I don't care!" she replied. "I'm not your damn chauffeur or some typist from the secretarial pool. Why didn't you tell me you had spoken with the doctor? Why didn't I at least have his name? What else are you not telling me!?"

"Just like a split tail to get upset," he replied.

"A what?"

"A split tail. A babe, a chick," Litton rattled off more slang. When he was done he sat back, satisfied with himself for getting Laura flustered. She sat looking at him.

"From what rock did you crawl out from," she said. "You ignorant little troll."

Litton took another cigar from his pocket, but left it wrapped. He pointed it toward his partner, "You better watch that pretty little mouth of yours, it might get you in trouble, Laura." He saw her eye the cigar, and he placed in back in his pocket.

"Bite my 'pretty little mouth'! I'm a Naval Investigative Service Agent just like you. I don't enjoy being out of the loop."

Litton watched her for a moment. She had never stood up to him before, and he didn't like it. "This isn't some law school class trip. I am your superior here, Agent Wilson," he said. He could feel his ears turning red. "That means you'll know what I want you to know, and do what I say you are to do."

"You may be my boss, but no way are you in any way superior. Look at you," she said. "I know how you treat the other women in the office. You're a walking sexual harassment suit!"

"Do you feel better now? Putting me down," Litton said. "Would you feel the same if I was six two and a bodybuilder?"

"You could be six foot four, without an ounce of fat and have the nicest ass in the world and I would still feel the same way."

"Uh, huh." Litton said. "Well, regardless, I am still your boss. And if you don't like it, take your law degree, and your looks, and get a job with some big law firm somewhere. But until you do that, I don't want to hear about how I am handling this case or any other!"

Laura thought about saying something, but she was so angry she could not think of anything. She threw the car into gear and pulled out onto the road.

"You just don't get it, do you, Missy? " Litton continued. "I've been on this base too long to take shit from some quota with a nice set of legs."

"I get it," Laura said gritting her teeth in anger. "Now can we just drop it?!"

"Fine."

"Fine," she repeated. The two rode in silence as they drove along the base golf course. Laura was so angry at herself for not saying something that she did not see the two men in the golf cart coming down the path toward the crossing. The two golfers were not paying attention either and they shot right out into the road.

"Look out!" Litton screamed, and Laura whipped the car around, barely missing the startled golfers. The white Ford Crown Victoria spun out in the grass, leaving muddy tracks in the soft soil of the fairway. As the car came to a halt, the two agents both took deep breaths.

"Are you trying to kill us?" Litton said.

"It wasn't my fault," Laura replied. "That cart came out of nowhere."

"Yeah, right. And if you weren't speeding..."

"I was only doing forty."

"In a thirty-five zone," Litton said. "That's speeding. I'll have to report this."

"What?'

"You broke the law," Litton said. "You just admitted it."

"Oh..Oh.. And you didn't?" Laura said, not believing what this righteous hypocrite was saying. "You just denied a guy his legal right to representation, then accused him of confessing to a murder?"

"What are you talking about?" Litton said, lighting a cigar.

"Don't act all innocent with me, you knew exactly what you were doing," she said, ignoring the smoke. "Cox doesn't know if he's killed someone or not, but he feels guilty just the same. It's natural and we both know it. But you and I both know that kid's death was not intentional!"

"We don't know that," Litton said, resting his head back as he sucked on the stogie.

"Yeah, you do." she said.

"No, we don't. And I'm just giving him enough of a rope to see if he'll hang himself."

"How?" Laura asked. "By denying him his rights or twisting his words so much that any lawyer in the country could have that tape thrown out?"

"I think he knew what he was doing."

"Say you're right," Laura continued. "Say he was negligent or overzealous or had somehow planned this whole thing; thanks to you, we can't use anything he's said." Laura placed the car in gear and slowly pulled back out on the road. She started to feel sick in the pit of her stomach. Laura was not sure if it was the smoke from Litton's cigar or that she felt she was somehow turning her back on her own morals. Either way, she needed some air.

"If you are going to smoke that thing," Laura said. "At least put down the window." Litton rolled the window down as they headed back to the office.

"Do you feel okay?"

She didn't answer, the knot in her gut had become tighter. Litton took a long drag on his cigar, then removed it from his mouth and threw it out his window, but blew the smoke at Laura.

"What do you have against that instructor?" Laura asked, coughing.

Litton shook his head. "Nothing," he said watching the traffic outside the window.

"Then why..."

"Is that what they taught you in law school?"

"What?"

"That trying to get a confession is a personal matter," Litton asked. "That you have to have something to gain personally to suspect someone of a crime."

"Do you mean was I taught that a coerced confession is not admissible and cannot be used in a courtroom?" Laura replied. "Yeah, I think we may have covered that somewhere."

"You're not in the college anymore," Litton said. "The real world is not as cut and dry as some class in criminal law. There are reasons things happen the way they do."

"Thank you, professor know-it-all."

"If you don't realize that now," Litton said, ignoring her

comment. "Your next job will have you wearing a name tag and aspiring for a promotion to french fries."

Laura looked over at what she was supposedly aspired to become. Had Litton started out this way, or was he always such an asshole. That stupid smirk of his told her the answer, and she was already regretting taking this assignment; in fact she was again regretting joining the NIS. She wondered how she would be able to do this job. Most of the people she worked with were professionals. But if she had to be side by side with Litton..why did it have to be a case like this? She didn't want to think about it. "Regardless of what you say, Litton. The law still applies to everyone."

"You've been in the NIS how long," Litton asked lighting another cigar. "Five months?'

"Six months," she corrected.

"Five, six, whatever," he said waving his stogie out the window. "The point is, you haven't been around the military much, have you?"

"No, not really. But I don't see..."

"I'll give you a quick lesson."

"Whoopee," she said.

"The Navy has their own laws. It's called the Uniform Code Of Military Justice..."

"I know the UCMJ," she replied. She did not need to hear this crap, but if Litton was happy hearing himself speak, she had little choice but to listen.

"The UCMJ has articles that people outside the military could never understand. Take article 134. It says that even if you do something that is not covered anywhere else in the UCMJ, you can be held accountable and punished."

"Yeah, but isn't that only used in combat zones."

"Is a sunburn combat? It's considered destroying government property, and you can get fined or worse," Litton told her as they drove past the hangers and flight line. The aircraft were lined up in neat rows, their white gloss finishes reflecting the sun. "People think that kings in the middle ages had power, but they are nothing compared to an Admiral in the modern military. It's amazing, really."

"So you're saying that these guys make their own laws?" Laura asked, "I find that hard to believe."

"They don't make them, but they are different," Litton continued. "They need to be. The commander of a submarine has enough power at his fingertips to destroy the world, and at sea his authority cannot be questioned. He must control the crew, so that power is not corrupted. Or take one of these pilots out here," he gestured at the rows of aircraft. "What is to stop one of them from flying over a city and dropping some bombs instead of going to the target range?"

"So," Laura asked, "You're telling me that by keeping tight control over the men in their command, and by letting the commanders have absolute authority over them, this keeps the men from making mistakes."

"Or worse, yes."

"But what happens when that power is abused?" Laura asked. "If they have absolute power, then those under them have no rights."

"Of course they do," Litton said. "They have the right to go above their commander's head."

"But what if the abuse comes from the top, then what?"

"It doesn't go that high," Litton said. "No one is going to allow themselves to knowingly place their command at risk. It doesn't happen. By the time men attain that rank and responsibility, they know better. They have too much to lose."

"But what if they didn't know better?" Laura replied. "Then some innocent person is made to take the fall, right."

"I'm not saying anyone would be given blame, or that they would do anything," Litton said. "You're the lawyer, you figure it out." They pulled into the NIS office parking lot. "It's three o'clock and I have some errands to run. I'll see you in the morning at seven sharp."

"Where are we going?"

"I'll let you know in the morning," Litton said as he walked to his own car. Laura didn't mind her boss leaving early, she had some of her own errands to take care of.

*

Hunt closed the door to his bosses office after saying goodnight. The Admiral waived at him and continued to listen to the speaker phone on his desk.

"Donald, you and I go back a long way."

"I know, Robert," the Admiral replied. As if the Senator did not remind him of it every time they spoke.

"And, Donald, you know there is not anything that I would not do for you to help you in your retirement next year."

"I know that, too."

"But," Senator Lee replied, "This was my son and your command is responsible for his death. I would hate to have his death reflect on you, Donald."

"I am so sorry this happened," the Admiral said.

"As well you should be!" Lee continued. "I entrusted him to you. You said you would look out for him. I never expected this!

"And this is an election year!" Tract heard on of the Senators aides say in the background loud enough for him to hear.

"I am so very sorry," Tract said. "But I am doing everything possible to find out what happened."

"We both know what happened! One of your instructors went nuts!" The Senator said. "Donald, how can I, in good faith, recommend you to sit on the corporate board of one of the largest defense contractors in this country when you can't even control those in your command?"

The Admiral leaned back in his chair and rubbed his temples. He knew this would come up. "I have the investigation going at full speed, didn't your people get the files Hunt sent up?"

"We got 'em," Senator Lee said. "I see that you haven't even arrested that son of a bitch yet."

"There's a problem, with that," Tract said. "Didn't you read my notes?'

"The only problem I see is that the man who killed my son is walking around free. And that is now your problem." Lee replied. "Now, I am flying down there in the morning. We leave Andrews at nine a.m. I will be arriving about ten."

"I will have a car waiting and the normal accommodations set up," the Admiral said. He pulled a pen from his desk and wrote down the times. "Is Sharon coming with you?'

"No," Lee said. "Just my two aides. We thought it be better if I were alone."

"You know what you need."

"We sent a press release out a few hours ago," the Senator said. "I don't see any reason that they cant be present at the funeral."

"I'll let my people know."

"See you in the morning, Donald." the phone disconnected. Tract opened his desk drawer and took out a bottle of aspirin.

*

The Velvet Club was well known in Pensacola, even though they never advertised. As the only openly gay bar in the small southern city, it was the subject of controversy. There was always some protest going on that placed the building on the local news. If it wasn't the religious right, then it was the neo-Nazis, or the Klan or some other outfit that wanted everyone to live in a free world, as long as they followed their specific point-of-view.

But what the protesters did not realize is that all the publicity had the opposite effect than they had intended. The clubs patrons came from all over to show their support, making the club one of the most popular and profitable in the area, which in turn allowed it's owners the money to fight the lawsuits. It was a never-ending battle.

But all the publicity and threats had one major advantage, at least as far as Litton was concerned. It had forced the management to scrutinize everyone who entered the club for security reasons. And the popularity ensured that there was always a long line waiting to get in.

The line moved slowly, giving Litton an opportunity to increase his knowledge of the customers, including photographs and detailed times and dates. The "Don't ask-don't tell" policy of the military did not make this information as valuable as it once was, but Litton still found that it had its uses.

His target of choice lately had been Ensign Davis. The young officer worked in base legal, and had access to all kinds of records. Litton had dropped hints that he knew the man's secret, but as yet he had not asked for any favors. So far, Davis had not acted on his impulses, but Litton knew that it was only a matter of time before he had some incriminating photographs.

As Litton watched his subject, he thought this might be the night. Davis had arrived with three other young men that the NIS agent did not recognize. He assumed they were military by their haircuts and freshly shaven faces, but who could tell?

The four men appeared to be drunk, and Davis had his arm around one of the men. All four were quite handsome, and it made Litton cringe at the thought of them together.

Litton aimed his camera at them and pressed the button, letting the auto-winder capture every moment. He shot film of all four men, just in case one of the others turned out to have a job that would interest the agent. He zoomed the lens in, but he could not get close enough to get the money shot. He would need to show lips on lips or some other incontrovertible proof. He placed the camera on his lap and unscrewed the lens.

He opened a case on the passenger floor when he heard a loud banging from behind. He looked in his rearview mirror and saw two young guys beating the trunk of his car with their fists.

"Hey, look at this pervert!" Litton's head snapped to the passenger side window. Willy was standing there laughing and banging a beer bottle on the glass.

"This faggot is taking pictures!" Willy said. He was drunk, as were the two other men with him. They joined him at the window. "Hey, faggot. Get your homo ass out of the car," one of them said to Litton.

"Get the fuck away from the car!" Litton yelled, trying to scare them off. But it didn't work. Willy kicked the door, and hit the bottle on the glass. It shattered into thousands of tiny fragments, startling the agent. Litton reached down and looked for the keys, but he was nervous and dropped them on the floor. When he leaned over to get them, he felt someone grab the back of his head.

"Hey, look! He must be used to this position," one of them said. He started violently shaking Litton's head up and down, each time causing his forehead to hit the parking brake handle in the center console.

But the pop of the window glass had drawn the attention of the Velvet's patrons waiting in line. They notified the club's security who called the police. The Velvet could not afford any violence. Davis and his friends started walking over to tell Willy and the others that the police were on the way.

Willy saw Davis and the others and tossed a beer bottle at them. They ducked out of the way. "Hey, you three better get the hell out of here, the cops are on the way."

"Hey, fuck you and the cops," Willy said and started laughing. Then the one who held Litton let the agent go and stepped away from the car toward Davis. "You want a piece of me, faggot?" He yelled. "You think I'm cute?!" Willy and the other kid started to laugh.

"Yeah, you want to do me," Willy yelled. Just then a police cruiser turned the corner and turned on his spotlight, shining it on Willy and the others.

"You have five seconds to clear the area," the officer said over a loudspeaker. Willy and the others stood for a moment of defiance, then turned and walked up the street. The cruiser slowly followed until they turned the corner.

Davis, meanwhile, had walked up to the car. Litton was leaning over into the passenger seat, puking. The ensign did not recognize him until he reached in and lifted Litton up.

"Litton?" Davis said, surprised. The agent had a large knot on his head, and a cut below his eye. A combination of vomit and drool ran from his mouth down his shirt and pooled on his lap. He looked over at Davis. "Get the fuck out of here!"

One of Davis's friends handed him a red bandana, and Davis leaned into the car to wipe Litton's face.

"Get that fucking AIDS blanket away from me," he yelled and pushed Davis arm back.

"I'm trying to help."

"I don't want you help," Litton said as he wiped his chin with his hand."I just need my keys."

"Where are they?" Davis asked.

"Down there," Litton said pointing to the passenger side. He leaned back and closed his eyes as Davis opened the side door and looked on the floor.

"Where, I can't see them with all this shit," Davis said. "What the hell were you doing here..." his voice dropped off as he found the notebook. He saw the last entry : *Ensign Davis, 3 others. Camera roll 159, photos 6-15 . Velvet Club 9 pm.* Davis then noticed the cameras and zoom lenses. "You son of a bitch!"

Litton smiled through the pain in his head. "Yeah, I know. I know it all, Davis."

The Ensign reached down and grabbed the camera. He opened the back and pulled out the film, exposing it. He looked on the cartridge. The number 159 was written on it.

"You can't find them all, Ensign."

"Damn you!" Davis said, and threw the camera at Litton. "Find your own keys!"

8

***

Tuesday, June 16

"Are we mailing *all* this stuff?" Nick asked.

"Why?" asked Rolo.

"Because I think we need more tape," Nick said. Rolo looked over at the various boxes scattered about Lee and Lorner's room. They were all overstuffed with Lee's things. Lt. Jackson had asked that everything be packed before Lee's father arrived in the morning.

"I'll go to the duty office," Lorner said, "And see if they have any." After he left the room, Daley closed the door.

"I think he's taking it pretty well," Daley said. "Thanks for helping out, you guys."

"Sure," Rolo said as he placed Lee's uniforms in a box. "I mean, he was our friend, too."

"Yeah, well I heard Lorn crying last night, but I didn't want to say anything."

"No problem, D." Nick replied, "We got it covered. Rolo and I are looking after him, too."

"We just need to keep Willy out of sight for a while, D." That they all agreed on. Daley used the last of the tape sealing a large box full of shoes, jackets, and winter clothing. He lifted it from the bed and stacked it against the wall before grabbing another empty box. Lorner came back in with another roll of packing tape and handed it to Daley.

"Hey Lorn," Nick asked, "if Lee's dad is coming, then why are they mailing this stuff?"

"'Cause his dad lives in Washington," Lorner said. "But this is going to their house in North Carolina."

"His family is pretty rich, huh?" Rolo asked.

"Not next to Lorner's," Daley said, embarrassing his friend. Lorner hated that people knew his family was wealthy. Almost as much as Lee had.

"Lee's father is a Senator," Lorner said. "Before that, he was a Navy pilot. Lee told me he flew with Admiral Tract back when."

"No shit?" Rolo asked. "Must be nice. My mom and I never even owned a house, just lived in apartments." He couldn't comprehend the life that Lorner and Lee had.

"Your lucky," Lorner replied. "I'd give anything to have my mom back. I'd live in a tent."

"Sorry," Rolo said. "I forgot."

"It's okay," Lorner said. "At least I have my dad."

They continued to pack as Lorner told them about their friend. Lee's father never gave a damn about his son--never saw him or contacted him. He had told Lorner that his father thought Lee wasn't his son, because he had been two months premature. His father had only been back from overseas seven months when Lee was born, and would not accept what the doctor's said. He constantly accused his wife of cheating on him, though he would never leave her. She was the daughter of an admiral, and he came from nowhere, just poor white trash, so his wife was his ticket to the big leagues.

When Lee's father left the Navy, and jumped into politics, he still needed his father-in-law's influence. But that changed when Lee was seven, about ten years ago, when the Admiral died.

"No shit," Rolo repeated. "This kid's life was like a fucking soap opera."

"Oh yeah, but it get's better," Lorner said. Lee's father had his own contacts by then, so he didn't need his wife. Lee had told Lorner that was when the affairs began. The Senator even brought them home for dinner, which showed he could care less about his wife. But she had no other family and wouldn't divorce or leave him. Besides, his father said she was a good homemaker and hostess.

"Damn," Nick said. "I'm glad I'm from a middle class home and don't have to deal with all that crap."

"No kidding," Daley added. "I guess he was a lot tougher than

I gave him credit for."

"I can see why Lee joined the Navy," Rolo said, "I'd want to escape from that, too."

"Escape from what?" asked a familiar voice from the other room. Willy strolled in, holding a beer, as usual.

"Nothing," Lorner said. "Get out of my room."

Willy looked at him and belched. "Who was talking to you, terd?"

"I'd watch it Willy," Nick said. "He knocked your ass out the other night." The others laughed. Willy did not like being the butt of jokes and gave them all the finger.

"Ha, Ha." Willy replied. "I'd like to see him try it now."

"I don't like to repeat myself," Lorner said with a little more confidence than normal. Willy ignored the comment and remembered why he was there. "Since class was canceled, I was wondering if you guys wanted to go to the beach."

"Where's the other two stooges you hang out with?" Daley asked.

"They got popped on a piss test, so they're restricted to base or some shit," Willy said.

"Your number didn't come up?" Lorner added.

"I don't do that shit, butt-munch," Willy held up a beer. "This is the only mind-altering substance I use."

"Give us about twenty minutes, and we'll go." Daley said. Willy nodded and sat down. He saw the boxes stacked against the wall, and watched the others packing boxes. "What are you doing?"

"Packing Lee's stuff," Nick said.

"Man, he had a whole bunch of shit," Willy said, and picked up a baseball mitt. Lorner reached over and grabbed it from him. "Relax, Cujo, I wasn't gonna steal it?"

"Don't touch anything." Lorner said. Willy shrugged, took a swig of beer, and relaxed. Daley opened a drawer in Lee's desk and carefully removed stacks of papers and photographs that had been jammed into it. He opened the drawer below it and inside were small bundles of envelopes, most of which were addressed to Lee. Below them were some magazines and videotapes.

"Lorn," Daley asked. "Did Lee have a girlfriend?"

"Yeah, back home."

Daley threw the unlabeled videotapes to Nick, who was sitting near Lorner's own television and VCR. Nick was caught off guard, but managed to catch most of them, though some fell to the floor.

"What am I supposed to do with these?" he asked.

"Watch 'em," Daley told him. "They don't have any labels, who knows what the kid taped. We wouldn't want his grandmother to expect to see a movie of him and have Debbie Does Dallas pop up."

It made sense to Nick, so he reached up and turned on the television. As he fiddled with the VCR, Daley tossed stacks of letters and photographs to the others. "We might as well read these, too."

"Are you sure?" Lorner asked. "I mean, some of this stuff is private."

"What does Lee care, he's dead," Willy said reaching into a cigar box full of photographs.

"Shut up!"

"Willy's right, Lorn," Daley said. "I'm sure we all have stuff we'd rather not have our girlfriends or parents see."

"No shit," Rolo added. "If my mother ever saw some of the pictures I took when I was at spring break, she'd have a freaking conniption."

Daley handed Lorner an opened letter. "We're just doing this to keep his memory clean."

"What are we supposed to be looking for anyway?" Willy asked as he looked at each picture from the box, then neatly stacked it on the nightstand next to the bed he was sitting on.

"Anything that could piss someone off."

The five of them began reading each and every item in front of them. Although they did not know it, they had embarked on a long military tradition of honoring a comrade's memory. They all took it seriously, even Willy; which had surprised the others. As each completed a stack of letters, Daley would take it and place it neatly in a box, just as if it had never been touched. He would then give them a new stack.

"Most of these are to his dad," Nick said as he examined a stack of envelopes. They had been bundled by a string which he had removed. "I don't think they've been mailed."

"What do they say?" Lorner asked.

"I don't know, they're still sealed." Nick held up one of the envelopes to show the others. It was not even stamped, just addressed. "Should I open it?"

Daley took the envelope from him and checked the seal with his finger. He looked over and saw that Nick held probably ten more just like it. "What do you guys think."

"Open it."

"I say open."

"Me, too."

"I agree," Daily said. "Lorn?"

"I don't care," he answered. "But isn't opening someone's mail a federal crime." Daley thought about it for a minute. He told the others that, at least he thought, if there was something disturbing, it would probably be in a bunch of letters that Lee hadn't mailed. Or why else wouldn't he have mailed them. Even Lorner agreed with his logic, he just didn't know if this was going too far. He didn't want them all to end up in trouble.

"This isn't mail yet," Daley said after a few minutes. He held up the envelope and pointed to the empty left corner. "No stamp."

"Yeah," Nick agreed. "They could all be Christmas cards or something!"

"Christmas cards?" Rolo threw a pillow at him. "How does your mind work?"

"No, Nick has a point," Lorner said. He agreed that they should be opened.

Enclosed with the first letter was a photograph of Lee in a Naval Reserve Officer Training Corps uniform. "What's this?" Nick said. He unfolded the letter and began to read silently.

The others passed the photograph around, then asked Nick what the letter said.

"It's to his mom," Nick said. "Basically, he just talks about how he likes UCF-whatever that is..."

"The University of Central Florida," Lorner cut in. "It's where Lee went to college."

"Yeah, that's what he talks about mostly." Nick continued. "It says he joined N.R.O.T.C., like he promised his father. That explains the picture. Let's see." he scanned the paper. "Oh, and that he likes Orlando a lot better than North Carolina... yadda, yadda, yadda. That's it."

"I wonder why he never sent it," Willy said. "It doesn't seem too bad to me."

"What's the date?" Lorner asked.

Nick looked. "It doesn't have one."

"He probably didn't send it," Lorner said, "because his mother died during his freshman year. Maybe he thought there would be time to send them." Nick picked up the envelope and read the address. "But this one look like he was going to send it to his dad?"

"Who knows," Daley said. "Open the next one." Nick took another envelope from the pile. He opened and read it. "Just a standard letter home to his mother," Nick said. "Nothing important. It said he was taking flight lessons at some airport so that he would know how to fly, giving him an edge in flight school. He's met some friends. That's it. He seems pretty happy."

Willy looked at his watch while Nick read. When his friend had finished reading, Willy let out a loud, exaggerated yawn."I've had about all the excitement I can take for one day." He scooted off the bed and stretched his arms. "There's nothing interesting here, I'm going to the beach. Anyone else coming." They all said no, and after some teasing, Willy left.

The four sailors went through the other letters one by one. They all had the same upbeat tone, though it seemed strange that the letters were addressed only to Lee's mother, while the envelopes were addressed to his father. Nick picked up the last one, and opened it.

"This is different," he said after reading it. "It's a letter to his father, listen up..." Nick read the letter out loud.

"I think we should hold on to these for a while," Daley said. "Let's get the rest of this stuff packed and over to the school."

"Is that legal?" Lorner asked.

"I don't know, but I don't think we should just hand them over to Lee's father," Nick said. "This is way above our pay grade."

*

Litton had not showed up at seven, and Laura had been waiting all morning for him to arrive. It was close to lunch time and she thought she would check one more time. She strode down the hall towards his office. It wasn't really a hall, just a clear aisle between cubicles, most of which were empty. Most of the agents were out in the field, which was where Laura thought she should have been. Instead, she had sat around the office not getting much of anything done. She strode quickly down toward Litton's office. As the senior agent of the division, he had a private office at the far end of the building. It was enclosed by soundproof glass partitions, of which the top was visible over the cubicle walls from where Laura was walking.

When she could finally see into his office, she saw his little fat face and round body behind the grey steel desk. The phone was to his ear, his feet were up on the desk, and a lit cigar stuck from his mouth. She noticed a bandage on his forehead, and his eye had an ugly purple and black bruise around it. The smoke was thick in his office, and the odor caused Laura's nose to wrinkle as she tapped on the glass. When he looked up, she pointed to her watch, but he turned away. She hated going in his office, but she hated being ignored even more. She went to his door and pulled on the handle. It was locked. "Damn." she said, growing more impatient.

She went to the window again, and saw as Litton hung up the phone and grabbed his sport coat. She met him at the door, but he all but pushed her aside.

"I'm late," he said.

She ran to catch up, grabbing her purse they passed by her cubicle. "What happened to your face?"

"Don't worry about it," he said huffing as they walked outside and into the sunshine. "I fell." He hurried over to the car. He opened it and jumped in behind the wheel. She ran to the other side, unlocking the door herself. She had just opened the door, when Litton threw the gear into reverse and started to back out.

"Hey!" she yelled as the door almost knocked her down. He hit the break.

"Get in the goddamn car, already!" he said. She jumped inside. He did not wait for her to close the door as he sped out of the parking lot.

"Where are we going?" she asked as she buckled her seatbelt, after closing the door.

"Can you go into my briefcase and find that tape recorder," he said, ignoring her question and searching the pockets of his coat. "I need you to put in...Dammit, I left them on my desk!"

"What?"

"New batteries for the tape recorder," Litton said. "Shit!" He thought about going back, but he was already late.

*

Rick was still wearing his khaki shorts and blue T-shirt with the small RSS insignia and the word *instructor* on his left breast. It was the uniform of the day when he was with his class. But today he had no classes. Lt. Jackson had phoned just as he was leaving and told him about the decision. It was just as well for Rick. He had not told Jackson about the down chit yet, he was hoping that he could get the doctor to change his mind. He had already called the base clinic, but they said Craft wasn't due in for another two hours.

He flipped through the channels looking for something to take his mind off his situation. He stopped on the local TV news. Same old shit. Some trade agreements, some congressional hearing, some country in turmoil. People shot, floods, and so on and so on. His problem should seem small in comparison, but it didn't. Not to Rick. His stomach growled, and he looked up at the clock on the wall.

With the door propped open, Rick stood and stared into the refrigerator. A two week old gallon of milk, a half loaf of bread, an uncovered bowl of creamed corn that was turning brown was all he saw. He wasn't hungry, but he just did not know what to do with himself. He closed the door and grabbed a glass from the pile of dirty dishes in the sink. After washing it, he filled it with ice and water and went into the small living room of his one bedroom apartment. He went out onto the small balcony and looked down at the parking lot.

It was still early as he watched the strangers that lived all around him come outside, get in their cars and leave for work. He used to pity the poor fools in the world who went in every day to a place that had no excitement, no danger, no rush. Why would anyone settle for a job that was the same day in and day out? But today he would give anything to be one of those people.

Actually, he wished he at least knew some of the people he saw. Rick had no one to talk to, nowhere to go, nothing to do. Rick thought about what Lt. Jackson said when he had called earlier --don't come in, and don't talk about this to anyone, especially anyone in the command. Harding's orders. They were trying to keep this as quiet as possible.

Rick understood, the military didn't need any more black eyes. Between Tailhook, those Army Rangers dying in the swamps, and all the sexual harassment charges, it appeared that all discipline in the military was breaking down.

Rick couldn't sit still. He picked up the phone but with no family, no woman in his life, he had no one to call. He placed the receiver back down. Looking around the apartment, Rick figured he needed to do something to take his mind off of this damn situation he was in. Something productive. He went into the bedroom and grabbed the laundry basket.

*

Litton parked the car in handicapped parking. It was the only open space near the massive brick and marble U.S. Navy Schools Command building. He jumped out and quickly crossed the manicured lawn with Laura in tow. They walked in front of a 1970's vintage F-4 Phantom fighter plane that had been turned into a multi-million dollar lawn ornament after a twenty year life as the navy's premier fighter. The plane was painted up with the Schools Command insignia, and on the side of the fuselage, below where the pilot sat, the name *Rear Admiral Donald W. Tract, USN* was painted in black, block letters.

They climbed the steps and entered the lower level of the building. Once inside, Litton just about ran down the hall. They passed the administrative and support offices, and continued until they were at the wing containing the flag offices. This was where the various admirals and their staffs worked. The floor was carpeted, and the hall was paneled with wood, instead of the standard gray painted plaster like the rest of the building. The doorways had wooden headers, and Laura thought it felt more like an upscale law office than a military headquarters. The doors had names engraved in brass, and she could tell the offices were much bigger, because there were fewer doors leading out into the hallway.

She had never been here, but Litton seemed to know just where to go.

*

There were no other customers at Suds & Soap, the combination pub and twenty-four hour laundromat where Rick stood separating his clothes. He usually just threw everything in together-whites, colors, whatever. But he was drawing this out as long as he could. The attendant sat over near the door, behind a scarred wooden counter top. He was reading the local paper which he held up in front of him, but his eyes occasionally wondered around the edges towards Rick.

Finally, with all the clothes separated, and lying out in neat piles, Rick started going through the pockets. He pulled notes and change from a pair of jeans, a ten dollar bill and receipt for motor oil from a shirt he hadn't worn in a month, and dumped some sand from a pair of shorts he had worn at the beach. As he emptied the pockets, he threw the garments in the washing machine.

He had filled three machines, and was working on the fourth when he picked up his dress uniform bell bottoms he had worn the day before. They didn't need washing, in his opinion. He had only worn them for a few hours, but they were here. He reached into the pocket and felt something. He pulled out a small white card. It was Laura Wilson's business card. He had forgotten all about her giving it to him. He stuck it in his wallet and finished loading the machines. After they had started their cleaning cycle, Rick took a quarter from the pile of change he had, and took the card from his wallet.

*

After passing several offices, Litton stopped at a large oak door that had a brass plate affixed to it. A small brass bell hung from the wall next to the door. On the plate a single star was engraved, along with the same name as the aircraft outside, *Rear Admiral Donald William Tract, USN.*

Litton adjusted his coat, and brushed his hair with his hand before opening the door. He stepped inside and was immediately greeted by a large red-haired naval officer. The officer was about thirty years old, over six feet tall and muscular. His hair was close cut, and he looked more like a Marine drill sergeant than anything else. He wore the rank of Lt. Commander on the collar of his khaki uniform, and an aiguillette that denoted his assignment as the Rear Admiral's aide.

"Jack," the officer said. He did not shake hands. "What the fuck happened to your face?"

"Lt. Commander Hunt, I see you're still charming as ever," Litton said. Hunt nodded as his attention was drawn to Laura, who had followed her boss into the office.

"Who's your friend?" Hunt asked, as he eyed Laura.

"She's with me." the NIS agent said. "Agent Wilson, say hello to Lt. Commander Hunt." She smiled. Hunt gave her the once over. Laura felt like she was being inspected, and immediately decided that she did not like this man at all. He gave her chills, and it seemed that he could see right through her.

"This meeting was for you, only Jack," Hunt said. He turned and opened another door, which Laura presumed was Admiral Tract's actual office. She looked past Hunt, expecting to see a man who looked like he could be her grandfather. Instead, sitting behind a overly large mahogany desk, sat a handsome officer who, she guessed, could be no older than forty-five. She could tell by the gold on his shoulder boards that this was the Admiral, but she would never had guessed it if he was in civilian clothes.

She could also see a pair of legs jutting out from one of the large back chairs in the office. But legs were all she could see, because the angle of the chairs faced away from her and toward the Tract's desk.

She saw Tract stretch his neck to see around the chair. "What's the problem out there?" he called.

"Mr. Litton has a guest with him, Admiral," Hunt replied. Litton stepped around Hunt and into the Admiral's office.

"She's not a guest, Admiral," the agent said. "She's with NIS and she's working with me on the investigation."

"This meeting was only for you, Jack," Tract said, as he looked at the clock on the wall. "And you are already an hour late."

Litton turned and went out to the other office to where Laura was standing. "I didn't think this would be a problem," he said. "But evidently, it is."

"If this has to do with the investigation," Laura said and gestured toward Tract's office. "Then I should be in there."

Litton turned and looked at Hunt's expressionless face, then back at Laura.

"I'm already on Tract's shit list," Litton seemed nervous, and that was strange to Laura. "I will tell you everything that happens. I promise."

"Uh-huh," she said, not quite believing him. But, he was acting strange, too strange and she thought maybe he was on the level for a change. She grabbed his arm, "You tell me everything, okay."

"Fine, fine," he said and headed into the office. Hunt closed the door behind them.

"Great," Laura said to the empty reception area.

*

Rick looked up at the clock on the wall, then walked over to the attendant and asked him if he could leave his clothes. The attendant told him he would be charged the regular price for wash and fold service. Rick said, "Fine." He told the guy he would be back in a few hours, then went out to his truck. He was still dressed in his shorts, T-shirt and running shoes.

He headed over to the base hospital and asked to see Dr. Craft. A few minutes went by before Craft came out to the waiting area.

"I said a few days," the doctor replied.

"Listen, Doc. I feel fine."

The doctor took a long look at Rick. He asked him a few questions about sleep and appetite. "You seem okay, but I want to wait a little longer."

"Sir," Rick said. "I need an up chit to keep my class."

"I said a few days," Craft replied.

"Sir, I can accept the fact that somehow I probably screwed up," Rick said. "But I did the best I could and it was an accident."

"Petty Officer Cox, I never said it was your fault," the doctor replied. "In fact what you did had very little to do with that kid dying."

"I was there. I felt his body go limp," Rick said.

"Regardless. It doesn't matter. You just aggravated a condition that was there," the doctor explained. "He would be just as dead if he were sitting in the chow hall or on the beach. His heart gave out. I've practiced medicine for well over a decade, I know what I'm talking about."

"But the kid was only eighteen years old?'

"It was genetic, he was born with it. He should never have been in the water with you. Hell, he should never have been in the Navy. Whoever cleared him for the school killed him, not you."

"So I didn't have anything to do with it?"

"Well, yes and no," Craft said. "But I would not say that he died because of what you did. You had no reason, no way of knowing. Wait here a minute okay?" The doctor walked over to the sick call desk and took an up chit from the corpsman. He filled it out, and postdated it three days. He walked over and handed it to Rick. "Here," he said. "Now relax a few days and call me if you need anything."

"Thanks, Doc," Rick said, still wondering how a screw up like this could have happened. At least he better call those NIS people and let them know. He went out into the lobby and found a pay phone on the wall. He pulled out the card Laura had given him.

"I'm sorry," The NIS receptionist said. "But Agent Wilson is not in her office. Would you like to leave a message?"

"No thanks," Rick said. "I'll call her home.". Rick turned the card over and dialed after depositing another quarter. After three rings a machine answered asking him to leave a message.

"This is Rick..Cox. I spoke to you the other day, about the student who died. Anyway, please call me at home. I wanted to talk to you..." He left his number.

*

Inside the office, Litton took a seat across from Tract. He looked over, but did not recognize the man sitting in the other chair.

"I'm glad you could join us, Jack," Tract said. "This is Senator Robert Lanford Lee. I don't believe you two have met." Litton nodded to the Senator, who showed little reaction. "The Senator has a problem with the way you are handling this case."

"I'm sorry but..." Litton stopped speaking when Tract held up his hand.

"I wasn't done speaking, Jack," Tract said. "I think the Senator has some things he would like to talk with you about. I have a staff meeting I need to attend, but you gentlemen feel free to use my office as long as you like." Tract stood up and then left the room. That left Hunt, Senator Lee, and Litton. Hunt went over and sat down in the Admiral's chair behind the desk. "The Admiral wants to give you his support, Jack. He really does. We all like to see others move ahead in life. But you need to give us your support."

"How exactly do I do that?" Litton replied, skeptical of where the conversation was heading.

" I think you know who killed my son," Senator Lee replied. "I think it is fairly obvious."

"Oh yeah? Who's that?"

"An overzealous instructor," Hunt answered.

"How did you come to that conclusion," Litton asked. "Without any facts or even speaking to a witness."

"I reviewed your case file," Hunt said."It would not look good to draw this investigation out any more than it has to be, Jack. Not good for you, not good for the Command."

"How did you get a hold of my files?"

"It's in your computer," Senator Lee said. "You are on a network I have friends in your office in Washington. The same friends that can get you that promotion."

"I see," Litton said. He didn't like surprises, unless he was the one holding the cards.

"I do have a concern though," Hunt said. "This agent--Wilson--I can't find out much about her."

"Not much to tell- she's green. Been with NIS a few months."

"The Admiral would like this to be handled personally by you."

"So would I," the Senator added. "I don't need no woman looking into the affairs of my family."

"She's doing her job, Senator."

"Let her do it somewhere else," he replied. "You just nail that son-of-a- bitch who killed my son."

"What if he didn't do it?" Litton said.

"Hell, he admitted he held my boy under," Senator Lee said. "What the hell else do you need, boy? It sounds like he confessed to me!"

"I'm sure you can prove it was intentional," Hunt said. "I have confidence in your abilities. We both know it was the instructor. That's where I'd concentrate my efforts."

"You would, huh," Litton said. He did not like being told how to do his job.

"I most certainly would if I wanted that job in Washington and knew it would be handed to me."

"I understand you don't have many friends there, Mr. Litton?" The Senator asked. "It's nice to have friends."

"I could use a friend, Senator."

"I do all the time."

"So how do we handle this? I'm open to your ideas..."

*

Laura walked out the main entrance and across the grass. She was frustrated. What the hell was she supposed to do for the next God knows how long while the "Good Ole' Boys" talked about the case she was working on. She shook her head in disgust. This was bullshit, and everyone knew it. She should be there. Besides, she knew that Litton would not tell her everything that was said. Probably not even half of it.

She looked across the street and saw the Aircrew School building. She decided if Litton wanted to investigate without her, she would do her own detective work.

*

Rick was standing at the start of the obstacle course. No one else was around, and the rain from the night before had erased any footprints in the ankle deep sand of the "O" course. It was fresh and new. With a stop watch in his hand, Rick was tensed. Focusing his concentration, he leaned into his stance and drew a breath. He let it out, then drew another. He was ready. His finger clicked the start button of the timer as he exploded toward the first obstacle. His breathing was hard, rhythmic. He hit the six foot fence, and went over easily. His adrenaline pumping, he approached the twelve-foot wall and grabbed the rope. As he climbed, he saw Robert Lee's face. Underwater, the air releasing from his mouth, the eyes rolling back. Rick reached the top of the wall and flipped over, landing in the sand.

With his calves burning, he ran toward the next obstacle and saw the faces of the two pilots he had recovered. Only now they were alive and screaming for him. Rick ran across the balance beam made of logs as he heard the men screaming in his head.

Through the tires he ran, as he saw the two pilots sink under. Across the monkey bars Rick watched Lee struggle, surrounded by other instructors. He reached out to save him, but suddenly the face was that of his older brother, but Tim was just inches too far. He reached out with both hands trying to save his brother's life. Reaching. Reaching. Watching as his brother said goodbye and closed his eyes.

Rick's outstretched arm, sweat soaked sand stuck to the skin, crossed the finish line, stop watch in hand. His body was airborne as he dove. Rick slammed into the sand, landing on his shoulder shooting pain through his body. The second hand on the watch is still at 4:08. His chest was still heaving, trying to pull in oxygen as he lay between two wood poles. Eight feet above him a wooden board, chipped and weather-beaten connected them. The plywood board was covered with coat upon coat of dark blue paint. Numbers and letters painted in gold formed a chart of various events and notable times covered the side facing the RSS building. Along the bottom of the chart, in large, intimidating letters was written: COURSE RECORD 4:17.

But Rick didn't look at the sign or at the stopwatch. He slowly climbed to his feet, his breath still labored. He did not wipe the sand off, but held his shoulder, and slowly walked over to one of the large steel light poles just off the sand. He stood next to it, then violently slammed his shoulder into the pole, while he let out a scream as flesh and metal contacted. The separated shoulder slipped back in place. Rick took the watch and threw it at the sea, then fell to the pavement. The sound of his scream still echoed off the surrounding buildings.

Laura heard the scream as she walked out of the Aircrew Administration Building, but could not tell where it came from. After listening for a moment, and hearing nothing else, she headed back to meet with Litton. It had been three hours, and she hoped he was done.

*

"Times-Press news desk."

"I was wondering if you realized a sailor was killed during training at the Naval Air Station?"

"Who is this?"

"Don't worry about who this is. Do you have a pen?"

"Hold on!"

*

As Laura crossed the road, she saw her boss standing near the car. She whistled, and he turned and saw her. He walked over, meeting her halfway.

"Where the hell have you been?" Litton asked.

"Been waiting long?" she asked, sounding genuinely concerned. Litton didn't answer, but looked down at the stack of copies she was holding in several manila files.

"What's that?" he asked, reaching. She turned away, just out of his reach.

"You first," she said. He reached again. She avoided him again. "I said, you first."

Realizing she was going to get her way, Litton replied, "Nothing much. Just met the kid's father. He wanted to know what was happening. Nothing new."

Laura looked at him disbelieving. "And I wasn't allowed to witness that? You've got to be kidding."

"His father was concerned with how the investigation was going, had we charged anyone yet with the boy's murder."

"Charged anyone?" She replied. "We don't even know if there was a crime. And besides, since when do we answer to someone's parents about how we conduct investigations? "

"Since the kid's father is a U.S. Senator," Litton replied. "And his grandfather was a highly respected Admiral."

"I see," Laura said. "So that's why you are pushing so hard? This is some political bullshit, that's what you were explaining to me."

"Now, listen..." Litton started to say.

"No," Laura interrupted. "You listen, Litton. I'm not playing politics. If there is a crime here, then we'll find out and make an arrest. But I'm not going to rush this because of who the victim's relatives are."

She didn't wait for him to say anything, but headed over to the car. She unlocked the driver's door and got in. Litton followed. They said not a word between them for the ride back, and her outburst had made Litton forget about the files she had with her. As soon as they returned to the office, Laura went right to her car and headed home.

She checked the machine and heard Rick's message. She tried to call, but there was no answer. After a shower, and a quick dinner, she went into the bedroom of her beachfront condo. She slid open the drapes of the sliding glass door and watched the colors of the sunset as she spread the files out on her bed and began to read.

9

***

Wednesday, June 17

It was still dark when Rick walked out to his truck the next morning. His shoulder ached, and there was a large bruise where he had slammed the pole. His arm hurt when he moved it, as did his ribs from hitting the sand. He was so stupid yesterday. He knew better than to get hurt, but at least the pain kept his mind from his other problems.

Rick slowly climbed into the truck, and started the engine. He pushed in the clutch, and groaned as he moved his arm to shift gears. He should have gone to sick call at the base hospital yesterday, but he didn't think he had hurt himself that bad. This morning he would go, as soon as the meeting with Lt. Jackson was over.

Rick reached over and turned on the radio. Jimmy Buffet filtered out the traffic as he turned up the volume. The sun started peaking over the horizon, and the sky was turning red, reminding Rick of a childhood rhyme.

"Red at night, sailor's delight;
Red in morning, sailor take warning."

"No matter what color the sky is," he said to himself. "You'd better watch yourself."

The pickup truck pulled up to the gate. It was six o'clock in the morning, but there was already a line of cars waiting to drive on to the base. The gate guards saluted or waved through each car individually, and everyone patiently waited as they drove through the rows of orange cones that divided the lanes of traffic. Finally it was Rick's turn and he was waved passed by the civilian gate guard.

As he pulled through, the music on the radio stopped and Kim Christen, the station morning news reader came on the air. After some ribbing by the disc jockeys, she started with the weather, then traffic, and then moved on to the national headlines. Rick turned down the radio and started singing Buffet to himself as the news reporter talked about the recent Midwest floods. He was still singing as she began talking about some local news.

"...According to the Times-Press, a new development has surfaced in the death of the U.S. Senator Robert Lee's son during training a few days ago." Rick stopped singing and turned the volume back up. "Sources close to the investigation say that they are looking into criminal charges against some of the instructors at the Navy's Rescue Swimmer School, where the sailor was in training."

"What the hell?" Rick said to himself out loud. "What instructors?" He pulled over to the shoulder and stopped as he listened.

"Sources said that at least one instructor had admitted to the intentional drowning of the eighteen-year-old, but no other information has been released, and no arrests have been made. Although a spokesman for the Senator has told us that Senator Lee has no comment at this time, he did say a statement would be forthcoming in the next few days. Senator Lee is the Chairman of Appropriations Committee in the Senate."

Rick sat behind the wheel while the reporter continued with other news, but he didn't hear a word she said. The only thought he had was of Litton and how the NIS had assured him that it was just a normal investigation. When had the NIS known about Lee's father? When had Harding? Rick had been in the military too long to believe that the death of a politician's son would be treated in the same fashion as any other investigation.

The car horn blared behind him, shaking the instructor from his thoughts. Rick checked the rear view mirror and saw Giles' car, with his friend waving. Rick put the truck in gear and pulled out into traffic.

*

Watson and the rest of RSS staff were already in the duty office when Rick and Giles entered. Except for the instructor on duty, they were all wearing shorts and SAR school T-shirts, and feeding off a box of donuts and pastries that someone had brought and left on the table. It was a typical morning muster with the standard horseplay, jokes, and stories of what everyone had done the night before. Most of the men had been questioned by the NIS, and that was the conversation de jour this morning. Especially comments about Agent Laura Wilson.

"And those legs," Giles said. "She could interrogate me anytime!"

"I wouldn't mind a strip search!"

"I think she was hot for me!"

"Get out of here!" Giles said, as the others laughed. Rick ignored the conversation and went right over to the morning paper. He opened it and searched the headlines.

"Did you guys hear the news this morning?" Rick asked still looking. The somber tone of his question quieted the others. None of them had.

"Why?" Watson asked.

Rick did not answer right away but continued flipping pages, until he had double checked both the national and local sections. He placed the paper back down on the table.

"What did they ask you guys?"

"Shit," Giles answered, "Lots of stuff, why?"

Rick rubbed his chin, and a worried look took hold of him. "I just heard they were looking into criminal charges against some instructors who confessed." He let the last word come out slowly as if it had soured in his mouth. The look on the others told him they all had reason to worry.

"Hey, I didn't confess to shit," Watson replied.

"I just told them what happened," said one of the others.

"I wasn't there!"

The denials came from them all until the room was silent. The mood of the room had changed one hundred-eighty degrees, as they all looked at each other, searching for an answer.

"This is like survival school," Giles said. "Remember in SERE school when they took everyone in for interrogation, and they would try to screw with your mind saying that everyone else said this and that, so we might as well tell them, too." Giles looked at the others and saw agreement. "This is just a bunch of bullshit because there's nothing to confess, because it was an accident, right?"

Rick and Watson both quietly nodded. "See," Giles continued. "This is just some bullshit because of the kid's dad."

"You know who his dad is?" Rick asked. Most of them nodded.

"How do you think he got into Aircrew School," Watson said. "He had a problem with his security or medical clearance or something, but a few calls from dear old dad and-Boom!-everything cleared right up!"

"Yeah," Giles said looking at Rick, "I thought you knew. I was on duty-this was when you were on leave because of that ejection thing and I had to walk him through. Master Chief Russo didn't want anymore problems. But his med record was missing."

"Are you saying he checked in here without any medical records?" Rick asked. "How?"

"I told Jackson and he said he would handle it. I never heard anything back so I figured everything was fine."

"But he had them," Rick said. "That doctor was holding them in his hands. He was looking at them."

"I'm just telling you what I know."

Rick rubbed both his eyes. He had suddenly developed a massive headache and it felt like his stomach was slowly tying itself in knots. Giles watched as the color drained from his friend's face.

"Are you okay?" Giles asked. "You look like you're about to pass out." Giles motioned for Watson to get up from the chair he was sitting in, and Rick sat down.

"I'm fine." Rick said. He looked up into the others concerned faces. "I just don't like what's going on. I'm getting a very bad feeling."

"About what?"

"This whole thing with the NIS. It's the same feeling I got yesterday when they read me my rights it's just..."

Giles interrupted, "They read you your rights? When?"

"Yesterday- When they questioned me." The others looked at each other. "Why? Didn't they do that with you guys?"

They all shook their heads no. Now he really felt sick. "I think I'm gonna head over to sick call."

"Do you need a ride?"

"No, just tell Jackson I went over.."

"That's Lieutenant Jackson, Cox," Jackson said as he entered the room. He was in his khaki work uniform. He came in and grabbed a donut. He was almost one of the guys, a rare thing for many officers, especially junior officers. When he saw their worried looks and noticed no one talking, he wondered what was up.

"What's with the faces?" Jackson asked them. No one spoke up.

"Okay guys, what's going on? I know that a student's death is a wake up call to everyone, I certainly don't like it, but it was an accident." The instructors looked at each other. So even the officers are saying it's an accident.

"Did you hear the radio this morning, sir?" Watson asked.

"No, should I have?"

"Supposedly the Navy says the kid was murdered and one of us," he spread his arms, "has *confessed to the killing*."

"Yeah, right," Jackson said. Then he looked around and saw that this wasn't a sick joke, and that the men, his men, believed this. "You guys are professionals. We all know that's bullshit. Don't worry-no one thinks any of you are murderers. Believe me." But he could see that they weren't buying it.

"But what if..." one of the instructors began to ask.

Jackson took a breath, then shook his head. "LOOK, GUYS! IT WAS AN ACCIDENT!" The outburst caught his men by surprise. Looking around, Jackson was embarrassed by his show of emotion. "I'm sorry for yelling. I didn't get much sleep either," he said and unlocked the door to his office.

He disappeared inside, placing his briefcase on his desk before walking back out to where the instructors were standing. "They canceled classes for the next few days, so you guys can knock off early unless you have duty. But hang around a while, some NIS people are coming over to talk to you all."

Rick stood and walked toward the bathroom. "Where are you going, Cox?"

"Just making a head-call, sir."

"Come on back, sailor," Jackson said. "That is one of the things that the NIS wants from us this morning."

"Are you serious?"

"You got it. A little liquid sunshine for Uncle Sam."

"Well, I still need to take these," Rick said holding up a plastic amber prescription bottle. Jackson nodded and Rick went into the men's room or head as the Navy called it. He went to the sink and turned on the faucet. He placed his hands in the cool water and splashed some onto his face, it felt good. He wiped the water off with a paper towel, then poured two pills from the bottle and swallowed them. He took a sip of water and walked back out to the others.

Outside the SAR School building Litton's car pulled up. The NIS agent stepped out. He moved to the rear of the car and opened the trunk. A second man, even shorter and more bald than Litton, and wearing a white lab coat over his suit reached into the trunk . He pulled two aluminum cases from the trunk, then followed the NIS agent inside the school.

Rick walked back in the room just as the door opened and the two men came in. "Good morning, Gentlemen," Litton said as he placed a case down on the floor. He walked over to the table and helped himself to a couple of donuts. He poured himself a cup of coffee and stood in the middle of the room feeling important. The man in the lab coat silently cleared off the duty desk and opened the other metal case.

Inside were fifty to sixty small plastic jars, all empty. They were neatly lined inside the case, each inside its own little pocket surrounded by Styrofoam so they would not spill or touch. Each had a little yellow lid and a blank label on it that had a number that matched the number on the label on the bottle. It was very sterile.

"I'm Special Agent Jack Litton with NIS, this is Mr. Ritter from NAMI." The Naval Aeronautical Medical Institute was familiar to everyone who flew in the U.S. Navy. It was *the* only medical opinion that counted for anyone on flight status. NAMI's determination as to whether someone was fit to fly or not was the first, last, and only word in the Navy. This was a relief to Rick, because he knew that there was no way for Litton to influence this test. Ritter picked up a small box and started to hand out pens and blank labels.

"Gentlemen," Ritter said when everyone had a container, "Please fill in your name, social security number and sign the card. We are taking a urinalysis today. If you need a drink, either Agent Litton or I will escort you down to the coke machine or water fountain. From here on out, no one leaves this room by themselves until I get a sample."

"I hope you all studied," Lt. Jackson replied.

"You too, Lieutenant," Ritter said and handed him a pen and label to the chagrin of his men.

"Why do we need an escort to get a drink?" Rick asked. "We never needed to do that before."

"You never had someone die before either, Petty Officer Cox." Litton replied. "People, this is not a joke. There is a young man dead." Litton looked over at Rick. "Some of you were there when it happened.

We at NIS want to ensure that there was no physiological reason for that death to have occurred. Let me ask now, all of you: Is there any of you who are using any substance--legal or Illegal? This is the time to come to Jesus! Comprende?"

Everyone stayed silent "Good, then this should not be a problem."

"If there are no questions, then let's get started," Ritter said. "Lt. Jackson, you first please." Jackson followed Ritter out into the hall toward the head.

The instructors each filled a cup with some coffee and started drinking. Giles and the others spoke quietly to each other, as Litton stood in the center of the room, trying like hell to make himself seem imposing. But these men were not easily impressed or intimidated. The agent pulled a cigar from his jacket and chewed the end, he placed it in his mouth and searched his pocket for a lighter.

"Hey, Litton," Rick said. "There's no smoking in here."

"Fine," he replied. "Then we will all go outside while I smoke." One of the other instructors walked up to him and stood in front of the much smaller man. They were so close that the cigar touched the instructor's chest as Litton clenched his teeth on the other end.

"I don't think so," the instructor said. "The regulations say there is no smoking in here. Period. And we follow regulations." Litton did not back away but held his ground.

"Don't fuck with me, sailor," he said then backed away. He took the cigar from his mouth and put in his pocket.

"Speaking of fucking with people," Cox replied. "Why was I the only one questioned who was read his rights?"

"And what is all this shit about some confession, Agent Litton?" Giles added. Litton looked at Cox, then at Giles.

"What confession?" Litton asked. He removed his sportcoat and placed it on a chair before grabbing another donut.

"That's what we want to know," Rick said. "What confession?"

"I don't know what you are talking about."

"Uh-huh," Cox replied. He didn't knew where the story came from, but he was now convinced that either Litton knew or said it himself. "It was on the radio."

"What the hell kind of investigator are you?" Watson asked. "It's been all over the news all morning."

Litton stopped sipping his coffee. "Unlike you gentleman, I

investigate facts before I make a statement. I don't worry about what the media says."

Jackson and Ritter entered the room. Ritter placed the partially filled container in the box and gave a slip of paper to the naval officer. "Who's next?"

"I'll go," Rick said.

"I'll take this one," Litton told Ritter. "You can get the next one."

Rick started walking down the hall. "You got a hard on for me, don't you, Litton?"

"Maybe I do."

"Well just promise you won't try to show it to me when we get in here," Rick said as he pushed open the door to the head.

Once inside, Rick walked over to the urinal and Litton handed him the plastic container. Rick filled it halfway and handed it back to the agent. He made sure to miss slightly.

Litton took the container and nearly dropped it as his hand slipped. "God damn you, Cox." He placed the cup down on the edge of the sink and washed his hands. "You did that on purpose!"

"Maybe now you know what it's like to feel pissed on, Mr. Litton." Rick washed his hands and walked out and down the hall with Litton close behind while trying to screw the cap on.

"I hope I'm not pregnant," Rick said when he walked back in the room.

"You better hope it's positive," Giles said."It's the only way anyone would marry your ugly ass."

"Where's Agent Litton," Ritter said as he cleared a space in the tray.

"Hey piss boy?" Rick called out as Litton entered the office. "There you are. C'mon, let me sign this so I can get out of here."

*

Laura Wilson was sitting at her desk looking through the transcripts of the meeting with Rick when her phone rang.

"Agent Wilson."

"Sorry, Laura." It was the receptionist. "But I have someone on the line from a Senator Lee's office? He said he was supposed to talk to Jack, but he isn't here. I think it's regarding that sailor who died. You are working on that, right?"

"Yeah, put it through. I'll talk to them." Laura hit the speaker phone button and went over to the file cabinet to get the forms to requisition the medical files of Airman Lee. Great, now, not only was she not allowed to sit in on meetings, she also had obviously become Litton's secretary taking messages.

"Hold on," the receptionist said. There were a series of clicks and then an unfamiliar voice came on the line.

"Jack, this is Jimmy at Senator Lee's office..." The man spoke so fast that Laura did not have time to respond. "The Senator wants to know about the test results and also he said to thank your for the info regarding that asshole's brother. If you dig up any more dirt, feel free to give me a ring. You have the number." Laura just sat there and looked at the phone. So that slime ball was responsible for the press reports.

"Hello?" the voice said. Laura did not make a sound, what would she say. "Hello?" the voice said again. "Is there anyone on the line?....That goddamn stupid receptionist can't even transfer a phone. Shit!" The phone went dead.

Laura quickly hung up and then dialed the receptionists extension.

"Hi," she said when it was answered. "This is Laura. That call hasn't come thru yet. Did you transfer it to me?"

The receptionist thought she had, she told her. But the phone system is so confusing anyway, maybe not.

"Don't worry about it," Laura told her. "If the person calls back, just send it to Litton's voice mail." Laura had somewhere else to go.

*

"Hey, Lieutenant," Rick said as he poked his head in Jackson's office. "Can I go now?" Jackson looked up from the stack of paperwork and waved for him to get out. Rick closed the door behind him, grabbed his bag, and headed out through the instructor's office.

"Where're you goin'?" Giles asked.

"Sick call."

"Petty Officer Cox," Litton yelled out after him. He followed Rick outside.

"What?" Rick said without slowing down. Litton pulled a cigar from his shirt pocket and stuck it in his mouth while trying to keep up.

"Why were the students singing the National Anthem?"

"Didn't we go over this before," Rick said still not slowing down.

"Tell me again," the agent said, tripping over the curb. He was getting winded.

"It's standard procedure," Rick replied speeding up his step. "It's normal!"

"Really," Litton said, coughing and out of breath. "Because I don't see it that way necessarily." Rick stopped and turned toward the agent. Litton noticed the instructor wasn't even sweating. Son of a bitch.

"And how do you see it, necessarily?"

"I think it's sick. It could be looked at as a way for someone to distract the other students from what was really going on."

"Oh yeah, and what was really going on?"

"You tell me," Litton replied, finally able to smile.

"You know what? You are a fucking psycho, you know that?" Rick replied as he swung his gym bag down off his shoulder and placed it on the ground between them. "How did someone like you get into a position of authority. That boy's death was a fucking accident, dipshit. Pure and simple. Take that goddamn Conspiracy Theory, Third Man, Area 57 on the grassy knoll head of yours and shove it up your ass!"

"You have a problem with authority, don't you?" Litton replied.

"No," Rick replied. "I just have a problem with you. Now, I am going to sick call because you make me so fucking sick to my stomach that I can't think." He leaned over and grabbed his bag. "If you have something to say, then say it. If not leave me alone."

"I think you killed him. I think you hated him because he wasn't the perfect macho bullshit intimidator that you are, and so you killed him, right there, with everyone looking."

"Think what you want," Rick said walking away. "I know it was an accident."

"One more thing."

Rick turned around and squared up on him. "What?"

"You wouldn't happen to have a lighter would ya," Litton said smiling with the cigar in his mouth. "Mine's in my coat."

Rick grabbed the cigar from his mouth and threw it down on the pavement, then crushed it with his boot heal. "I just saved your life, Agent Litton. Those things will kill you." And with that, he turned and started to jog over to base sick call. Even though he felt even worse now, it was better than speaking with that little troll Litton.

"Don't go anywhere!" Litton yelled at him.

Rick turned and ran backwards a few steps, "Where would I go? I'm in the Navy!"

Rick was sweating as he walked through the automated sliding glass doors of NAS Pensacola's infirmary. It was crowded as usual, and he grabbed a drink from the water fountain before walking over to the sign in desk. He waited in line and signed his name, turning over his military ID card to the corpsman sitting there. He was instructed to sit down and wait for his name to be called from the Records Department.

He looked around and realized that he was sitting in the same chair that he waited in the day Airman Lee died. After a moment of thinking about that, Rick stood up and moved to another seat. It was then that he spotted the familiar face walk by.

"Laura," he said loud enough for some other patients to turn and glare at him. Agent Wilson turned as well, and smiled as she walked over to Rick. She sat down next to him just as his name was called by a corpsman in records.

"Hold on, I'll be right back."

"Okay," she said. He ran over and signed out his medical records. She stood up as he returned over to her.

"How are you doing?" she asked.

"Okay, I guess," he replied. He held up his records. "My stomach has been aching a lot lately."

"That's understandable."

"What are you doing here?" Rick asked. "If I'm allowed to know"

"Oh sure," she nodded. "Just doing some research, nothing special."

"I just spent some quality time with your partner."

"Oh yeah? Where was he?"

"Over at the school. He just gave us a piss test..," Rick stuttered, "I mean a urinalysis with some guy Ritter from NAMI."

"How'd it go?" she laughing at his uneasiness. It was an embarrassing subject and she thought it cute the way that Rick was squirming around like a little kid.

"Uh, okay I guess." Rick told her. "I mean. I passed. So anyway...was Litton born an asshole or does he work real hard at it?"

She laughed, "I think its natural talent with a lot of practice."

Rick was feeling better, but didn't even notice. Laura had his full attention and he missed his name being called.

"Oh, by the way, since I have you here, do you have the name of that doctor? I was going to look it up in the transcripts, but...you could save me a lot of time."

Rick looked at her eyes, and tried real hard to think of why he should help her; after all, she and Litton were partners. But those eyes of her's were lethal, and he just couldn't say no. He pulled his wallet from his pocket and searched through it. "I know it's in here somewhere.".

He held out a stack of business cards and rifled through them a few times. "I don't have it with me...damn."

"That's okay. I'll dig it up somewhere," Laura said. "There has to be a record somewhere."

"Wait a minute!" Rick said. "I have his name right here!" He leaned his leg up on a chair and opened his medical record. He flipped through some pages. "Here it is-- Commander Craft, Benjamin Craft. USNR-Medical Corps." He held the file open as Laura copied the information.

"Why is his name in your medical record?"

"Because he gave me some pills to take," Rick replied.

"Maybe that's what is making you sick?" Laura asked as she finished copying the file notes. He closed the record.

"No," he said. "It's just some over-the-counter stuff."

"Then why did you need to see a doctor?"

"Because of these," he said pointing to the gold wings on his shirt. "I'm on flight status. Everyone who flies needs a flight surgeon's approval for any meds. I'd bet at least half our washouts at the school are because they are found medically unfit to fly."

"Can a student do anything about it?"

"Not really," Rick said. "You can't be on medication all the time. Altitude sickness or decompression, safety of flight for the FAA, being alert, whatever. They all become dangerous when other people's lives are at stake."

"So what do the students who can't make it physically do?"

"Some try to get waivers," he explained. "But that's rare anymore. I guess if you knew someone you could get by, but that's only until the next physical or until you get to another command. Then you'd be grounded anyway, so there's no point in fighting it. Most just get sent out to the fleet, scraping, painting, mopping and waxing." As he was talking a corpsman came out from a door across the room. "Cox! Last call!"

"That's me," Rick said. "Gotta run. It was nice speaking to you like a regular person, Laura."

"You too."

Rick walked over and handed the corpsman his record. The corpsman opened it up and scanned some pages, reading notes. "Sick call?" he asked.

"Yes, Aircrew, " Rick said.

"Back through this hallway, second door on your left for blood work."

As Rick disappeared down the hall, Laura walked over to the receptionist and asked where she could find the flight surgeon. The woman sent her down a maze through the hospital to the nurse's station. A lone nurse was sitting behind the large counter, along with two corpsman. Laura walked up to the counter and placed the files she was carrying on it. The nurse looked up and asked if she could help.

"I'm looking for Dr. Craft," Laura said. "I was told I could find him here."

"Sorry, but Dr. Craft is not available right now."

"Do you know where he is?"

"He's unavailable," the nurse said slowly. "Is there something I can help you with?"

Laura pulled her NIS identification out. "I really need to speak with Dr. Craft," she told her. The nurse examined her ID as Laura continued. "He was on duty here a few days ago, when that student swimmer was brought in."

"Hold on," the nurse said as she picked up a logbook and began paging through it. "Let me find out who was on duty."

"I know who was on duty," Laura said. "Dr. Craft."

"I am sure you are correct," the nurse said. "But let me just make sure. Okay-- let me get Lt. Spring up here to talk with you." She picked up the phone and dialed.

"I don't need a nurse," Laura said.

"I know, I'm gonna let you talk with Lt. Spring," the nurse told her, then waited for someone to answer the phone. "This is Joan, station twelve, I have..." the nurse looked at Laura.

"Agent Wilson," Laura said, handing her the NIS ID. "Naval

Investigative Service."

"I have an Agent Wilson to speak with Dr. Craft...Oh, he is...okay, hold on," The nurse turned to Laura. "She says he's been temporarily reassigned, and they don't know when he'll be back."

"Ask them where he went," Laura said. The nurse repeated the question, waited then turned to Laura.

"They don't know where," the nurse replied. "He went on convalescence leave yesterday, no one knows why."

"Okay, thanks," Laura said. "Which way to your Administration Department?"

*

Litton was in his office reading over Lee's hospital admission notes when a large manila envelope was delivered to him by the receptionist. He placed it on his desk and planned to go back to the notes when he noticed who it was from. He quickly opened it and withdrew the contents. Reaching into his back pocket, he pulled out his wallet and then retrieved a piece of paper. He grabbed the phone and dialed the number on the paper. It rang only once before being answered.

"I know I shouldn't have called," Litton said.

"Then why did you?"

"I just got the file," he said. "Where did you get this?"

"What's the difference? I had it. Now you do."

"Yeah, but Craft is gone?" Litton replied. "He signed this out."

"I know he's gone," Hunt replied. He placed his feet up on the Admiral's desk. Tract was off playing golf, and the Aide enjoyed the use of his boss's office.

"Are you insane?" Litton asked him. He picked up the file and slid it back into the envelope."People will start asking questions."

"I had no choice."

"Do you realize that I can't use anything from this record now?"

"Why not?"

"Because it was signed out by the guy," he replied. "If I say I had it, then people would assume I knew where Craft is, which I don't!"

"And you won't either," Hunt said twirling a pencil in his fingers. "No one will except me."

"I don't like it."

"It's not your decision. I saw no alternative after reading his admission notes," Hunt said. "Besides, he already knew too much about this before."

"I know."

"Is there anything else?" Hunt asked.

"Well," Litton replied. "Wilson's becoming a pain in the ass."

"How so?"

"I just have a gut feeling she knows more than she tells me," Litton said. "I think she has been talking to some of those idiots at that school."

"So tell her to stop talking," Hunt said. "Or just kick her off the case."

"I can't just kick her off. But I will think of something." Litton replied as he placed the file in a drawer. The metal filing cabinet had a combination lock on the front, and he spun the dial after closing the drawer.

"We can't have a loose cannon on this," Hunt said.

"That's what I'm afraid of," Litton said.

Hunt was getting tired of talking to him."Is that all?"

"What if they find Craft?"

"They won't, I told you." Hunt replied. "But if they do, he is working in a medical capacity on a nice little black project in the Caribbean that I would love to tell you about, but don't have the time. If there is nothing else?"

"Nothing."

"Good," Hunt said and disconnected the call.

*

Giles was sitting in the duty office when he heard the knock on the door. He put down his magazine and walked over. Outside, Daley and Nick were standing.

"Sorry to bother you," Daley said.

"What's up?" Giles asked as he walked back over to the duty desk. Daley and Nick followed inside.

"We got Lee's stuff packed," Nick told him.

"Where is it?"

"Out in the duty van," Daley replied and tossed a set of keys onto the desk. Giles picked them up and placed them on a nail in the wall behind him.

"I guess we should bring it in here," Giles said. "I'll give you guys a hand."

The three sailors went outside and over to the dingy, gray, Chrysler van. The doors were opened, and a stack of white bankers boxes filled the back of the van. They were filled with the dead student's personal affects. Giles held a clipboard with a list that Daley had prepared.

"Everything here?" Giles asked. Nick looked over at Daley before answering.

"We kept some letters and a diary we found."

"We thought we would go through them first," Nick said. "You know, make sure there's nothing that his girlfriend wouldn't want to see, shit like that."

Giles nodded and understood. "Just make sure they end up where they should." The others answered "No problem," and started unloading the van. They opened the boxes and showed their instructor the contents as he checked them off. When they were finished the boxes were stacked behind the truck. Giles signed the inventory sheet, as did Daley and Nick. "Who has the letters?"

"Lorner," Daley replied. "They were best friends."

"Okay, but I am holding you responsible for them," Giles told Daley. "Why don't you guys go bring the boxes in the office for the time being?" The instructor walked back to the RSS duty office leaving the two rescue swimmer students with the boxes.

*

Laura walked into Litton's office after coming back from the clinic empty-handed. Litton was listening to the tape of his interview with some of the witnesses to the events in the pool. The walkman was turned up loud and his eyes were closed so he jumped when Laura tapped him on the shoulder. He pulled the headphones off and threw the walkman down.

"What the hell are you doing!" he said startled.

"I came in to tell you that the doctor who examined that kid is gone." she said. "Disappeared. Even his records are gone."

"So?"

"So?!" She replied. "So he's gone which means we can't talk to him. Don't you think that's odd?"

"No," Litton said, mad that he underestimated her. He had told her not to go checking and she did anyway. The senior agent was not accustomed to people ignoring what he told them. But he was glad that

Hunt had beat her. "Agent Wilson, we don't need to speak to the doctor right now. If I determine that we do later, I will find him. Don't worry."

"What the hell kind of investigation is this?" she asked out of frustration. The moment the words left her mouth she regretted saying them. She waited for a Litton tirade about how he runs his investigations and who was she to question.

"I really need to listen to these," he said and put the headphones back on. For once she was happy he ignored her. She went back to her office and saw the time. It was too late to start anything else. She went to the ladies room and changed into her running clothes.

*

Giles and Daley sat in the air conditioned duty office as Nick walked in with the last of Lee's stuff. The boxes were stacked high in the corner, and Nick strained to lift the last one to place on top of the pile.

"Is that it?" Giles asked. Nick nodded as he pushed the box in place. Nick finished, wiped the sweat from his brow and collapsed into a nearby chair. "Thanks for the help, D."

"Petty Officer training," Daley said smiling. "Assign authority but not responsibility. The law of command in the military."

"Yeah right," Nick said. "Shut up and give me some change for a coke!" Giles reached into the small refrigerator near the desk and took out a can of soda.

"Hey!" Giles said and threw the can at Nick who barely had time to react. He fumbled with it for a moment, almost dropping it. "Nice catch," the instructor said.

"Thanks."

"No problem," Giles said. "You guys know the service for Lee is tomorrow, right?'

They both nodded. "We thought we'd go over as a class." Giles said he thought that would be a good idea. They sat around in silence for a couple minutes just relaxing before Nick belched loudly, causing all of them to laugh.

"Hey, Petty Officer Giles," Nick said as the laughter died down.

"Hey, what?"

"We've been hearing some rumors."

"Rumors?" Giles asked , the smile disappearing. "Rumors about what?"

"That Petty Officer Cox confessed to killing Lee," Nick said. "Murdered him. On purpose."

Giles became suddenly totally serious. "That's bullshit. Where'd you hear that from?"

"Willy said he heard it," Daley asked.

"Yeah, well, consider the source," Giles replied. "I'll have a talk with Airman Wilson. Lee's death was an accident. You both were there, so was I."

"But, Cox..."

"Petty Officer Cox," Giles said correcting Nick.

"*Petty Officer Cox* always seems like he hates us. Not just our class but all the students. He never talks to us like you or some of the other instructors. He always seems pissed off about something."

"Petty Officer Cox doesn't hate anyone," Giles said. "He just thinks that if he makes this course hard, it will make you a better SAR swimmer."

"But does he have to be...I don't know how else to say it...an asshole?"

"When we go through instructor training they tell us don't be a friend, be an instructor," Giles replied. "Some people can be both, some can't. Petty Officer Cox is a pretty good guy, but he is a hard ass. If after you leave here, you end up stationed with him, you'll find out what I mean. The guy would do anything for you."

"I guess I'll take your word for it," Nick said. "But I just wish he'd lighten up."

Daley looked at his watch, then stood up. "Chow hall opens soon."

"You guys go eat," Giles said. "I don't know when class resumes. But you should stay ready."

"We are," Nick said. "We've been practicing the 'O' course and swimming."

"Good." Giles said standing. "Now get out of here! That door says Instructor's Lounge!"

Giles was relieved by another instructor, and signed off duty a little while later. Walking out to his car, he saw Rick's truck pull into the base auto hobby shop across the concrete parking lot from the school. The hobby shop was a full service garage that the Navy provided on each base to give sailors a place to work on their cars. Giles laughed to himself. That old truck of Rick's seemed to have a permanent place there. Giles jumped in his car and drove over to where Rick was parked.

"Whatcha doin'?"

"Nothin' today," Rick said as he lifted some boxes out of the truck's bed. "Tomorrow I'm gonna pull the tranny and put a new seal in, and put new brakes on." Giles grabbed some smaller boxes from the bed and followed Rick inside. He went to the desk to make a reservation for a workbay, but was told the only bays available would be outside, without a lift. Rick reserved a jack and asked if he could store the parts there. When he was done, the two instructors walked outside.

"Want to go eat?"

"No," Rick said. "I thought I'd go run the fitness trail."

"Oh," Giles replied. He started to walk to his car, but turned around after a few steps and came back. "Hey, listen. I was talking with some of the students today..."

"Yeah?"

"Rick," Giles said. "I know you are a hardass-- and that's cool-- there's nothing wrong with that. But could you do me a favor?"

Rick looked at him with contempt as he pulled his gym bag from the cab of his truck. Giles was a good friend, probably his best friend, but the two were very different. "What is it?"

"Could you lighten up a bit?" Giles said. "Not in class, maybe. Just, like if you see some of these guys out of class. Just try to let them know you're human." He smiled. Rick looked over.

"Human?"

"Yeah, just a human being."

Rick turned and started walking back into the Hobby Shop. "I'll think about it," he said as he neared the building.

"That's all I ask," Giles said.

Rick held his arm up and flipped his middle finger at Giles. "C'mon, Rick. I mean it."

Rick changed his gesture to a wave goodbye as he kept walking away. "How's that? Is that enough for ya?"

An hour later, Rick finished running and was cooling down near the bay. The fitness trail was crowded this time of day, and Rick had scraped his arm while passing another runner. The tree branch had whipped back and drawn some blood. Rick was nursing the wound when he looked over at the obstacle course a few hundred yards away.

"Human," he said out loud to no one.

"How's it going?" Rick said as he walked over to the beginning of the obstacle course. Nick, Rolo, Willy, Lorner and Daley were resting near the water fountain. The late afternoon sun was starting its final descent on the horizon, but the air was still hot and humid enough for beads of sweat to form as the men stood there. They had seen Rick standing over near the seawall earlier, but all were surprised to see him come over to them.

"Who's got the best time?" Rick asked. Every student pointed at Daley, who was still bent over trying to regain his breath from his last attempt.

"A couple seconds off the record," Nick said. The instructor looked up at the old weather beaten record board that sat over the entrance and nodded his head. "You'll beat it. Keep trying," Rick told him.

"Then they'll put my name up there," Daley said.

"Record's are made to be broken."

"Petty Officer Cox," Lorner asked. "I heard you're not going to be our instructor any longer?'

"Where'd you hear that?"

"I heard it," Willy said defiantly. Rick turned and looked at him. "Where'd you hear it?"

"That NIS guy told me."

"Why would he tell you that?" Rick said.

Willy shrugged. "I don't know, he just did. When he was questioning me."

Rick looked at the others, "I didn't realize they were gonna talk to all of you." They all said they were told they would be contacted, but so far only Willy had been called. Rick thought that was strange, but everything about this accident was strange to him. But they questioned the instructors, why not the students? "Contrary to what Agent Litton may tell any of you, I haven't been told that I would not be your instructor."

"So you still are?" Nick asked.

"As far as I know," Rick said. "But that may change."

"Petty Officer Cox," Daley said. "We know that this wasn't on purpose. We were there. We don't blame you."

All the others, except for Willy, echoed Daley's words. Rick thanked them for the support then told them they'd better get back to practice. They would probably stay on the class schedule and test the "O" course the first day back. He turned and walked back to the seawall as Lorner took his turn.

"Maybe Giles was right?" Nick said to Daley after their instructor walked away. "When he isn't an instructor, maybe he is cool."

"Don't get excited," Willy said. "I think the guy just knows the shit's coming down on him, and he's just playing it cool."

Rick took a seat on the marble base of the statue and took a deep breath when he saw her come around the turn on the fitness trail. She slowed her run to a jog, then to a walk before stopping. Rick did not know who she was at first. All he noticed was her tanned body dressed in spandex shorts and a sports bra that seemed painted on. Her hair was up in a bundle and it wasn't until she let it down and walked closer that he recognized her from the other day.

Laura did not see him sitting there as she leaned over, placed her hands on her thighs and tried to catch a breath. She then stood straight up, stretching her back, and pulled out a small water bottle. She took a sip, then poured some of the cool water over her head and neck, letting it run down the front of her body before she noticed him watching her.

Her expression changed when she saw him to that of child caught drinking milk right from the carton in the fridge. He smiled at her. Embarrassed first, but too thirsty to care, she wiped the water from her chin and sauntered over to the statue.

"Hey sailor," she said trying to sound coy. Rick smiled, and she watched his eyes as they followed the stream of water down between her breasts.

"Hey you, I'm up here,"she said playfully placing a finger to his chin and tilting his head up.

"I'm sorry," Rick said, now it was his turn to be embarrassed.

"It's okay, I'm used to it," she replied. "Mind if I sit down?"

Rick shook his head and slid over after wiping the dirt from the statue base. She sat down, closed her eyes and leaned back against one of the granite horse's legs. The two sat quietly for a few minutes, listening to the water from the bay splash against the sea wall.

After a short time, Laura opened her eyes and stared up at the statue looking over her. "So who's your friend?" she asked, still looking up at the sculpture above her head. He turned and looked at it.

"I'm not sure," he replied.

"Probably some famous admiral or general," Laura said, tracing her finger around the horse's hoof. "He probably died defending the base from attack during the Spanish American War or something."

"I doubt that," he said turning to face the life size monument.

"Why?"

"Look at it."

"I am," she told him as she searched for the clue that was obvious to Rick. He turned back and looked over the water. She gave him a puzzled glance. "I don't see anything?"

"The horses legs," he replied. She looked at them closer for some words or sign of what he was talking about.

"I don't get what you mean?"

"If a statue of a person on a horse has all four legs on the ground," Rick said, "like this one, the person died of natural causes."

"Yeah, right," Laura said. She wasn't sure if Rick was pulling her leg or not. "Then what does it mean if the legs are in the air?"

"If a statue has both front legs in the air," he said, "the person died in battle; if the horse has only one front leg in the air, the person died as a result of wounds received in battle."

"What would Airman Lee get?"

"I don't know," said the instructor. Laura was sorry she asked as they sat in a very uncomfortable silence.

"What if the horse has all four legs in the air?" She asked. He looked at him and playfully leaned against him. There had been too much sadness lately. He didn't answer. "Well, smart guy?" she said again and bounced her shoulder sideways into his and smiled at him, forcing him to turn away. "Ah, you're not that smart," she said. "You don't even know what it means when all their legs are in the air!"

"Okay," he said finally. "What's it mean?"

"It means the man died while riding a carousel at an amusement park!"She said and started to laugh. Rick shook his head, "That is so stupid!"

He turned away so she wouldn't see him smile. She leaned down and around to look at him, but he kept facing away. He couldn't fight it. They both started to laugh.

"You almost impressed me," he said. "Where do you learn that stuff?"

"I know all kinds of stuff!"

"So do I," Rick said.

"But I have a college degree."

"So what does that mean?" he said teasing.

"It means I can read," she said laughing.

"I read!"

"I meant books *without* pictures!"

"I'll have you know I was offered a scholarship to college."

"Oh yeah?"

"Yeah!"

"I'm impressed," she said still laughing. "Not only do you have a body, but you also have a mind." Rick playfully placed his finger on her chin and tilted her head up till they were face to face.

"I'm up here," he said.

"I know," she replied and the laughing suddenly stopped, replaced with the soft, gentle touch of his hand. Their eyes locked for a moment too long before she turned away. Her face was flush, he swallowed hard. "Your girlfriend is a lucky woman."

"I guess she would be if I had a girlfriend."

"I figured someone like you," she said. "would have women throwing themselves..." she stopped talking as Rick stood up and walked over toward the seawall. "I'm sorry, did I say something wrong?"

He stood there looking out over the water. "No, it's not you. It's me, I guess."

"I don't understand?"

"It's not something I like to talk about," he said. She watched him. He was no longer relaxed, and the confidence that he seemed to have overflowed with since she met him had simply disappeared in an instant. She tried to look at his face, but his eyes would not meet hers.

She turned to walk back to the statue to grab her water bottle and bag. "Maybe I should go," she said. She did not get too far before he spoke.

"I have trouble trusting people," Rick said. The words just came out, his expression did not change, and it wasn't as if what he said was even directed at her or anyone else. It was a confession, as if he was trying to tell himself. But she turned and walked back to him. "I don't let people get close to me. I don't trust them." He said still looking away.

"Most people aren't bad,." Laura said. "We're not like a pack of dogs fighting among themselves for scraps."

"A dog you can trust," Rick said. "But people...No, they play too many head games. People end up hurting each other."

"Huh?"

"I would like to be able to get close," he turned to Laura. "But what's the point? I get asked out by women. And I go occasionally, but I know it won't last, and it doesn't."

"Maybe it doesn't last because you don't expect it to," Laura replied.

"Everyone I have ever trusted..." Rick said turning back to the water. "..everyone I ever trusted, they left me or worse."

"What do you mean?" She asked moving over next to him and looking out into the distance to try and see what he saw.

"My father left us when I was born," Rick said. "He couldn't handle two young boys. My mother passed away later, when I was in high school."

"I'm sorry," she said. "That must have been rough. But at least you had a brother, right?"

"Yeah," Rick said. "There was always Tim."

"Are you two close now?"

"No," Rick replied. "He died a short time later."

"I'm sorry," she said. "That must have been hard."

"It was."

"How old was he? Or don't you want to talk about it?" She asked. For once he found someone who he did not mind talking to. Rick told her of the events surrounding his brother's death. Of how he quit football and turned away scholarships. Of why he joined the Navy, thinking that he should have done what that swimmer on the news did. Laura could not believe that Rick was as well adjusted as he was after all the sadness he'd gone through. No wonder the guy never trusted anyone. He had seen so much, so young, she thought.

"You know it's funny how things work out."

"How?,"she said expecting anything. "What things?"

"I met the guy a few years later," he said.

"The guy?" Laura asked, confused for a moment. "You mean the swimmer? The kid from on that news report?"

"Yeah."

"Did you tell him about all this?"

"Yeah," Rick said. "I started to, but he didn't want to hear about it. The guy was an alcoholic now. He said that the mother had stayed in touch with him, writing letters about the kid for close to two years."

"Sounds like she was grateful."

"Yeah," Rick replied. "So grateful that she was arrested for child abuse in Florida after police found the kid dead from malnutrition and neglect "

"My God!"

"She had apparently beat the kid so bad that his jaw broke and he couldn't eat," Rick said. "The child had just turned four years old. So the guy started drinking and blaming himself for what happened to the kid."

"But it wasn't his fault?" Laura said.

"He said that if he never rescued the kid, that child would never had suffered all the abuse."

"But the baby would have been dead!"

"The child is dead now," Rick said. Laura could not think of anything to say. She stood there trying to find some words, but she did not even know what to think. Was it better to have let the kid die at the hand of his mother or in car wreck?

"I don't know either," Rick said, reading her mind.

"Look," Laura said. "There's a lot of bad things that happen in the world. And I know that you haven't had the best of luck, but you can't go around worrying that everything is going to turn out badly or that everyone you meet is going to leave you."

"Why not?" Rick said. "I don't get close, I don't trust anyone. I don't get hurt.'

"But that's not living. That's just surviving."

"Sometimes, just surviving is enough," Rick said.

"You need to learn to trust people."

"Trust people?" Rick said with a sarcastic laugh. "You're the lawyer. In fact your whole job is to not trust what people say!"

"That's not fair!"

"It isn't? Let me tell you about lawyers!" Rick said. "When my brother was killed, it seemed as if every damn lawyer in the world told me I should sue the county, the state, the kid who was driving the jeep, the girl who was in the jeep, my brother's friends and girlfriend, the store that sold him beer, everyone at the party. You name it!"

"What does that have to do with anything?"

"It has everything to do with it," Rick said. "I refused to sue anyone."

"But the driver was at fault!"

"You sound like the prosecutor," he replied. "When I refused to sue anyone, the State of Florida went after the kid driving the jeep. But what was the kid supposed to do?"

"I don't follow you?"

"The kid comes around the corner and suddenly he sees what looks like a body in the middle of the road, so he steers the truck to the only place where he is sure not to hit someone."

"The water," Laura replied. "But there was your brother in the water. And the pile was not a body."

"I know that now! And so does everyone else," Rick said. "But on a dark road at night? What if it had been someone passed out on the road and my brother was not in the water? Then the kid would be a hero!"

"Why do you defend the person who killed your brother?" Laura asked. "I would think you hate him, not the lawyers?"

"I never said I don't hate him," Rick told her in no uncertain terms. "I hate him with all my heart for taking away my older brother. But I don't blame him, and there's a difference."

"You're a better person than I am," Laura said. "I would have wanted to put the son of a bitch away."

"That's why you are on the side you are."

"What does that mean?"

"Let me ask you this," Rick said. "The doctor told me that there was some kind of damage to Lee's heart, and that I was not to blame for his death. That he'd be dead anyway. In fact I called you and left a message about that."

"I got the message. I called back but you weren't home." she said. "What doctor said that? Craft?"

"Yeah," Rick answered. "But the kid died while in my arms, while I was doing what I thought I was supposed to do."

"So you are saying that the doctor said that even if you wouldn't have held Lee under, he would have died?"

"I don't know if that's what he meant," Rick replied. "You should ask Craft. But what I am asking is if he died as a result of me doing something that anyone else in my place would have done, without knowing that someone would die as a result, was I wrong?"

"Are you asking me as a lawyer or a person?"

"As a human being," Rick said.

"You are assuming that I agree that with you that the kid driving the jeep...wait a minute," she said. "Your brother was not going to die anyway, right?"

"Yeah, but if Lee had not signed up to go in the Navy and instead become an accountant then any physical ailments would not have been a factor in his life either," Rick replied. "All I'm asking that you assume the situations and circumstances were not the choice of me or the kid in the jeep, since we are being blamed."

"Are you sure you're not a lawyer, cause you sound like one?" Laura said smiling. She managed to break some of the tension. If at least for a moment. "Okay, as a *human being* I would not say it was your fault."

"Okay," he said satisfied.

"But as a lawyer, not a human being..."

Rick started to laugh as Laura realized how she had phrased her statement. "You said it," he told her. "Not me."

"As a lawyer," she said as she restarted her sentence. "As a lawyer, I would say that you are both to blame. At least partially."

"I know you would," Rick said. "I know most lawyers would. I know Litton does. And I am sure that Senator Robert Lee does."

"I don't know why Litton is preoccupied with you, he's certainly *not* a lawyer," she replied. "But the Senator has a right to feel the way he does. You said yourself that you hated the kid who killed your brother."

"I can understand hate," he replied. "But he also blames me, I'm sure."

"Why do you say that?" She asked. "You don't know that. Maybe he thinks like you?"

"Maybe."

"Although," she teased, "I would find it impossible to believe anyone thinks like you."

"He's a politician," Rick replied seriously. "They're worse than lawyers. Politicians never blame themselves."

"I don't know if I like you placing me in with politicians like that," Laura said. She sat down on the grass and started removing her running shoes.

"Why not?" He asked. "You do work for the government, and you are a lawyer."

She had one of the laces in a knot and Rick bent down and took the string from her hands. He worked on taking the knot out as she spoke. "True. But, Rick, not all lawyers are out to get people."

"Yeah? Well, most are."

"I'm not," she said as he pulled her shoe off her foot without removing the knot. She took off her socks and stuck them in her shoes and walked back over to the seawall. "And neither is my father." She sat down on the cold concrete, and threw her feet over the side. Rick removed his shoes and followed suit. The waves danced at their toes. The water was warm, but felt good to both of them after working out.

"Your dad's a lawyer?"

"My father's a lawyer, his father was a lawyer," she told him. "So I went to law school."

"How'd you end up here?"

"I wanted something more than Macon, Georgia," she said, watching some fishing boats go by. "I wanted to travel, to experience life to see what else was out there."

"If you come from a family of lawyers," Rick replied. "Then I'm sure you had enough money to travel and do things, didn't you?"

Laura looked at him and then down at the ground. "You don't know what being in a family of tax lawyers is about,"she said laughing to herself. "You would think so."

"I thought all lawyers had money."

"Money wasn't the problem," she replied. "No. It's time. My father works ten hours a day now. Growing up it was twelve or fifteen. The only places he traveled to were tax seminars, and most of the time I couldn't go."

"But you did sometimes?"

"But even then, it was Chicago or Washington or New York."

"So, what's the problem?" Rick asked. "In a city there's a lot to do."

"I had to stay in the hotel," she said. "There was no way daddy was going to let his little girl out into the city alone."

"What about your mom? Didn't she go with you?"

"No," Laura replied. "My mother is afraid to fly, and since dad never had time for a car trip..."

"I get the picture," Rick said. "Poor little rich girl."

"Oh no," she told him. "Don't get the wrong impression. I am very close to my family. And they gave me everything I could want. A great home life, my education. My dad is my best friend."

"You just never got to go anywhere."

"Right," she said.

"So what does your dad think of you being in the Navy?"

"When I told him I was going to work for the government, he didn't take it too well," she said.

"Why?"

"He's a tax lawyer, remember?"

"Oh." Rick replied. "I guess he wouldn't be too happy about *that*. But at least you're not in the IRS or FBI, right?"

"That's what I thought," she said. "But then he asked why I joined the Navy instead of something like the FBI."

"What did you tell him?"

"In the Navy, I get to see the world!" she replied as if reading a recruiting poster. "Plus, my dad was in the Navy Reserves for a few years, a long time ago."

"So have you seen much?" Rick asked.

"Ahhhh... no... not yet," she replied. "But I am out of Macon, and that's a start."

"Well, I've been all over the world," Rick said. "But I have never been to Macon."

"So I guess I'm one up on you then," she said. "It's not a bad place, just small town."

"At least you have a home to go to," Rick said. Suddenly Laura felt guilty about her home life. She placed her arms around his shoulders. "When this is all over, I'll take you there!"

"It's okay," he said gently pulling away. "I am glad one of us had a nice childhood."

She leaned against him. "I'm sorry," was all she could say. The two sat there against each other. No thoughts of the investigation, they both sat quietly trying to make the other feel better.

It was Rick who moved away first, when one of the tugboats on the water blew its whistle. Laura felt his arm drop off, and felt him ever so slowly slide over. She looked out across the bay, not acknowledging what he'd done. She did not want the moment to end yet. So peaceful, the sun was not completely set, but the small green and red lights on the ships passing back and fourth made them seem alive on the calm water. The moon was becoming visible to the east, and the sun was setting on the other horizon. The wind was blowing slightly, and some gulls were chatting away in the sky. There was no need to speak. They both felt something had changed between them. But right now it did not matter.

When the last rays of the sun finally disappeared Laura stood up. "Thank you," she said.

"For what?"

"For this,"she said looking out at the water. "For the sunset, for letting me get to know you better. It was nice."

"You're welcome," Rick replied. He couldn't think of anything else to say. She smiled at him, and quietly picked up her gym bag and walkman. He then watched as she turned and walked away without a word.

He couldn't help but think of her as he walked back to his car. He wished he had told her how much he had liked talking with her, too. But he couldn't. It was nice. But more than the moment, he had the same feeling that he had when he had met her that first time, in Harding's office. It seemed like years ago. It was a feeling he had not had for some time with anyone. A feeling that he could say anything to her. A feeling of trust. *But she was still a lawyer*, he reminded himself.

*

"New orders, Commander," the Duty Officer said. Commander Benjamin Craft came out from his room at the Bachelor's Officer Quarters, Naval Air Station Roosevelt Roads, Puerto Rico.

"What the hell are you talking about, Ensign?" Craft said standing there in his boxer shorts, his face full of shaving cream. "I just got here?"

"Sir, you have a flight leaving in two hours," the young officer replied..She had only been in the Navy a couple weeks and had already seen her share of quirky assignments. "The orders came in a few minutes ago."

"Dammit!" the doctor said as he watched the Caribbean sun dip down below the horizon. He looked at the tanned woman in front of him. He hadn't even had time to get to the beach on base yet. "Fine! Fine! Wait out here!"

*

Laura had just stepped out of the shower when the phone rang. She wrapped a towel around herself and walked out to the kitchen. She pulled the phone from the wall and answered. It was Litton. She looked at the wall clock. It was eight-thirty at night.

"This better be important," she said.

"Any time I call you it's important," Litton replied. "I wanted to know if you were planning to attend the funeral tomorrow?"

"Not really, why?"

"Good," Litton remarked. "I just figured that since I will be there anyway, there is no reason we both should go."

"Why is that so important?"

"It's not really. I just want to make sure that we both can get some work done," he said. "Oh, yeah another small thing. I think that you should look at the administrative aspects of the case, do the research and leave the interviews to me."

"What's that supposed to mean?"

"I'm just saying that you need to learn how to do the research and that there is no need for you to sit in on the depositions."

"Are you saying I can't speak to witnesses involved in the case?" Laura asked.

"The next case we work on, you can do the interviews," Litton said. "I just want you to get your skills up to speed on the research end of the job."

"Does this have anything to do with the other day when we spoke with those instructors?"

"No, Agent Wilson," Litton answered with some agitation. "But now that you bring it up, I don't want you speaking with Petty Officer Cox. I was told he stopped by to see you."

"Yes, he did, but I wasn't here."

"The man's a murderer, Laura. You need to stay away from him."

"He's not a murderer, Jack," she replied. "In fact, you should cut him some slack. The man's had a hard life..." She told him the story of how Rick's brother died. Litton listened intently. "I doubt he intentionally hurt anyone," she added after she was done with the story.

"So he just stayed on the bank of the lake while his brother was suffering? Doesn't sound like a man with much conscience to me."

"He was held back!"she said. "Weren't you listening to me?"

"How do you know all this?" he asked.

"I was out jogging and ran into him."

"Just like that?" Litton replied. "He just happened to be out where you were jogging and then you two just sat down and he gave you this heart wrenching story."

"I parked near the Rescue Swimmer School like I always have," she said. "But yes, we sat and talked. Why?'

"I don't want you near this guy."

"He's a decent guy," she said. "I think you're reading him all wrong."

"Okay, maybe I am not being clear enough," Litton said with much more authority. "You, Agent Wilson, are not to go near Petty Officer Cox. You don't talk with him, you don't phone him, you don't anything with him. No contact!"

"Why?!" She said. "This is bullshit!"

"Because I said so," Litton told her. "Because I think the guy is fucking dangerous. And because I am your boss, and the Agent-in-Charge of this investigation. That is reason enough."

"Oh, this is a bunch of crap!" Laura said.

"Do I have to put this in a memo?" Litton replied. "If you contact him, you are off the case. Period. In fact, I will have you arrested for obstruction if I find out you have been speaking to him. Got it?"

"Yeah, I got it! And I do want it in a memo!" Laura said and slammed the receiver down, pulling the phone off the wall. "You are such a bastard!"

*

The twin-engine turboprop's gleaming white and gold paint contrasted sharply with the dull grey fighter and attack aircraft parked on either side. The small Navy King Air transport plane's red strobe light cut through the hazy evening as its only passenger climbed aboard.

"Howdy, Commander," the pilot said as Craft climbed on board. The doctor handed his bag over, and it was stowed in the back of the cabin, under a cargo net. The pilot handed Craft a cup of coffee, and gave him the rundown of the flight to NAS Key West, where the doctor would then catch a plane to Miami, and then overseas to his final destination.

"Sounds like you're in for a long trip, Sir?"

"You got that right," Craft agreed. "Do you mind if I log some seat time on the flight?"

"No, sir, as long as your quals are up," the pilot replied. He checked to make sure that the flight surgeon was familiar with the type aircraft and other necessary requirements before they took off.

"Thanks," Craft said from the right seat up front. "I need the hours for my flight pay, who knows when I'll be up again."

"No sweat, sir," the pilot said. "We'll get the hours back to your command so they log 'em for you."

"Don't worry about it," Craft replied. "I'll have the duty office fax it when I get to Suda Bay."

10

***

Thursday, June 18

Rick woke up to the phone ringing. He looked outside, it was still dark. He reached over and turned the light on. It was only four-thirty in the morning. He wasn't on duty. *Who calls people this early in the morning?* he wondered.

"Hello?"

"Is this Richard Cox?"

"Who's this?" Rick replied still half asleep.

"Is this Petty Officer Richard Cox?"

"Yeah, this is Rick," he said as he laid back down on the bed and closed his eyes. "Who's this?"

"Chandler Hanson, Times-Press. May I ask you a few questions?"

Rick sat up, "Times - what?"

"Mr. Cox, is it true that you were holding Airman Robert Lee, Jr. under water at the time of his death?"

"What..yeah..wait," Rick said confused. He was quickly waking up now. "What is this?"

"It is true?"

"Who are you again?" Rick said as he rubbed his head trying to wake up. He swung his feet off the bed and sat on the side of the mattress. "What is this for?"

"I'm a reporter, sir," the man said. "I'm trying to verify some facts about the death of Senator Lee's son. I have information that you caused the Senator's son to die by drowning."

"I didn't cause anyone to drown,"Rick said.

"What about your brother?"

"What about him!" Rick said.

"I have information that said you sat by and watched him drown a few years ago, do you have any comment?"

"This call is over!" Rick said and hung up. The phone rang agin, and Rick pulled the cord from the wall, and threw the phone across the room. What the hell was going on? Rick laid down and tried to go to sleep, but it wasn't going to happen. Every time he closed his eyes, he saw his brother, he could see the headlights under the water. After an hour had passed, Rick decided to just get up and eat breakfast. The funeral was at nine, and he was going.

*

Laura was up and awake at seven, as usual. She walked out into the pantry and grabbed a coke from the fridge. She threw some frozen waffles in the toaster and went into the living room. She sat on the couch and turned on CNN. The Atlanta-based news network reminded her of home, and she always checked to see what the weather would be like, knowing her parents were already awake since Pensacola was an hour behind Georgia.

While waiting for the weather, the morning show always gave the top stories. She barely had time to read the newspaper, so this was Laura's window into what was happening around the rest of the world. While waiting for the weather, Laura paid little attention to the news, until she heard them mention the death of a student at the Navy's Rescue Swimmer School.

"CNN has just confirmed that the Pensacola, Florida Times-Press is reporting that Navy Petty Officer Richard Cox, the instructor who was in charge of Airmen Robert Lee's training, has admitted holding the young sailor under water at the time of his death."

"As you may recall," the anchorman continued. "We reported yesterday that the young sailor was the only son of Senator Robert Lee, Chairman of the Senate Appropriations Committee. The report also stated that Petty Officer Cox had a brother who also drowned." A still photo of Tim was shown on the screen. It was a Florida State University team photo, with Tim's face circled.

"Apparently, Tim Cox, the Navy instructor's older brother, drowned during a party at which Petty Officer Cox was present." The image then cut to a live shot of the reporter in front of the Main Gate for NAS Pensacola. "According to Naples, Florida, police reports during the drowning which happened a little over twelve years ago, Richard Cox made no attempt to rescue his brother. We will be investigating more into this tragedy."

"Was that before or after Petty Officer Cox had joined the Navy, Ted?" the anchorman asked.

"We believe it was prior to Cox's entry into the Navy," the reporter replied. "But we are still checking on that. The funeral for Airman Lee is in a few hours here at NAS Pensacola. We understand that Senator Robert Lee, as well as some other dignitaries, and his classmates will be attending."

"Will any of the instructors be there?"

"I have no word on that as of yet," the reporter replied.

"We will certainly continue to keep you informed of the events unfolding in Florida. In other news, Wall Street had a busy day yesterday..."

A few miles away Rick shut off the television set and went outside on his patio. He sat on the steps and thought about what had occurred that night, the worst night of his life. And now he was forced to relive it just so so damn reporter can get face-time on television. Damn him for trusting Laura. Damn him for trusting anyone. He felt more alone than ever.

*

Laura went into the base clinic and over to the records department. The sailor on duty was sitting at the counter reading a magazine. Obviously a slow day. Laura introduced herself and showed him her credentials. She told him she was looking for Commander Craft's records and that he was a staff officer there as far as she knew. He went to a far wall and opened a large file drawer. He looked through from front to back, then back to front. He closed that drawer and searched the drawer below it before returning to the counter.

"No personnel records here, " the sailor said. "They must be checked out."

"Who checked them out?" Laura asked.

"I don't know," he replied.

"There is a checkout record isn't there?"

"Yes, ma'am."

"Then who signed the checkout log?"

"Hold on," he said and reached under the counter. He pulled a green logbook out and placed it on the counter. He searched through pages covering entries from the last few days. “Looks like the commander checked his own records out,” he told her.

“When?”

The sailor turned the book around so she could read the entries. “It looks like two days ago.”

“I thought that people weren’t allowed to check their own records out?” Laura asked.

“They can’t.”

She looked around. “I don’t see them anywhere, do you?”

“No, ma’am.”

“Well, where are they?”

“Ma’am,” the sailor replied reading from the log. “It says here that they are checked out to Commander Craft. That is a full Commander, ma’am. See this?” He pointed to the crow and chevron on his shirt. “I’m only a Third Class Petty Officer. If a Commander wants his records, I give him his records.”

“Did you give him his records?”

“No, ma’am”

“Who did?”

The sailor looked at the log book.“I don’t know,” he replied. “No one initialed the logbook.”

“Did he take all his records?”

“This is just the sign out for his personnel records, ma’am.”

“How about his medical record?” Laura asked. The sailor placed the logbook back under the counter and told her he’d be right back. He disappeared through a door. A few minutes later he returned. “Not here either, ma’am.”

“Is there any record that this man exists?” she asked exasperated.

“You might want to try finding his NATOPS jacket.”

“What is a NATOPS jacket?”

“Naval Air Training Operating Procedures Standardization--its a file listing all the Commander’s training and qualifications for flying.”

“May I see that?”

“I don’t have that here, ma’am,” the sailor replied..

“Where is it?”

“It’s at base ops.”

“That’s N-A-T-O-P-S?” she asked, writing down some notes. “Why does base ops have it?”

"Because," he replied. "That's where all the flight records are kept for base personnel on flight status who are not assigned to a squadron."

"Wait," Laura said. "I am talking about a doctor, not a pilot."

"Yes, ma'am, but Commander Craft is a flight surgeon,"the sailor told her. "He's a doctor and a pilot, ma'am."

"Oh." Laura said. "Well, I guess I am off to base operations then. You've been a great help." The sailor was already back to reading his magazine before she stepped outside.

*

Giles arrived at the funeral for Lee a few minutes before the service. Spotting his students, he went over and greeted them. The class were all wearing their dress blues. Only Willy was missing.

"Where's Willy?"

"He said he was too upset to come," Daley told him.

"Uh-huh," Giles said. "I didn't think they were friends."

"They weren't," Daley said.

*

Laura left base operations and drove over to the base chapel. She needed to speak with Litton, but saw Rick's truck in the parking lot. She pulled in and parked in the back. She walked around the church and past the press set up in front. The services had already started. She slipped into the back and scanned the rectory. She spotted Rick sitting in the back and made her way over to him. He did not see her until she was next to him.

"What do you want?" he said, not even looking at her.

"I was hoping you'd be here"

"You have a lot of guts coming over to me now," Rick said.

"So you saw the news?"

"What do you think?" He replied. She tugged at his arm and pulled him out into the hall, which was crowded with mourners. She looked around and then motioned for them up a narrow set of stairs and into a small empty room. In it a row of small pews faced a window that overlooked the chapel's main hall below. After closing the door behind her, she turned and faced him. Rick was standing defiantly, not looking at her, but past her out a stained glass window that faced the parking lot of the church. Through the open pane he could see some reporters waiting out there.

"Is that your work, too?" he said nodding at them.

Laura turned and looked out. "Rick, I didn't call anyone last night. You need to believe me."

"I'm sure."

"Listen," Laura said grabbing his arms with hers, staring up into his face, which would still not meet hers. "There was one person I told, and I did not tell him to hurt you in any way."

"Yeah?" Rick said. "Who was it?"

"Litton."

Rick backed away from her. "Now I know you are lying to me! You're going to sit there with a straight face and tell me that you honestly want me to believe that you repeated what I told you about the night my brother died...about how this was making me feel...about how helpless I felt that night to the one single person who is trying to take away everything I have?!"

"I ..."

"I don't know which of us is more stupid," Rick said. "Me for telling you or you for thinking that Litton would help me?!" He went over to the pew and sat down, placing his head against the glass and watching the oblivious mourners below. She sat down next to him.

"You're right, I should have known better," she said. "And I can't undo this. But it does tell me that Litton isn't alone."

"What do you mean?"

"I mean I received a call from one of Senator Lee's aides the other day," she explained the call that was sent to her office instead of Litton's.

"Then you knew he would do this," Rick said quietly. "Do you have any idea how hard this is for me?"

"I know it is," she said. "Rick, I am not trying to hurt you. I believe it was an accident, I do. But you can't do this alone. I think you may need a lawyer."

"Why?"

"I just do, that all."

"No," he replied. "Only guilty people need lawyers. I did not do anything."

"Rick, you need help."

"I don't want anyone's help," he said and turned his attention to the ceremony starting inside the church. Laura gave up talking to him for the moment.

The chapel was packed with mourners and the press. A flag-draped coffin was on the alter, and in the first row sat the Senator, alone. In the opposite pew sat Admiral Tract, Hunt, Harding, and the Senator's staff. Behind them sat Litton. Lt. Jackson sat with other junior officers from School's Command.

The priest started his eulogy and the organ played. The choir sang. After the initial prayer, the chaplain invited Senator Lee to address the chapel.

"A little over three months ago, Robert entered boot camp in Great Lakes, Illinois," his father said. "I could not have been more proud. During his time there, I am told he distinguished himself in the tradition of our family..."

The words were touching and caring and written and well rehearsed. The Senator paused when he should have, and sobbed when appropriate. He was followed by the chaplain, and a few words by Admiral Tract. Those who knew Lee were not asked to speak. It would not have been proper. The sound bites were there, and to the Senator's staff, that was what mattered. They took no chances in letting someone else say words that would appear in the press. This was the Senator's time.

"I need to get out of here," Rick said. The service was ending.

"Where will you be later?" Laura asked.

"Why?"

"I wanted to talk with you," she said. "Some things are going on and I wanted to ask you about them."

"What things?"

"I can't talk about them here," Laura said. "What are you doing for dinner? We can meet and eat someplace."

"I don't have any transportation," Rick said. "I have to leave here and work on my truck."

"How long will that take?"

"It's a two day job," Rick answered. "Besides, after last night, tell me why I should even talk to you?"

"Okay," Laura said. She took her beeper from her waist and handed it to him "I need to prove to you I had nothing to do with this press thing." She reached into her purse and pulled out her keys. She also handed them to Rick. "Here, take my car."

He stood there holding everything in his hand. "What's all this for?"

"You saw the press out there, right?"

"Yeah?"

"If you walked outside," Laura asked. "How long do you think it would be before a reporter saw you? I saw your truck parked out in the lot. How many other people do you think saw it?"

Rick shrugged. He hadn't thought about it until now.

"Take my car," she said. "It's parked right out back. You can be in it and on your way in less than thirty seconds, and I know no one is staking out my BMW."

"So what are you gonna do?" Rick asked, still wondering why he should trust her.

"I have some people to talk to on base," she said. "I'll beep you when I'm done. Then you can pick me up and we'll talk."

"I don't know why I'm agreeing to this."

"Because," she said, "you know that you did nothing wrong. And you know I know it, too."

"Do me a favor," Rick said. "Give my keys to Giles and ask him to get my truck over to the hobby shop?"

"Which one is Giles?" she asked. He pointed his friend out to her. She said she would as Rick started to move out of the pew. But before he got too far, she grabbed his arm. "Rick.?"

"What?"

"I think it would be a smart move to get a lawyer," she said.

"You know how I feel about that," he said and turned. He left unnoticed by any of the press. Laura waited until the mass was ended and found Giles as he was walking out.

"Petty Officer Giles?"

"Yes?" he said turning around. He had been talking with Watson. His eyes told her he remembered them meeting before. "You're that agent..."

"Hi," she said. "Yes. The name is Laura." She reached her hand out and Giles took it, but then felt a set of keys.

"What's this?"

"I can't explain right now," she said. "But would you drive Rick's, I mean Petty Officer Cox's, truck over to the hobby shop?"

"Rick's here?" Giles said looking around for his friend.

"No," she replied. "He was. But he will meet you there, okay? Thanks." She was gone as quick as she had appeared.

Laura walked out of the base chapel. She stood at the top of the steps and saw Litton alongside Admiral Tract and the Senator. She quickly made her way past the press and others surrounding the dead sailor's father and grabbed Litton. He turned and after seeing her tried to brush her off. But she pulled harder until he had to follow her away.

"Not only is Craft missing, but now his records are gone as well!" she told him.

"I told you not to worry about him!"

"Don't you think it is odd?"

"No," Litton said. "People go on convalescence leave all the time."

"This guy's not on leave, he's disappeared."

"He's in the Navy, no one disappears," Litton said. "Relax. He probably is TAD somewhere. If all his records are checked out, then what is so strange?"

"He isn't TAD, no one gets temporarily assigned that fast. Besides, he didn't check out all his records." Laura told him about the NATOPS jacket. "If he was checked out, the guy at Base Ops told me he should have taken the NATOPS record."

"I'm sure that someone knows where he is."

"Well, then they aren't talking."

"I think you are reading a little bit too much into this," Litton replied. "Maybe his wife is sick."

"He's not married."

"Maybe he's sick, himself."

"No record of it on sick call," Laura said. "And everyone he works with said he was fine the day before."

"What do you want me to say?" Litton replied. "Fine, he's not here."

"Look, I'm not an idiot. This is strange--admit it!"

"You know what?" Litton said. "You are way, way, way overreacting to this. So don't worry your pretty little self about the background checks. I'll do it myself."

"Wait a minute," Laura said. "First you tell me I can't interview anyone, because you'll do it. Now I can't research or investigate because you are going to do it."

"Yep," Litton said. "You got it."

"If I can't investigate or interview people," Laura asked. "Then why am I assigned to the case."

"That's the first valid point I have heard from you in a long time." Litton said. "And I can't think of an argument."

"So what does that mean?"

"I guess you're off the case," he said and shrugged his shoulders.

Laura could not believe what happened there. "Are you saying I am not on the case?"

"Did I stutter?" he replied. "You said it better than I could. I can't argue with the reasons you stated."

"Wait a second!" Laura said. "What just happened here?"

Litton walked back toward Tract and Senator Lee. "You have just given me the reasons to get you off my back. Be happy- you won't have to worry about this any more."

"You can't do this!"

"Oh, yes I can," Litton said and looked at the watch on his wrist. "In fact...it's done!"

"I'll fight you on this-- so help me!"

"No, you won't, Laura," Litton said. "Because if you do, I will win, and you will have wrecked a budding career."

"I will go over your head!"

"Go ahead," he replied. "And I will give them the same reasons you gave me and then some. You know, your actions during this whole investigation have not been what I would call 'professional.' Most prosecutors and investigators don't sneak around with the suspects of their cases." He turned his back on her and continued walking.

"What does that mean?" she said running around in front of him.

"I saw you in the church talking with Cox," he said. "So you go down to your office, and you call my boss, and you tell him whatever you want. But I won't hold anything back, do you understand? Now either let this rest or destroy your career. Your choice."

"You're a prick!"

"You may be right about that," Litton said smiling. "But I am still your boss." Litton walked around her, then stopped. "Oh, and Laura," Litton said lighting a cigar. "Don't let me find you speaking to anyone about this case or I will have you arrested for obstruction. Do you understand?" He blew a cloud of smoke and gingerly walked back to the car. He arrived just as the others were getting inside. Hunt pulled Litton aside. "Where you been?"

"Getting rid of our problem," Litton replied. "Wilson is done!"

Hunt pulled Litton inside the car with the others. They pulled away quickly and headed back to Tract's office.

"What happened?" Hunt asked.

"She has been talking with Cox," Litton said. "Then she went and got Craft's NATOPS records."

"Damn," Hunt said.

"So she has his NATOPS record, big deal," Litton said. "It doesn't mean anything."

"You idiot," Hunt said. "It shows that he flew down there on the Admiral's personal aircraft. Shit!"

"What about my plane?" Tract asked from the front seat. Unlike the Senator, he was not paying their conversation much attention. He had more important concerns to worry about and a command to run.

"Nothing, Admiral," Hunt answered. Tract nodded, turned around, and went back to ignoring the two men.

"But you said it would be fine if someone found out."

"Well, I did not mean for the only person on this base to find out is the only one who doesn't think that Cox is a killer?" Hunt replied. "Dammit, I knew Puerto Rico was too fucking close."

"I warned you it was."

"At least he isn't there now. You'll have to do something, Litton," Hunt said. "And quick."

"I kicked her off the case," he replied. "She won't be a problem now. I'm more worried about the Senator."

"Why?" Senator Lee asked. "My son is dead, Mr. Litton. If anyone has a right to ask questions, it's me."

"Because the press is involved," Litton replied. "I understand your position, and you're right, Senator. I'm sorry."

Just then Hunt asked the driver to stop. They pulled over, and the Admiral's Aide excused himself and Litton, and said it would be a good day to take a walk. The two men stepped out of the car and onto the sidewalk, leaving the others to continue along their way.

"It's hotter than the Goddamn sun out here," Litton said removing his suitcoat. "Nice day for a walk, my ass."

"Your fat ass could stand a walk, Jack," Hunt said as he began to stroll along, seemingly unaffected by the heat. "There are some things that do not need to be discussed in front of others. So what's the problem with the press being here?"

"The problem..," the agent explained, "..is I don't want a bunch of reporters nosing around. I told you before that the leaks might hurt us."

"I think the press is under control, besides we all know where the leaks are coming from," Hunt replied. "It's your girl who worries me."

"Well, don't be," Litton replied as they walked along the sidewalk. The canopy of trees at least allowed the shade to block some of the sun. But the heat was still intense. "I can handle her. She might be wide-eyed at the moment, but she's as green as they come. She will do what I tell her."

"I hope you are right about this."

"I am," he said. "She won't throw a career away over someone like Cox. She doesn't even know this guy. She just wants good evaluations. I'll give her busy work. Not a problem."

"It might help us if we could find a witness that would go against this guy."

"I'm working on that right now," Litton said.

*

Rick was sitting in Laura's light blue BMW. The little Z-3 Roadster was about as opposite of his truck as he could think of. He parked near the garage and waited for Giles. He thought about what she said. She did just save him from the press, but he could not think of why. Sometimes he felt like he could trust what she said, but he had made it this far without trusting anyone. And she did work with Litton.

Rick was quickly developing a headache when he saw his truck heading across the parking lot. When it pulled up, Giles climbed out, checking his dress uniform for stains and dirt. He saw Rick get out of the little sports car. "Nice wheels," Giles said. "Who's are they?"

"Laura's."

Giles was confused. "Laura, eh?"

"Yeah," Rick said. "Can we drop it?"

"First name basis huh?"

"I said drop it, please."

"What's going on with you two?" Giles asked, not letting go of the subject.

"Nothing," Rick said. "She's trying to help me, I guess." Rick was annoyed that he didn't have an answer. He liked her and he trusted her and he didn't. It was confusing enough for him to try and figure out.

How could he explain it to anyone else? "Hey, I don't know!"

"Just calm down," Giles said laughing. "Don't get all angry at me. I'm just happy you're talking with a woman. I was worried about you." Rick started bringing out parts ignoring the teasing. Giles stood watching. "Want some help?"

"Dressed like that?" Rick asked as he pulled off his shirt and placed it inside the trucks cab.

Giles looked down at himself, then over at Cox who had worn his civilian clothes to the funeral so he wouldn't be noticed. Dress Blues looked good on a Cracker-Jack box, Giles thought, but were not something you wore while working on a car. "I guess I'll go and change. You want me to come back?"

"No," Rick said. "I'm just gonna take the tranny out today," he said as he laid down on the concrete and slid under the truck. "Then I have to go to dinner with Laura."

"Life sucks for you, huh?"

"Shut up," Rick replied.

"Okay," Giles said. "I'll see ya later."

*

Laura walked back and watched Litton talking with Hunt. She turned and headed over to a small white wooden building a few blocks away from the chapel. The structure looked more like an old southern mansion than an office, but inside it had the same coldness of any government building.

The Pensacola Naval Air Station Legal Department was smaller than most civilian offices, yet just as busy. They handled everything from the wills of sailors to lawsuits from farmers who's chickens had heart attacks from low flying jets. Nothing surprised the lawyers here. And contrary to popular belief, the defense attorneys in these offices could hold their own with anyone. They had to. The lawyers here needed to know civilian as well as military laws.

Laura walked into the reception area and asked to see Captain Tom Reilly, then sat down in the waiting area. There were no fine leather couches here, instead the room was filled with art-deco furniture from the 1960's and 70's. Of course, the Navy had not purchased the stylish furniture to be in tune with fashion. It had just been in the office since the late seventies and was just now coming back into vogue.

It was not long before she was shown back to Reilly's office.

The door opened and she was greeted with the smile from a very handsome man in his early fifties. His salt and pepper hair was slicked back and his chiseled good looks screamed confidence. It was easy to see why Reilly was so successful in a profession that bases everything on convincing people of the truth. His voice was deep, but not too much so. He was someone who people instantly liked, yet he was imposing enough that it would be hard to argue with him.

"Miss Wilson, come in," he said

"Sir, I need your help," Laura said as she took a seat across from the career U.S. Navy lawyer. "I have a problem with the object of one of our investigations."

The senior officer leaned back in his chair and picked up the can of coke from his desk and took a sip. "Tell me what's going on."

*

Hunt and Litton arrived at the Schools Command building where the agent told Hunt he was still interviewing the sailors in the class. He was sure he'd find someone that would be able to help them, whether the student knew it or not.

Litton got in his car and drove over to his office where Daley, Willy Simms, and Lorner were waiting to be interviewed as instructed. The agent walked in, still soaked in sweat. He went right past the students and over to the receptionist, who gave him his messages.

"Oh shit," Willy said under his breath.

"What?" Daley asked. Willy told him about the other night in front of the gay bar. "I hope he doesn't remember me!" As he finished talking they saw the receptionist point in their direction. Litton said something back to her, then walked down to the three.

"I'm sorry but something has come up," he told them. "We'll need to reschedule this for later..." his words dropped off as he looked at Willy's face. He did not turn to the others, but continued to stare at Willy. "You two can go," he said without taking his eyes away from the familiar face. "But I think I will talk with Airman Simms after I change."

*

The 737 started its approach over the crystal clear waters surrounding the island. Craft looked out the window at the bleached white stone homes that dotted the landscape below. This wasn't such a bad deal after all. He was wearing civilian clothes, and there was nothing about him that would give away the fact that he was in the military, except for the color of his passport.

The plane taxied off the runway after landing and was soon stopped outside the terminal. The door opened and the stream of people exited down the stairs and onto the concrete tarmac. They were ushered over to the terminal where they were met by customs officials. Craft went through without a hitch, lost in a sea of European tourists on holiday, as vacation was known on this side of the world.

He was tired, but the sun and heat woke him up, defrosting him after spending the last twenty hours in the confined air-conditioned spaces of various airports and airliners. He had an idea of why this was happening, but had never realized to what extent they had meant for him to go.

He went outside and saw the taxis waiting for the tourists. But Craft wouldn't be going in a taxi. Off to his left, at the end of the terminal, a little white van sat parked along the curb. Next to it, two crew-cut men stood holding a large white cardboard sign with the doctor's name on it.

*

Cox had not been at the auto hobby shop long. He was under his truck, in the parking lot. He heard someone approach and saw a pair of shoes. "I see you're still in mourning for your victim."

Rick knew the voice to well. "Lee wasn't my victim. If you just came here to annoy me, I am not in the mood."

"That airman was not the first student you've killed, was it Cox?" Rick slid out from under the truck. Standing above him was Litton smoking a cigar. The agent had changed clothes from the funeral. Litton's legs seemed even shorter and stubbier in the white shorts. He was also wearing a white cotton polo shirt and white hat. Cox thought he looked like he should be selling ice cream.

"Don't mess with me today," Rick said.

"It's the truth, isn't it? You did cause the death of that student pilot, didn't you?"

"A bird caused the death of that kid."

"Oh, yeah," Litton replied. "That's what the report said. A bird caused the plane to go down. But wasn't that pilot alive when he hit the water?" The agent tapped his ashes so that they fell on Cox's shirt. The SAR instructor jumped to his feet.

"Yeah, and then he got dragged down by his chute," Cox replied without brushing himself off. "A parachute weighs three tons wet. He was tangled in it."

"You mean the great Petty Officer Cox couldn't untangle someone from their chute? Or did you think he was resting also?" Rick took a step towards the little round weasel, but thought better of it.

"Temper, temper, sailor," Litton taunted. Cox knew that Litton was pushing his buttons, and worse, it was working. He counted to ten in his head. Then fifteen, trying to calm down. After all, he didn't do anything.

"You probably enjoy it, don't you?" Litton said.

"Enjoy what?"

"Killing them," Litton said, waiting for the angry outburst that he was sure would follow. But Rick didn't give him the satisfaction, and decided to play the man's game instead. "There's a big difference between not saving someone and killing them," he replied calmly.

"It doesn't seem to be in your case."

"I don't expect someone like you to understand," Cox said and walked to the back of his truck. Litton followed. Rick reached in the back of his truck and pulled a spray can out. He took a bolt from his pocket and sprayed it with the industrial cleaner.

"I'm just stating a fact," Litton said. "When Petty Officer Cox is involved in a rescue, I wouldn't want to be the person he is rescuing."

"Well, don't worry about it," Cox said as he turned toward the NIS Agent. "I wouldn't need to waste my time pulling you out of the drink anyway- -shit floats." He squeezed the trigger of the spray can and the brown cleaner shot all over Litton's shirt.

"Dammit!" Litton said and jumped back, startled. Cox started to laugh, then reached over and grabbed the cigar from his mouth. "Give me that!" Litton ordered.

"I don't think you want to smoke right now," Cox said. "That stuff is extremely flammable. I'd go home and change if I were you."

"You son of a bitch," Litton said walking away. "I'm on to you."

"I'm on to you, Litton," Cox said to himself. "I'm on to you."

*

"Captain," Laura said. "I think he feels guilty over his brother's death, and maybe this is his day in court somehow. Maybe this is his way to find out if he should have done something twelve years ago."

"Are you a psychologist now, Laura?"

"No, sir," she said. "But he refuses to be helped by anyone. I'm trying, but I can't defend him. I'm NIS, and I'd be interfering with a government investigation."

"It is his choice," Reilly said. "With all the press around, I'm sure he will get a lawyer soon."

"He said he won't," Laura replied. "And he seems to do what he says he will."

"Why are you so worried about this?" Reilly asked. "I thought he was the enemy."

"Sir, I think we are making a big mistake," she said. "I don't think he's done anything wrong. I don't believe he caused any harm to that kid, at least not anymore than anyone expects in that world."

"Are you sure it isn't that Wilson heritage of yours? Fighting for the underdog is in your blood," he replied, smiling. "And maybe now it's coming out in you."

"My dad said the same thing, sir," Laura smiled. "Maybe you're both right, sir, at least in the beginning. But not now."

"Are you sure?" Reilly asked. "I remember when you were little, your dad would tell me there wasn't a stray animal you ever met that you didn't try to bring home and adopt."

"Rick is not a stray animal, sir," she replied. "Plus, this is just too strange. Too many coincidences."

"I'll look into it, okay?" Reilly said. "And don't let Litton scare you. He's not the only one who knows people around here."

"I won't."

They both stood, and he walked around his desk. He then leaned on the edge of it, in front of Laura. "You should come over the house for dinner. I'm sure my wife would love to see you."

"I will, I promise."

"You've been saying that for six months now," Reilly said. "I will hold you to it soon."

"Okay, sir," she said and turned around to leave his office

"Tell your dad and grandfather hello for me," he said as she opened the door.

"Yes, sir."

*

Giles walked across the parking lot and along the seawall. He was sweating in the heavy wool uniform and cursing every person who had anything to do with designing it when he saw Willy. The RSS student was skate-boarding along the concrete toward him, wearing a portable CD player, apparently oblivious to the outside world. As he came closer, Giles stepped in front of him. Willy lost his balance as he tried to avoid a collision, and flipped off the board onto the concrete. He got up yelling.

"What the hell are you doing asshole!?" he said. Then he saw who he was talking to.

"I see you're in mourning for your classmate," Giles said.

"No one said I had to go," Willy replied. He was right, of course. But Giles had another issue to speak with him about.

"I hear you're passing some rumors around," Giles said. "Now I know that wouldn't be true."

"They aren't rumors," Willy said. "So I don't know what your problem is."

"If they're not rumors," Giles asked. "Then you wouldn't mind telling me where you get your information from?"

"I'm not allowed to say."

"What the hell are you talking about?" Giles said. "What do you mean you're not allowed to say?"

"I can't." Willy said. "We are not to talk about it 'Not even among ourselves.' Skipper's orders, Petty Officer Giles. And unless my C.O. tells me to, to my face, I ain't saying a word."

"You know what, Willy?" Giles said. "It's a real shame that someone like Lee ends up dead, and that we keep having the pleasure of your company in class every day."

"Is that a threat, Petty Officer Giles?"

Giles looked at him and shook his head before walking away toward the RSS building. He walked right into the instructors lounge and pulled his shirt off. He sat down on an old recliner and closed his eyes and enjoyed the relief of air-conditioning. He hadn't been there five minutes when Lt. Jackson walked in.

"How's it hanging, Lieutenant."

"Where's Cox?" Jackson said, removing his dress uniform jacket and rolling up his sleeves.

"Working on his truck," Giles said. "Why, sir?'

"I need to talk with him," Jackson said. "Go get him."

"Can I get changed first?"

"I need to talk to him right now!"

Giles put his shirt back on and grabbed the duty van keys and went back outside. He drove the un-air-conditioned truck back over to the Auto Hobby Shop and found Rick under the truck. He told him that Jackson wanted to see him. Rick told him he would be there in a few minutes and went to clean up.

A few minutes later the blue BMW pulled up in front of RSS. Jackson watched him through the window and met him at the door to the instructors office. Giles was already back and in the office changing clothes when the two walked in. Jackson asked Giles to leave, then told Rick to come in and close the door behind him.

"What's up sir?"

"I have the results of the piss test, Cox."

"This quick?" Rick asked. "It's only been one day?"

"Yeah," Jackson replied. "Is there something you want to talk with me about?"

"No, sir."

"Your test,"Jackson hesitated. "It, ah, it came back positive."

"That's wrong, sir. It can't be mine."

"I called NAMI," Jackson said. "Ritter confirmed it was your sample."

"That's bullshit sir!" Rick argued. "I have never taken dope, not ever! Not even before the Navy. Give me a test right now- I'll prove it!"

"I can't," Jackson said. "You and I both know that. As an E-6 you don't get a second chance. I've also had to pull your request for the officer program. I'm sorry."

"But, sir," Rick said. "Ask anybody, sir. Ask Giles, he'll tell you. I don't do that shit!"

"Cox," Jackson said. "Do you know what the chances are of this test being wrong?"

"Sir, I swear.."

"Cox," Jackson said. "I want you here in the morning at seven. At that time I will have Master Chief Russo here and I have to make a report about this. I need to let you know that this is serious and that at the very least you will be going to Captain's Mast."

"Sir?"

"A Senior Petty Officer normally gets discharged over this," Jackson said. "You will be discharged, but it will be up to the Skipper if the Navy brings charges or just administratively handles it."

"Sir!"

"Dismissed, Cox," Jackson said. "I want to see you in the morning. It's only because I know you that I am not confining you to the base. Now go before I change my mind."

"Yes, sir." Rick said, he snapped to attention, did a perfect *about face,* then marched out of Jackson's office, slamming the door behind him. He marched through the instructor's office, and outside where Giles was standing.

"What was that about?" Giles asked.

"My piss test," Rick said. "It was positive."

"What?" Giles said falling back against a car and laughing. "You? Drugs? Get real!"

"It's fucking real," Rick said. "And Jackson said that I have to go in front of the old man--that I am gonna be discharged." Rick leaned back against the brick wall of RSS. He rubbed his temples with his hands. Giles went over to his friend. "Hey," he said. "This is a mistake--a snafu! I'll go in and talk with Jackson, tell him you've never done dope. Don't worry about it!"

As Giles spoke, the beeper Laura gave Rick went off. "Shit," he said. "I have to go pick her up. I can't believe that my career will end like this."

She saw the little blue convertible coming across the parking lot. Rick pulled up in front of Base Legal where Laura was waiting for him. He didn't recognize her at first, she had put her hair up. She looked over and saw him there. Bare-chested and without shoes on, his appearance caught her by surprise. He saw the look on her face and explained that his clothes were covered with grease and oil from working on the truck.

"I thought it better to throw them in the trunk, than get your seats dirty," he said. She didn't answer right away. "I need to stop at my apartment and change."

Laura was not prepared to see Rick like that. She hadn't really given any thought to what he looked like underneath his uniform, but it was hard for her not to notice now. Every muscle on his body was sculptured and cut. His farmer's tan did not take away from his rock hard body. His close cropped haircut only exaggerated his features. She could not believe she didn't notice before what ten years of exercise and fitness training will do to a man's body.

She filed her thoughts away and reminded herself of the problem at hand. "That's fine," she said. "We can stop there first--then go to my place."

The little BMW pulled up in front of Rick's apartment. He left the car running and told Laura he'd be right out after grabbing the bag of dirty clothes from the trunk. She leaned back, turned up the radio, and closed her eyes. He ran inside and quickly washed his face and hands before quickly changing into shorts and t-shirt. He was back outside a few minutes later and hopped into the car.

"Where to?" Rick asked. Laura gave him directions to her apartment and then sat back and relaxed as he followed them precisely from memory. Along the way he told her about the results of the piss test, and what Jackson said about a discharge.

"Test results like that don't usually come back that fast," Laura said. "Of course, this is an unusual case."

"Laura, I don't expect you to help me. I'm not asking anyone for any help," Rick said. "But I just need some answers to my questions. I mean honest answers."

"I have no problem with that," Laura said. "I promise I'll be honest."

"I know you are investigating me but..."

Laura interrupted him. "Actually, I'm not on the case anymore. I can't believe I forgot to tell you!"

"What?"

"Litton saw you and I speaking," she said. "I was kicked off the case. In fact, I was told not to even speak with you again. I'm not to contact you in any way."

"Then why are you doing this?" Rick asked, confused. She was there, in her car, headed to her house, then dinner. She shrugged. "I guess I want to prove to you that I am someone you can trust, that you can talk too."

"But.."

"Last night you told me things in confidence," Laura replied. "And this morning...I guess you were right, and I screwed up. I told Litton some things, thinking it would help. But it didn't. I guess I wanted you to know that you could trust me. And maybe I wanted to show myself that too." She took her sunglasses and put them on, let down her hair. They said not another word while they drove along and the Florida sun started to sink toward the horizon. He parked in front of her house, and they both went in.

"Make yourself at home," Laura said. She saw there were no messages on the machine, and headed into the back bedroom."I'll be right out."

"Sure," Rick said, and sat down in the overstuffed couch and searched the room with his eyes. He read the titles of the books on her shelves, and the titles of her videos. He thought of turning on the television, but the reality was he was much too preoccupied to do anything. It had been a long time since he was invited into a woman's home. So he just sat there.

A few minutes later she came out to the living room and saw him sitting there. She handed him the remote and smiled, "I do have electricity," she kidded.

He took the remote and turned on the television while she went into the kitchen. She asked him if he wanted a drink, and poured them each a glass of ice-water.

"Do you mind if I take a shower first?" she asked. "I have been running around in the sun all day."

"No, go ahead," he said turning on the news. "You know, we don't have to go out, we can eat here."

"We can go out," she said. "Unless you don't want to?"

"I just thought, with the warnings from your boss and all," Rick said. "I don't want to get you in any more trouble, that's all." She agreed it would be better if they didn't go out in public, just in case. He said he would go get them some take-out while she was in the shower.

"How about some wings?"

"Sure," Rick said.

"Hooters wings okay?"

"You like Hooters?"

"Yeah," she replied. "My best friend worked her way through law school at Hooters. The food's good. Why do you look surprised?"

"I don't know. You just don't seem the type."

"Are you saying I couldn't get a job there?" Laura said pretending to be insulted.

"Not at all," Rick said. "I don't know, I just..."

Laura laughed and waved him away. "Are you gonna get us something to eat or what?"

"I'm going, I'm going."

"Just don't get lost," she said. "I'm hungry."

*

"Mr. Jackson, I think I know where a lot of these rumors are coming from ," Giles said.

"What rumors?"

"About Rick."

"Petty Officer Cox is not your concern, Giles," Jackson said. "He's a big boy. He can take care of himself."

"Yes, sir. I know that, sir," Giles replied as he balanced oon the line between anger and subordination. "But that doesn't change the fact that we have a student who is mouthing off to anyone who will listen, spreading lies about an instructor in this school. And I won't allow that, even if you do, sir."

Jackson sat there looking out the window onto the empty obstacle course. He did not reply to the instructor. Giles waited, then continued. "Rick and I were taking the class through *sugar cookies* and *cracks* when Airman Recruit Willy Simms started mouthing off. He's taking some revenge on Rick for putting him to the mat."

"Giles," the officer said, interrupting. "The Skipper freaked out when he had smurfing explained to him. I can't go in and tell them that *sugar cookies* and *cracks* were the cause of his piss test results."

"Sir, you and I both know that Rick doesn't take drugs. But, if rumors are going around as revenge for a form of training, regardless of what they are called!" Giles said. "I am not going to watch my best freind's life be thrown away because our Commanding Officer doesn't like the names we use in training!."

Jackson turned around. "The problem is that you and I know what these things are and why we do it. But the public doesn't know and frankly doesn't give a shit! To them, forcing a bunch of men into the water, then making them roll around in sand until they look like sugar cookies and then run down the beach until the sand falls off sounds incredibly sadistic. And I don't even want to go into *cracks.*"

"The way you describe it," Giles replied. "It does."

"That's an accurate description, isn't it?"

"Yes, sir." Giles said. "But being able to perform while under a lot of physical stress is part of the training."

"I know that and you know that, but a kid is dead,"Jackson said. "So who else cares what we think?"

*

Rick returned from the resteraunt to Laura's townhouse. She was still in the shower as he went into the kitchen. He found plates and napkins, and got a glass of water before he sat down at the table to eat. Laura came out wearing a robe, her head wrapped in a towel and saw he was back. "I thought I heard someone," she said, then disappeared back into the bedroom. A few minutes later, she returned dressed in gray gym shorts and an extra large Winnie-the-Pooh t-shirt.

"Mind if I watch the news while we eat," she said. He took the food and drinks into the living room. The television had not been on three minutes when a story came on that made Rick start to choke on his chicken wing.

"The Times-Press is reporting that it learned that Petty Officer Richard Cox made a fatal mistake in a Search and Rescue operation just weeks prior to the training session in which Senator Robert Lee's son was tragically killed. During the earlier operation, Cox apparently let one Navy pilot trainee drown while trying to recover the body of his instructor, who according to sources, Cox already knew was dead. We spoke with the young wife of the Navy pilot trainee."

The television station cut to a taped interview of the dead pilot's wife and kids sitting on the steps of her parent's home in Virginia.

"That's a damn lie, Laura! I didn't know! I swear I didn't know!" Rick yelled as he went over and stood in front of the television.

"I know. Hold on, let me hear the rest of this."

"I can't believe this man had the guts to not only accept thanks from us," she said into the camera, tears streaking down her cheeks. "But to accept a medal for heroism in front of all of Jimmy's family and friends."

The camera slowly zoomed in on the faces of the two toddlers who were now with out a father. The two children stared wide-eyed into the camera for an uncomfortably long time before switching back to the reporter who was standing in front of the gates at NAS Pensacola.

"I didn't even want the medal!" Rick said and walked out onto the back porch. Laura continued to watch.

"We are also checking out a related story," the anchorman continued. "This one concerning Cox's Commanding Officer, United States Navy Commander John Harding. Stories are circulating that Commander Harding had known Cox's older brother, who as we reported earlier, had also drowned. We are trying to confirm this, but this we do know: both men played football for Florida State University, not at the same time though. But they both had attended some Florida State University functions, and may have met there. This leads to some interesting theories regarding cover-ups. We have tried to contact Petty Officer Cox for comment, but he has not returned our calls. Back to the news desk."

Laura came outside to join Rick who was sitting on the porch swing. His head was down and his face was in his hands. She sat beside him curling her leg under her, and rubbed his back. He did not look up, but he also didn't pull away. The two sat quietly as the sun began to set.

"I don't think you should go home tonight?"

"Why?" Rick asked.

"I've seen cases like this before with my dad," Laura said. "The news media is probably waiting for you to come home. They are probably out front of your apartment right now."

"I need my uniform for the morning."

"I'll get it," Laura said. "No one knows me. They won't pay me any attention. I'll just slip in and out."

"Where should I go?"Rick asked in almost a whisper.

"Why don't you stay here? "she said.

11

***

Friday, June 19

Rick arrived at six forty-five the following morning. He had never been in trouble before, and even though it was not requested, he wore his dress uniform. Giles met him in the parking lot of RSS. He couldn't help but notice that he was dropped off by Laura.

"I called your house last night but no one answered."

"I stayed at Laura's," Cox replied. He saw his friend's reaction. "On the couch," he added. The two went in the building together. They were met by Lt. Jackson who told them that Master Chief Russo was running behind and he would be there soon. Rick went out into the lounge to get some coffee leaving Jackson and Giles.

"Mister Jackson?" Giles said after Rick left the room. "There are some things I think you should be aware of, sir."

"Is this about Cox?"

"Yes, sir," Giles said. "I know that Rick would not tell you himself, but I think there are some things you should know."

"Like what?"

"Well..." Giles did not know where to start.

*

Laura walked into Capt. Reilly's office. He was on the phone, but the Commanding Officer of the base legal office waved her in. She entered and sat down. He cut short his conversation and hung up the phone.

"Laura," he said. "Thanks for coming."

"No problem, sir."

Reilly reached around and grabbed a manila folder off the file cabinet behind him. He opened it and handed Laura a paper off the top. "I did some checking on my own about your friend and the young airman who drowned."

"And?"

"And I agree with you that things seem to be moving very quickly for both the Navy and as a legal issue," Reilly said."And I wanted to share what I've found..."

*

"...and if you don't believe me, ask him yourself," Giles said. Jackson told Giles to wait outside the office, then went in and phoned the Schools Command building. He asked if Master Chief Russo was still with Harding, and when that was confirmed, Jackson asked to be passed though to his Commanding Officer.

"Schools Command, Commander Harding," Jackson's C.O. said answering the phone.

"This is Lt. Jackson, Skipper," he said. "Sir, Master Chief Russo was supposed to be here at seven regarding the urinalysis results for Petty Officer Cox."

"Sorry about that, Lieutenant," Harding replied. "I was hoping we could postpone that meeting until tomorrow."

"Yes, sir," Jackson said. "In fact, that was what I was going to ask for. If you don't mind me asking sir, why are we postponing it?"

"According to Mr. Litton," Harding said, "it would seem as if we have some new evidence against your boy. There is now a witness that saw him with what is suspected to be an illegal substance. And I also have had a complaint about one of your instructors threatening a student."

"What witness, sir?"

"I'll brief you about that at lunch time," Harding said. "I reserved a table at the Officer's Club. We'll be joined by Admiral Tract's Aide, Lt. Commander Hunt, and Agent Litton."

"Yes, sir, what time?"

"One o'clock."

"What was that other thing, sir?'

"I'll talk to you about that at lunch as well, Mr. Jackson."

"Yes, sir." Jackson said. "Goodbye, sir." He hung up the phone and called for Giles and Rick to get in his office. Rick came in and stood at attention. Jackson put him at ease, told them both to relax.

"I just got off the phone with the Skipper. It seems that you have a few days, Cox."

"Yes, sir," he said and did a perfect about face, and started to leave.

"Not so fast, sailor," Jackson said. "Get back in here and talk to me." Rick stopped and turned around with another perfect about face.

"Sir?" he said, eyes straight ahead. Jackson walked over and sat on his desk. "Okay, Cox," the Lieutenant said. "I'm duly impressed, now knock it off and talk to me."

"About what does the Lieutenant want to discuss, sir?" Rick said still at attention. Jackson stayed relaxed on the desk.

"Unless you want to stand there at attention all day, you'd better relax and talk to me." Jackson said. "I am trying to help you." Rick's eyes dropped over to the officer. "Yeah, I am trying to help you, Cox. Giles told me some things, but I want to hear them from you."

Rick thought about it a minute, then relaxed his posture, after giving Giles a much deserved scowl. "Yes, sir," Rick said. "There have been a lot of strange things happening recently."

"Like what?"

"Sir, remember when I met with Litton right after Lee died?" Rick asked. "You had to leave?"

"Yeah?"

"I was read my rights--Litton made a big deal of it," Rick said. He explained that he was the only person he knew of that had been marandized. He told Jackson of the accusations by Litton. Of the news reports. And of what Dr. Craft had said to him, and of what Laura had told him about the records.

"Sir, everyone in this room knows we don't get transferred anywhere and leave NATOPS behind," Rick said. "Sir, you're an NFO, would you ever go anywhere, even TAD without them?"

Jackson knew Rick was right. He was a Naval Flight Officer himself. He operated electronics in the back seat, but just like a pilot or aircrew, he made damn sure his NATOPS record followed him wherever he went. "But I'll bet someone who doesn't fly like we do would not even think of this, sir."

"Cox, even if what you are saying is true," Jackson replied. "It doesn't change the fact that your piss test was positive."

"Sir, if someone is doing this to me, then I would bet that they could manipulate a piss test," Rick said. "I mean, c'mon! They had a

Commander disappear!"

"But why would someone go to all this trouble?" Jackson asked.

*

"Captain," Laura said. "There is one other thing I need checked out."

"What's that?"

"Rick's urinalysis test," she said. She explained the quick and positive results. She explained the consequences even though he knew.

"So what do you want from me?"

"I need to have those results re-checked, sir."

"I can't do that," Reilly said. "I have no idea where the sample goes or where it is."

"If you find out where, would you have someone re-examine the results?" Laura said. "I need to know what those results say."

"Hold on a minute." Captain Reilly grabbed the phone and dialed a number. He waited for an answer. "Bobby, it's Tom. I need a favor from you..."

*

"I'll admit that all this looks pretty funky," Jackson replied. "But the Skipper says he now has a witness that saw you with drugs, and also said that an instructor threatened him!"

"Willy? It has to be Wilson! " Giles said. "Willy is their witness- Now the shit is getting deep!"

"I don't know who it is," Jackson said. "Evidently someone was talking with Litton and said they saw something and some instructor threatened them."

"I'll bet its Willy," Giles said. He explained the meeting he had with him on the seawall and the remarks about rumors.

"Is this the same guy who you caught smashing windows in town, Cox?" Jackson asked. Rick nodded. This was getting more interesting by the minute. "Okay, I'll tell you what. I'll ask around, to find out what's going on. But Cox, I have to confine you to the base. Harding's orders."

"But sir?"

"No buts, Cox," Jackson said. "I can't disobey a direct order."

"Am I charged with anything?'

"Yeah," Jackson replied. "Using an illegal substance, for now anyway. That's not me, that's the command."

"Shit, sir. "

"Unless you can find someone that has the authority to overturn that order, you need to stay on this base." The Lieutenant picked up the phone and dialed a number. "I'll call the BEQ and get you a room assignment. I'm sorry."

"Yes, sir," Rick said. "I don't have any transportation anyway right now. Is that all, sir?"

"Yeah," Jackson said. "You guys go out into the lounge. Just hang out until I get the room info." The two instructors went out to the duty office and sat down. Without classes, there was very little for them to do. Rick picked up the phone and dialed Laura's pager.

The NIS agent was walking out to her car when her pager went off. She took the cellular from her purse and called the RSS instructor's office. Giles answered and handed the phone to Rick. He told her what happened. "I'm in trouble," he said. She heard the tone of his voice. It was finally sinking in.

"Rick, I want you to contact someone," she told him. "He will help us. I know him."

"Is he a lawyer?"

"I trust him," she replied. "Now I need you to trust him too."

"Okay," he agreed. He wrote down the man's phone number and promised to contact him.

"Rick," Laura said when he had copied everything down. "I need to go over to NAMI and get copies of your test results."

"Why?" He asked. "Ritter said that they were mine. No one doubts him."

"Hold tight," Laura said. "I'll figure something out." Rick hung up and put the note in his pocket. He sat down.

"If you need a car," Giles said. "You can use mine after tomorrow."

"Don't you need it?"

"No, I have off tomorrow, then SAR duty the next four days," Giles said. "Since we aren't having classes." Giles sounded upset about it.

"Wanna trade places?" Rick asked.

"If I could I would, buddy," Giles said. "So Others May Live--that includes you."

"Thanks."

"I mean it," Giles said. Rick knew he did.

*

"Who the hell is Ensign Davis?" Hunt asked.

"Why?" Litton replied.

"Because he called for you a few minutes ago," Admiral Tract's Aide replied. "How did he know you were here?"

"It's about some pictures," Litton said. He forgot all about that and made a mental note to pick up the pictures from the store. He had triple copies made. Just in case. He looked up at the clock. There was still an hour before lunch. "I will meet you at the 'O' Club."

"Where are you going?" Hunt asked. "The Admiral will be here any minute, and he wants to talk with you."

"About what?"

"That leak last night!" Hunt said. "What do you think?"

"I thought we should have some insurance that Harding will play along," Litton said. *What was wrong with that? If the guy did what was expected of him, then another leak would clear his name- if not- Oh, well!.*

"Fine, I'll wait," Litton said.

*

"Giles, Cox, " Jackson said when he came out of his office. "I'm heading over the club to meet with the Skipper. I need you two to be together."

"Why?" Rick asked

"I need you to wait here until the BEQ calls back with your room assignment," Jackson said. "Just think of Giles as the one person covering both our asses."

*

Laura was in her car and headed back to NAMI when she passed the Officer's Club. She saw a familiar face get out of his car and did a u-turn. She pulled alongside Lt. Jackson who was walking on the sidewalk toward the club. She asked if he wanted a lift, but he declined the offer. She quickly stopped the car and hopped out. Laura caught up with him as he neared the steps leading inside.

"Can I help you?"

"I don't know if you remember me, Lieutenant," Laura said. He shook his head. "Agent Wilson, NIS."

"I remember. What can I do for you?"

She told him that she was trying to help Rick, and that she needed some time. He told her about the results of the urinalysis, and of Captain's Mast and that because of Rick's rank, he would be discharged. She told him of his hatred of lawyers.

"That's okay," Jackson said. "Lawyers aren't used in Captain's Mast. Only court-martial proceedings."

"Regardless, Lt. Jackson, your instructor needs one," she replied. "I need to take Petty Officer Cox away from here, away from the press, away from Litton. I need to get this straightened out."

"Miss Wilson, you're asking me to disobey a direct order," Jackson said. "To betray the oath I took."

"But if you don't give Rick an opportunity to defend himself, then you are betraying the men that you command."

"He will get his chance," Jackson said. "Just as everyone else in the Navy does. Through the Chain of Command. This needs to be by the book."

"Do you do everything by the book?"

"Yes," Jackson said.

"Then why did you decorate Petty Officer Cox for ignoring the order of his pilot when he tried to save those two men a few weeks back."

"Because what he did was dangerous, but he disregarded that to try and save those officers," Jackson said. "He was willing to throw his life away to save someone else."

"So how is that different from what I am asking you to do? You can save someone who desperately needs your help, Lieutenant," Laura said. "Let me ask you this, that motto over there..."

They both look at the RSS sign. "...So Others May Live. Does that mean anything to you, or is it only for the men of your command?"

"I don't get your point?"

"I want to know if that is just words to you?"

"No, ma'am," Jackson said. "I'm not a rescue swimmer, but I would try anything to save a man. It's one thing I've learned since being here."

"Lt. Jackson," Laura said as she stopped and looked at him directly, face to face. "One of your men is drowning. He's in trouble so far over his head that he can't save himself. And he doesn't know it."

"I know."

"I am asking you to put your career on the line for him, I am asking that you not betray your oath, but that you do what's right," Laura said. "Rick would never ask you. The men in your command have learned how to save others, but Rick has never learned how to save himself."

"I don't know. I have direct orders that he not leave the base..." Jackson said, looking away.

"Do you believe he intentionally harmed that boy?"

"What everyone is saying..."

"I know what everyone is saying," Laura replied. "But the question is what do you know deep in your heart? Rick has put his life in danger to pull dead men from water. You and I and everyone else know he would not intentionally harm anyone. We know he doesn't do drugs. We know that! You know that, Lieutenant, I know you do!" Jackson walked away without a word. He looked out and watched the waves lap at the concrete seawall. At the empty 'O'course. At the motto displayed on the building that was under his command.

"My father never saw the sea," Jackson said. "We grew up in Tuskegee."

"Alabama?"

"Yeah." Jackson replied. "My grandfather had moved there during the war. He was a mechanic for the Army Air Corps. My dad would sit outside in the field when he was little and watch the black pilots fly around." Jackson picked up a stone and threw it out into Pensacola Bay. "We weren't poor, but we weren't rich either, Miss Wilson."

She said nothing. But he knew she was listening. "Both my father and grandfather retired from the Army. Both were enlisted men. So when I graduated from college, and entered the navy, I thought they'd be...well, let's just say not as happy as if I had gone into the army."

"What did your father say to you?"

He turned and looked at her. "When I received my wings, I'll never forget. I looked up at the two of them sitting in the bleachers on this very base, and the look they had...it was the same look they had when they would tell me about those Tuskegee pilots."

"I guess they were proud of you, huh?"

"Miss Wilson, I had never felt so proud to be my father's son in my entire life. And after the ceremony, when they came running over to me on the field, both my dad and my grandfather snapped me the most perfect salute I had ever received."

"Sounds like they were just as proud of you as you are of them."

"Yes, Ma'am," Jackson said. "But the thing that I remember now is what my grandfather said to me. He told me that there were two kinds of officers. There are officers whose men show them respect because of the rank on their shoulder, and there are officers that get rank on their shoulders because of the respect they have shown their men. I always thought I was the latter."

"From what I've heard from your men," Laura said."You are." Jackson turned around and adjusted his cap.

"I will give Cox a forty-eight hour liberty," he told her. "That's all I can do without asking Harding's approval. It's the best I can do. Any more than that and the skipper would need to authorize it. Especially after that story on the news last night."

"Your men are very lucky to have you," she said. "There may be a way to have it so you're not on the hook for him leaving." She told him her idea. He agreed it was worth a shot, then looked at his watch. "But you'd better hurry because I'm supposed to meet Harding and your boss and God knows who else in about two hours." She gave him a hug.

"You're doing the right thing," she assured him. "Your grandfather would be proud."

"I hope so," Jackson said. "Because if I do this, I doubt I'll ever get another command."

"Look, I'll make a deal with you," Jackson said. "You take responsibility for Cox and I'll let him go in your custody."

"I can't do that," Laura said. "I'm no longer a member of the investigation team.'

"Well, I'm sorry," Jackson said. "But my hands are tied."

"Will you keep him in your office for thirty minutes? I have an idea."

"Do you have a phone?"

"Yes," she said and quickly handed it to him.

"Thirty minutes," he said as he waited for an answer.

*

The hands that picked up the fax from the desk were seventy-two years old, but they were as steady and nimble as a thirty-year-old's. The eyes behind the framed glasses read each word, each page as it fed out of the machine. The smoke from the pipe that sat in the small metal holder curled up along the window as the information on the documents was filed away in the man's mind.

When the paper stopped printing, he took them all and went out of the small office and into the next room. He had some phone calls to make.

*

Rick and Giles arrived at the base legal office just as Laura had asked them to. She met the two instructors in the parking lot, and told Rick to get in her car. She gave Giles her cellular phone number and beeper number. "What's this for?" He asked writing the information down.

"Rick and I are going on a trip for a few days," She explained. "I need some time to figure things out. I may need to get a hold of you, and you me."

"For what?"

"I can't go through my office for information," she said. "Litton is bound to find out."

"So you want me to be an errand boy?" Giles said.

"Basically, yeah."

"I can do that," Giles said. At least he was doing something to help his friend. "The only problem will be Jackson. I mean, he might start asking me where Rick is?"

"It's taken care of," Laura said. Her smile told him all he needed to know. He said a quick good-bye to his friend before the two sped off toward the main gate. Laura looked over at Rick as they sped across the bridge and away from NAS Pensacola. She saw the muscles in his face relax.

"Why do I feel like I am doing something wrong?" he asked her as they drove past the tattoo parlors, used car dealerships and bars that lined the streets leading to the base.

"Don't worry," she said. "You are about the only one involved in this plan who actually should not be worried."

Rick leaned back in the seat. "That makes me feel a whole lot better," he said sarcastically as he closed his eyes. It was not long before he was asleep, and she realized how exhausted Rick had been. He did not wake up when they arrived at her house, and she let him sleep as she packed. She quietly strapped her bags to the luggage rack on the tiny sports car, and pulled away without waking Rick. She had only one stop before heading out of town. She pulled into the gas station and filled up. She also went over to the Fed Ex box and dropped in two next day air packs. She looked at her watch as she pulled onto Interstate 10. It was a few minutes after one. Now it was her turn to worry.

*

Jackson was a few minutes late arriving at the Officer's Club, but he was still the first one there. He was led to and seated at Admiral Tract's table. Some senior officers turned their gaze at the Lieutenant who sat alone at the Flag Officer's section. Jackson was relieved when Harding and the others came in, even if Litton was with them. Tract arrived and after visiting other tables, eventually sat down with the officers of his command. Jackson looked down at his watch and saw the time. It was almost two. He took a deep breath and tried to calm his nerves.

Lt. Cdr. Hunt introduced Jackson to the Admiral and generally took charge of ordering drinks. There was small talk, but most of it was between Litton, Hunt, and the Senator's aides. Senator Lee said very little, as did the Admiral who sat there observing, like a bored king watching his court jester at play. The food arrived, very quickly Jackson noticed.

The group ate and drank. They were not obnoxious, but noisy enough that other officers looked over to see what was going on. The Senator finally whispered something to Tract who then cleared his throat. The others quickly quieted down and as the empty plates were removed from the table, the Admiral took a sip of water, then directed his attention to Harding.

"So, Commander," Tract said. "How's the investigation coming on your end. I heard you have some news for me?"

Harding looked lost. "News, sir?"

"The piss test results, Commander," Hunt said. He turned to the admiral. "I believe that the test came back positive, gentlemen. As you all know, a Petty Officer First Class or above that has a positive urinalysis recieves an automatic separation from the military."

The men all nodded. They knew. Hunt turned to Harding. "But what I was thinking, gentlemen," Hunt continued, "is that under normal circumstances the offending sailor would be given a Captain's Mast."

"What is that exactly?" Lee's aide asked.

"A Captain's Mast is like court for minor infractions," Harding explained. It was used for smaller offenses such as unauthorized absences or dereliction of duty. For things that didn't require a full blown court-martial, but were serious enough to warrant punishment. The sailor would be brought in front of his Commanding Officer who would decide his fate. It made sense on ship to hold a Captain's Mast instead of sending offending sailors to shore every time regulations were broken. Of course, the accused could request a court martial, but most didn't.

"But in this case," Harding said. "I would not be surprised to see Cox request a court martial."

"Why is that?" Tract asked

"Because, Admiral," Jackson cut in, "Petty Officer Cox is a man who takes things to the extreme."

"Obviously," Senator Lee added. Jackson ignored the comment and continued. "The Navy is his life, his blood, Admiral. The man has no family. This is his family. He feels that he is innocent of this charge and of the other issues that are surrounding him right now. I think he would want the opportunity to fight for his name."

"He's fighting a losing battle," Litton said. "He knows he'll be discharged. It doesn't matter to me or my investigation either way."

"Harding?"Tract said. "You've been quiet, considering this is one of your men."

"Admiral," Harding replied. "I believe Mr. Jackson is correct. I think that Petty Officer Cox will fight us the whole way. And that is his right. And if that is his decision, I will encourage him to get legal counsel and make his case."

"Yeah, well don't encourage him too hard, Commander," Senator Lee said.

"Excuse me?" Harding replied.

"I think what the Senator is saying," Tract replied, "is that since this sailor seems to go off the deep end, or go 'all out' as you say, that we should try and keep control of this investigation. I think that a man like this needs to be watched, or better yet, supervised closely."

"He ought to be locked up!" the Senator added. After the remark, Tract stood up.

"Now that you all know how the Senator and I feel," Tract said.

"We must excuse ourselves. We have a tee time to make." The other officers stood, but Tract put them at ease. He told them all that they should stay and have dessert, and that Hunt had some more ideas regarding control of the current situation. "And lunch is on me, gentlemen." He and the Senator's party left for the golf course. After they were gone, desserts were brought in. Litton immediately ordered the most expensive one on the menu.

Hunt asked what was Cox's current status. Harding said he had ordered the instructor to be confined to the base, and that he was currently in the Bachelor Enlisted Quarters.

"At least if the son of a bitch can't be locked up," Hunt said. "He's around where we can watch him."

"That's not exactly true," Jackson said and swallowed a spoonful of chocolate ice cream..

"What do you mean?" Litton asked.

"He was released in custody of Base Legal around eleven this morning."

"What?" Litton said. "Who?!"

"An Ensign Davis came and took custody," Jackson said. He noticed that the only person not upset was Harding.

"God dammit!" Hunt said and took out his cellular phone. "I'll take care of this."

Captain Reilly was discussing recent cases in the meeting room when the message came in that Admiral Tract's Aide was on the phone for him. He placed the call on speaker. He and the other five legal officers listened as Hunt's voice filled the room.

"Captain Reilly, I don't know what your people think they are doing over there, but we have a problem."

"What's that, Commander?"

"One of your officers has taken custody of a sailor by the name of Petty Officer Richard Cox. He's an instructor at the Rescue Swimmer School."

"Is that so, Commander?" Reilly said. "So far I don't hear a problem." This drew hushed laughter from the other officers in the room.

"The problem," Hunt said, "is that this man was being held because he is suspected of dealing in drugs. This is a very high profile case, as I am sure you know."

"Mister Hunt. High profile or no profile, I am sure that if one of my officers took custody of someone, it was all above board and perfectly legal."

"Captain," Hunt replied. "I think it would be best that Cox be returned to his command immediately!'

"I'll take that under advisement, Lieutenant Commander Hunt," Reilly said. "Taking in your vast knowledge of law, and of the years practicing after passing the bar..."

Jackson and the others at the Officer's Club could not hear what was being said to Hunt, but the Admiral's Aide had a look of confusion on his face. "I'm sorry, Captain," they heard him say, "but you have me mistaken for someone else. I'm not a lawyer, I'm Admiral Tract's Aide."

"Oh! You're not a lawyer?" Captain Reilly said in mock surprise. "Well, in that case I suggest you not tell me about any legal issues; because Commander, you see--I am a lawyer."

"Dammit Reilly..."

"And I am also a Captain in our little Navy, Lieutenant Commander. You watch how you address me or you will have your own legal problems."

"Captain, do you realize who my boss is?"

"Yes, I do," Reilly said. "Do you know who my boss is? Maybe you should call Washington and find out. Goodbye, Mr. Hunt." The lawyers laughed out loud as soon as the connection was terminated.

"Dammit!" Hunt said.

"What?" Litton asked.

"Jackson," Hunt said. "You have a hell of a lot of explaining to do!"

"Mr. Hunt," Harding cut in. "You address me, not any of my officers."

"Fine, Commander. If that's the way you want it!" Hunt said. "Expect to hear from the Admiral, shortly!" He stood and left with Litton in tow. Harding did not say a word to Jackson. The C.O. left a few minutes later. Jackson sat alone and looked at his watch. It was a little after four o'clock. Time to go home. A waiter came over and placed a shot glass on the table.

"I didn't order this?"

"The Commander sent it to you," the waiter said. "He said someone should buy you a drink!"

*

"So how did you get permission for me to leave the base," Rick asked. "You did get permission, didn't you?"

"Yes, it's perfectly legal," Laura said. She hoped that wasn't a lie. He settled back in his seat, not convinced what they were doing was within regulations, but for the first time in a long time he was relaxed and letting someone else do some worrying for him.

The little blue sports car continued heading east along Interstate 10, the bungee cords on the back holding the bags that wouldn't fit in the small trunk. An hour or so into the trip Rick awoke and asked where they were headed. She told him she really hadn't thought too much about it. She just knew they needed to get far enough away so that she could work with Rick without worrying about being seen together, and without interference of Litton or others. "Even Giles could be a distraction," she told him.

"So why East?"

"Your Lieutenant said you had a place where you liked to go relax in Panama City," she replied. "So I figured that was as good a place as any."

"He's a good guy, Jackson," Rick said."Yeah, I know a little place."

He gave her directions to the resort. It was still a couple hours away and they used the time to go over what had happened in the pool, and also to just get to know each other better.

"I thought you said little?" Laura replied as they pulled in. Cars were lined up all along the circular drive. The valet came over and helped Laura from the car. She looked at her watch. Almost three in the afternoon. The hotel was obviously elegant, but crowded with kids and families. It was the last week of June and she hadn't thought about summer vacation and school being out.

"Wow!" she replied looking around at the palm trees and waterfalls, the busboys and valets. She had grown up with money, but they never traveled to places like this, or, if her parents had, they had never taken her. "They must pay you more than I thought," she teased.

They checked into a bungalow that faced the Gulf of Mexico. There were two bedrooms. Rick had offered before Laura had said anything, and she was glad that he had not misinterpreted why they were there. But she also felt just a little insulted that he had not asked if she wanted her own room. For Rick's part, he had wanted to ask her from the moment they left, but he had decided there would be no point in it. She was a lawyer; he was just a sailor in the Navy who would probably be kicked out anyway within a few days.

Rick tipped the valet after he left their bags in the room. During the ride, Rick had learned that Laura loved chocolate, the Beatles, and watching the Simpsons' reruns on television, though he had said little about himself. He called room service and asked if they had truffles, then ordered some when they told him they did. He made a dinner reservation at the resort's restaurant, it would be a late meal.

He hung up the phone and said he was going to take a shower quickly, then he wanted to take a walk and show her the resort. She thought that would be nice, but she wanted to start working before the base shut down for the weekend.

When Rick disappeared into the bathroom, Laura called her father's law firm. She was put through right away, and told her dad what had happened. She told him her plans. He offered his help, as only a father could. He asked her about Rick. She told him of the talks at the seawall, of his record, of the night he spent at her house.

"Dad, he's a nice guy, an honest guy," she said. "I don't know how he got in the position he did, but he needs help."

"It sounds like he's found it."

"Dad, please..."

"I'm just worried about my little girl," he replied. "That's all."

She had told her dad about the conversation they had during the ride earlier. She told him what she knew about Rick, which wasn't much. He collected Hot Wheels toy cars, had a twenty-eight-year-old teddy bear that his mother had given him when he was born, and that he still treasured, and of Rick's love of movies. She also told her father more about Rick's brother. "Dad, he doesn't have any family. His home is nothing like what you gave me."

"Just make sure you are acting in his best interest," he replied. "Not yours. That is what a good lawyer does."

"I promise," she said. He said she could call when she needed advice and she said for him to say hello to her grandpa, and also said Captain Reilly had said hello. She was off the phone and changed into a light summer dress by the time Rick was ready to go.

The two walked around the property and while they admired the grounds, they also talked about some aspects of Naval Aviation that Laura wasn't familiar with, including a hundred acronyms that she hadn't heard of. And one she did.

"What is a NATOPS Jacket used for?"

"NATOPS? It's basically the Bible for anyone who flies in the Navy. It spells out requirements to fly, from flight surgeon's medical clearances to what type of life raft to deploy from a helicopter to what a pilot should do if his landing gear malfunctions."

"And a NATOPS Jacket is a folder that has all that stuff in it?"

"A NATOPS Jacket is a personnel record that has things like certifications, such as what type of plane someone can fly in, or any schools or courses someone has had. It has copies of the NATOPS training exam scores and a record of any flight equipment the Navy gave you."

"You said it had medical stuff in it?"

"Yeah, it has copies of any time a person was cleared to fly, we call 'em up chits," Rick explained. "And of any time someone was grounded. Why the sudden interest?"

"I was thinking if we could get a copy of Lee's - what do you call them--Up Chits?" Laura said. "We could see if there was a problem anywhere."

"That would be hard to get a hold of," Rick said.

"Not really," Laura said. "I got Craft's."

"You have Craft's?!"

"Yeah," she said. "But a lot of good it will do us now."

"Maybe it will do more good than you think," Rick said. "Where'd you get it from?"

"Base ops, why?"

"Because," Rick said. "It might just help us find that slippery son-of-a-bitch!" They agreed that the first thing they needed to do was find out if any new hours were called in for the flight surgeon. And if there were, they needed to find out where the information had come from, so they could find Craft. They needed the doctor to collaborate Rick's story. But they also needed to somehow stop the Captain's Mast.

Laura called Base Operations on her ever-present cellular, and asked if any more flight hours have been added to Craft's NATOPS record. She was asked for her clearance number, which she gave to them. She was transferred to the Officer of the Day. After explaining who she was, he told her the only information he would give over the phone was that there were new hours faxed in.

"...but, as of now, we can't seem to locate his record."

"Do you know where they were faxed from?" Laura asked. "It's important!"

"Ma'am, I don't know if I can give you that information over the phone," he said. "But I would be more than happy to supply you with a copy if you stop by and show me the proper identification."

She thanked him and said that someone would be by before hanging up. "How am I going to get a copy of that record?" Rick sat there waiting for the explanation.

"They wont fax it?"

"Not to a hotel," she said. "I can assure you of that. And I can't ask them to fax it to my office."

"No one at NIS would get it for you?"

"No," Laura said. "We are on our own with this one."

"Why don't we get Adam to go," Rick said. "Just call the guy and say you're sending someone to get a copy."

"What if they ask for I.D.?"

"Why would they, one sailor looks like another," Rick said. "It's nothing classified." She agreed it was worth a shot. Rick paged Giles. It was about an hour later that the instructor called back. Rick explained what they needed and why.

"But they know me there," Giles said.

"Is there someone who can help?" Rick said. "How about Watson?"

"Those guys know every one of us," Giles said. He was right. The staff at RSS flew so much, that they couldn't risk getting caught.

"How about one of the students?" Laura asked. Rick hadn't thought of it, but it might just work. He knew that the possibility of anyone at base ops recognizing one of the students was remote.

"I'll grab Daley," Giles said after thinking about it. "There's no classes yet."

"Thanks, buddy," Rick said. "Call me when you got 'em." He hung up the phone, and handed it back to Laura. He then leaned over and kissed her on the cheek.

"What was that for?"

"Just in case I forget to thank you later."

*

Back at NAS, Giles drove over to the student BEQ. He saw Daley and the others outside near the grill. They were having beer battered catfish. Rolo was cooking it up and the smell made Giles stomach growl as he walked up to them.

"How's it going?" Giles said. "Daley, can I talk with you a minute?"

"Sure."

Daley walked over and away from the others. The two men stopped near some steps that led into one of the BEQ buildings. Giles sat down, and Daley followed suit.

"I think you know Petty Officer Cox is in trouble."

"Yeah," Daley said taking a sip of the Coke in his hand. "It's kinda hard not to notice." Giles waited to speak as he put his thoughts in order. "Daley," he said. "I think you know we all have a healthy respect for you."

"I know," he said without sounding cocky. Of course he knew, everyone had his whole life.

"So," Giles continued, "what I am going to ask of you, do not feel obligated in any way to do...But Petty Officer Cox needs help and I am hoping you will help us out."

"What's this about?" Daley asked. Giles explained the whole thing to the young sailor. He listened with an open mind, but as intensely as he had in any football huddle. When Giles was done, Daley sat back on the steps. "When are we supposed to do this?"

"As soon as possible," Giles said. "Listen, I will understand if you don't want to. If we get caught..."

"Then we get caught," Daley replied, interrupting. "I don't like what is happening. I would not want it to be happening to me, and I know if it was, Petty Officer Cox would be there fighting for me."

"He would." Giles said. He hadn't underestimated the kid.

"You guys put on this attitude," Daley said. "But you are just like my old coaches. Deep down you really give a shit, or you wouldn't try so hard!"

The two went up to Daley's room so he could get dressed. He would need to wear his working whites, since that's what most of the Administration-type Petty Officer's wore. He wasn't going to lie to anyone; he made that clear. He would just go in and say he was there to pick up the records. If no one asked, he wouldn't say a word. If they did, he was picking them up for Special Agent Laura Wilson.

"If they just assume I'm with legal, I won't say any different," Daley said when he was ready. "Let's go!"

*

Capt. Reilly sat at his desk reviewing the letter that Laura had left for him earlier that afternoon. It was for the best, he knew, but it still caught him by surprise. His secretary buzzed him and told him that Chief Lawrenz from the base medical clinic was on the line, as he requested.

"Steve," Reilly said. "I need some information."

"Yes sir," the Chief Corpsman replied. As the top enlisted man in the lab on base, he was accustomed to answering the legal officer's questions. "What can I help you with, Captain?"

"I need some time frames, Chief."

"Okay?"

"If a sailor came into sick call, how long would it be before his blood work would be finished?

"It depends on how sick he was?" Chief Lawrenz replied. "If it was the flu or food poisoning or an ulcer..."

"Nothing like that," Reilly said. "Not really sick at all, a hurt shoulder, general aches."

"Oh," the Chief replied. "Not long then. Maybe a week."

"Anyway to get it back sooner without seeing a doctor?"

"Not that I can think of, Captain," he replied. "Is there something you are waiting on that I can check on sir?"

"No, just asking," Reilly said. "How about a urinalyses?"

"Piss test are about a week too," the Chief said.

"What if a doctor rushed them?'

"It would still be a few days, sir," the corpsman replied. "We send them out to a lab. It takes at least a day to get there, a day for testing, and a day to come back."

"Could they be done next day?"

The Chief thought about it. "It would have to be a real special case, and they'd have to know what they were looking for in advance to cut the testing down. I would say they could, but it would have to be for a damn good reason."

*

"Dammit," Laura said looking at the log entries.

"What?" Rick said. He took a sip from his drink and leaned over the table. The sun glared off the glass surface, but the umbrella blocked most of its rays. This was the same bungalow that Rick had stayed in many times before. They worked outside, where the afternoon sun was warm, but the slight breeze from the Gulf and the unseasonably low humidity was too hard to resist. They couldn't work indoors, not today.

"All this does is list an aircraft type and serial number," she said. "It doesn't say where the flight originated or anything. I will never be able to track this down in a day, not from here."

"Let me see," Rick said and took Craft's NATOPS jacket from her hands. The new entries that Giles had faxed them were lose inside. "There must be a record somewhere--some data base that would cross reference it."

"All there is on it is this log number here," she said pointing along the edge of the faxes. The number ran along the side of the original and started with 011. "That's not a log number," Rick said. "That's a phone number."

"No, it's not."

"Yes, it is! But it's an overseas number." Rick told her. "Believe me, I've been around enough to know an overseas phone number. But I've never seen that country code before."

"I can find that out," Laura said. She called the operator and asked for the country code listed. "It's Greece?"

"I'll bet that is the fax number where Commander Craft is," Rick said.

"So we've narrowed it down to a country anyway" Laura replied. "But how many bases are there in Greece?'

"I have no idea," Rick said. "Why don't we just call that number? Maybe it's a phone." Laura dialed her cell phone, but all she heard was the screeching handshake tones of a dedicated fax line. She hung up. "Okay- now to plan B."

She went into the resort and made a cover sheet for a fax. She took a copy of Rick's medical record, blacked out the name, and asked the concierge desk to fax it to the number listed.

*

"This sucks," Willy said as he mopped the floor of the Aircrew School's quarterdeck. "It's not like we have anything else to do," Rolo said. He and Nick had also drawn swabbing duty. Mop, wax, buff. Rolo looked up at the clock on the wall.

"I guess we can cut out a few minutes early, guys," he said. "It's Friday." They put the mops away and cleaned up the buckets.

"You guys going to eat?" Willy asked.

"Yeah, you?"

"I forgot my chow card, I'll meet you over there," he said. "I need to go back to the barracks and get it."

"Okay," Nick said. Willy ran out of the building toward the barracks. When he was out gone, Nick asked Rolo if he thought Willy had acted strange the last few days. Rolo said he had noticed Willy had been quieter, "But I'm not complaining!"

"Me neither!" Nick said.

Willy quickly found his chow card and headed back toward the mess hall. He passed the RSS school as he took a shortcut. Lt. Jackson had just stepped outside when Willy ran by. Jackson called to the sailor. Willy stopped an turned around.

"Yes, sir?"

"Airman Simms, come in here, please."

"I was just going to eat, sir."

"I want to talk with you," Jackson said and held open the door.

*

The fax machine at the Suda Bay duty office came to life. It was late. The Junior Officer of the Deck, known as the JOOD, stood up with a loud groan, and walked over to read the incoming cover sheet. It was from a law firm in Georgia to a resort in Florida. "Some one has no idea what they're doing," he said to himself.

It was obvious the document had nothing to do with the US Naval Detachment on the small Greek Island in the Eastern Mediterranean sea.

But the twenty-two-year-old petty officer was bored, and there was a message on the cover asking that if anyone received the fax in error to contact a number since the document was important and confidential.

He showed the Duty Officer, a new Lieutenant Junior Grade, who was the same age and just as bored. "Mind if I call, sir, and let them know." the JOOD asked. "I haven't talked to anyone in the states in a while."

"Go ahead, but don't make it long, okay."

*

"Airman," Jackson said. "Something was brought to my attention recently and I want to find out exactly what is going on."

"About what, sir?"

"I understand that you made some accusations against one of the instructors at this school, accusations that you know to be false."

"I don't know what you are talking about," Willy turned around to walk out.

"Stand at attention, sailor," Jackson said. "You are not dismissed." Willy turned around and stood at attention. "Do you know it's a crime to make false statement's about your superiors in the military?"

"No, sir."

"Then you don't know everything?" Jackson said. "Do you sailor..."

*

Laura's cell phone rang a few minutes later. The JOOD told her that her firm had somehow sent them a fax by mistake. "Thanks for calling," she replied trying to sound as sweet and surprised as she could bear, ignoring Rick who rolled his eyes. "Where did those idiots send it?"

"Crete, Ma'am."

"Crete?"

"Yes, Ma'am, Suda Bay. It's in the Greek Isles."

"Wow," she said, making funny faces at Rick as she spoke.

"I have no idea how that happened," Laura said. "To be honest, I really don't know about fax machines much. What's the phone number I sent it to?"

The sailor told her. "Oh geez. That's the case number. I'm so sorry about that."

"No problem," the sailor said. "Where are you?'

"Florida," she replied and talked a few minutes before telling the guy she needed to get back to work.

*

"Sir, I stand by my statement."

"Simms, let me tell you what happens when you are sent to a federal military prison," Jackson said. "It's a bit more than spending your days making big rocks into little rocks, then cementing the little rocks back to make another big one. There are military guards--typically Marines- -and as you can imagine they do not treat you as nice as we do here."

"I can hold my own, sir," Willy replied.

"Probably, for a while anyway," Jackson replied. "But the thing about the military is that there is no parole. There are no televisions, no workout rooms. You work. You eat. You sleep. Period. The military uses prisons for punishment, not rehab." Jackson thought he saw something change in Willy's expression. A small increase in his attention. "But, like you said, you have nothing to worry about. I'm sure you'd do fine. Of course, you'd learn what the meaning of alternate lifestyle is."

"I know what that means, sir." Willy said. "It wouldn't happen to me."

"You're that tough, huh?"

Willy did not answer. Jackson turned and sat down. Willy stood at attention, waiting. After a few minutes Jackson had not said anything and Willy's knees started to hurt a little. His posture slacked, his feet started to hurt. "Sir?"

Jackson did not look up from his desk. "Yes, Airman Recruit Simms?"

"Sir, permission to leave, sir."

"Tired at standing at attention?"

"Yes, sir."

"Permission denied," Jackson said. "You're much too tough to let an officer like me wear you down so quick. I think you can take it a little longer. And stand up straight, stop slouching."

A few more minutes went by. "Sir, permission to use the head?"

"Permission denied," Jackson said without looking up. "You've only been standing for...," he looked at his watch, "...five minutes? Come on."

*

"He was really homesick," Laura said.

"I'm sure he was," Rick said. "You never lived overseas, right?"

"No," she said. "I told you that."

"You'd be surprised how good it feels to talk with anyone from the states when you're on deployment, Rick said. "Especially a beautiful woman who is flirting with you."

"I wasn't flirting."

"Oh, please..." Rick said."I said I hadn't dated a woman in a while, not that I was dead."

"I wasn't!"

"Oh, okay," Rick said laughing. Laura had not heard him laugh since they met on the jogging trail. Maybe things would work out after all.

"Well, now its your turn, stud."

"My turn?"

"Yeah, here," she said and hit the call back button, displaying the last number that called into the phone. She wrote it down, then dialed it and gave the phone to Rick. It took a few moments for the call to go through. It was answered by the same sailor. "Naval Detachment Suda Bay, This is a non-secure line, Petty Officer Sacks, can I help you?"

"Petty Officer Sacks," Rick said. "I need to speak with Commander Benjamin Craft. He's a flight surgeon who is on it is TAD there. Arrived a few days ago."

The JOOD looked up at the clock on the wall. "Sir, it's past midnight here. May I take a message?"

"Who am I speaking with, sailor?" Rick demanded.

"Who am I speaking with?" the JOOD replied.

"This is Special Agent Litton from the Naval Investigative Service! Are you going to get Dr. Craft or do you want me to charge you with obstruction? This is a federal investigation!"

"No, sir. I mean yes, sir- I'll connect you to his quarters! Please hold."

Rick gave Laura the thumbs up, and covered the phone's mouth-piece with his hand. "He's there!"

Laura looked over at him wide-eyed. "I don't believe you did that!" Rick just shrugged. "It worked, didn't it?"

*

"Airman Simms," Jackson said. "This is the time for you to speak up. If this is true, then you need to be prepared to back up your statements. If it's false- you better tell me now while I can still help you."

"Sir, I stand by my statement."

"Airman, I have known the instructor that you are speaking about, and I find it hard to believe what you are saying about him."

"Then don't believe me sir, I don't care one way or the other."

"That's the problem. It doesn't matter what I believe because the NIS evidently does believe you." Jackson. "As far as you not caring what I or anyone else thinks, that's a problem that I can address."

"Is that a threat, sir?"

"Why is everything a threat with you, Airman?" Jackson replied. "No, it's not a threat. Do you know what this school demands of its graduates?" Willy did not answer. He just stood there, defiant.

"I didn't think you do," Jackson said finally. "It demands that its graduates care. Care so much about others that you would risk your life for someone you never met."

*

"I knew there was something odd about this assignment," Craft said. "But I didn't think it was a cover up for anything. Are you sure?"

"I am sure, Commander," Laura assured him. "So they did not tell you?"

"Tell me what? They said that Cox confessed," the doctor replied. "Hunt asked me if it was plausible that he could have held the kid down. I said sure. It was possible. Then he said that they did not have enough evidence to hold the instructor, and that an assignment was coming anyway. They wanted me out of Pensacola for my own good."

"And you believed him?"

"I had no reason not to," Craft said. "Besides, I knew that the guy was pissed that I grounded him. At least he was when he came to see me."

"Who was?" Laura asked. "Hunt?"

"No, Cox. He was extremely upset," Craft told her. "That's why I gave him those sedatives."

"When did you give them to him?"

"I gave him a prescription right after the kid flat-lined." Laura asked him what drug he prescribed and she wrote it down.

"Who authorized you to be transferred?" Laura asked. "Hunt doesn't have the authority to do that."

"The Admiral--Tract. His office cut the orders."

"Didn't that seem odd to you that the Admiral would be so

concerned about this."

"To be honest this whole thing is odd!" Craft replied. "Talking with you about this in the middle of the night. Traveling halfway around the world in less than a week. None of it makes sense. But when I found out who the kid's father was-- then it was to be expected."

"Who told you?"

"What do you mean who told me? You know who told me," Craft said. "Your boss, Litton. Called me the night the kid died."

"Are you sure?"

"Yeah, Litton," he said. "Look I have got to get to bed."

"Commander," Laura said. "I need to bring you back here to Florida. I need you to speak to someone here. Give a deposition.".

"With all due respect, I just got here," the doctor said. "I am not gonna come all the way there voluntarily to give a statement. Besides, this is about the most beautiful place on earth and I haven't had a vacation in a long time."

"Doctor..."

"If you want," Craft interrupted. "I would be more than happy to write this up and fax it to you."

"Would you have it notarized by the legal officer there?"

"If you want- sure.".

"I would appreciate it if you could do it first thing in the morning!"

"Not a problem."

"Do me a favor--fax it to this number," she gave him Base Legal's fax number. "Send it to the attention of Captain Reilly." She hung up and asked Rick if he had used the prescription. "Yeah, I finally got it filled, and took some that morning before I went to the base. Then another right before the test."

"Then it should have been in your system when you gave that urinalysis, right?"

"I don't know?" Rick said.

"I hope it was in your body long enough to get into your bloodstream. I have to make a call." Laura said. "I need to get your medical records. I wish there was a way to match the results of that piss test Litton gave you to something that we knew was from your body."

"How about a blood sample?"

"That would be great, but it's too late," Laura replied. "It would have to have been taken that same day, and after the urinalysis to help us."

"Do you have any medical record release forms?"

*

"Litton, I swear this better work," Hunt said.

"It will. If we get his ass kicked out, the Senator will be happy, he'll get off Tract's ass, we'll close this investigation, and I can get my promotion and go to Washington."

"If someone else opens this up, I don't know what they'll find," Hunt said. "And I don't want to know."

*

"One down--one to go!" Rick said.

"Don't get too excited," Laura said. "Things may clear you for the drug test, but that's only half the battle. We still need to deal with the accident investigation."

"I know," Rick said. "But at least now I'm fighting with equal footing."

*

"Lt. Jackson?" Willy said. "Sir, can I ask you a question?"

"Depends on the question."

"Sir, what if a sailor was told by one officer that if he did not make a statement he knew was false, that he would be arrested," Willy asked. "And now the sailor was told by a different officer that he would need to tell the truth or he would be arrested. What is that sailor to do then?"

"Is that what happened?" Jackson asked. "Did someone tell you to lie about this?"

"I'm not saying someone did or they didn't," Willy replied. "I'm just asking what if they did.. And what if that other officer outranked you."

"Why would they have you do that?"

"What if I was involved in an incident off-base, and by lying the first time it could make that go away?"

"If that was the case, why didn't you come to one of the instructors?" Jackson said. "Or come to me?"

"Like you or they would give a shit, sir?" Willy said. "I would be out of school so fast and then what? A destroyer or an oiler or some shit detail in a desert or Iceland or something."

Jackson put him at ease and told the young sailor to sit down. "Who was it, Airman?"

"Sir, if I told you then I am history!"

"I won't let that happen, Willy," Jackson assured him. "But if you don't tell me, it will be a lot worse. It will come out, I guarantee it. Then you won't have anyone helping you."

"So now you are threatening me again?"

"Fine, Willy," Jackson said in frustration. "Yes, I am threatening you! With legal action. If that's all you understand."

"You are all the same!"

"I don't understand you!?" Jackson said. "Do you understand a thing about what this school teaches you? You're not dumb. I know you know !"

"It's about rescuing people from crashes and stuff, sir."

"What does the sign in front of this building say on it?"

"Rescue Swimmer School, sir."

"What else?" Willy sat there, clueless. The Lieutenant told him to go outside and read it and come back in. Simms did what he was told.

"What did it say?" Jackson asked again.

"So Others May Live?"

"You know what that means?"

"We save people who are drowning."

"You just don't get it," Jackson said. "*So Others May Live* does not just mean rescuing some poor guy who finds himself in the drink. It means putting others before yourself."

"I get it, sir."

"No, you don't," Jackson said. "If you did, you would have never found yourself in this position."

"Yes, sir," Willy responded spitting out the sarcasm.

"Willy," the Lieutenant said. "Go get some chow, but report back here in one hour."

"Just great," he said. "Another cleaning detail."

"Not hardly," Jackson replied as he picked up the phone.

*

Rick read through copies of Lee's personnel file. He wanted to get to know the young kid and the more he read, the worse he felt about what had happened. But it also raised more questions than it answered.

"Why the hell would he go to a flight surgeon in Jax? He went to boot camp in Chicago, at Great Mistakes?"

"Where?"

"Great Lakes, it's in Illinois. But he would have gone to Glenview Naval Air Station if anywhere."

"Maybe they don't do that anymore?" Laura said. "Maybe the doctor there wasn't available?"

"They wouldn't fly one kid down to Jacksonville, that's for sure," Rick said. "Something's not right here." Rick asked Laura if she would call the training facility located just off Lake Michigan, near Chicago. She was told there are no flight surgeons stationed there, that all recruits are sent over to Naval Air Station Glenview. She got the number for Glenview, and was transferred to the switchboard at the small medical facility there

Laura was told that the flight surgeon who had originally seen Lee was not there, and asked if she would like to speak to the doctor who was on duty.

"Sure," she said. After a short wait, the doctor picked up. He said he doesn't remember Lee, but he remembered a Senator's kid who came through and failed the flight physical about that time.

"It was strange," he said. "We tried to send copies of the physical to Great Lakes, but they said they didn't need them. I figured the kid was dropped from the Navy. According to Bob, the doctor who examined him, he should have been. That kid was in bad shape." The doctor asked Laura to hold on a few minutes and he would get Lee's records.

He returned a few minutes later. "That's strange," he said. "But the records are gone. I'm sorry, there's not much else I can do for you folks. You should try calling Jacksonville."

Laura called Naval Air Station, Jacksonville in Orange Park, Florida, along the St. Johns River. She was surprised to find the doctor who treated Lee there, at least the corpsman who answered the phone thought he was there. It was the first good break in a while, but it didn't last long.

"Commander Shilling," he answered, "How can I help you?"

"Commander, my name is Laura Wilson," she said. "I am a Special Agent with the Naval Investigative Service in Pensacola, I have some questions I'd like to ask you."

"Don't you people ever stop!" he replied abruptly. "I said I have not spoke to anyone about this already!"

"Sir," Laura asked. "Have you already been contacted by someone from the NIS?"

"You know damn well I have," Shilling said. "Tell Litton I don't need these head games! I think the orders are enough to convince me! Okay?! You win!" Laura heard the desperation and anger in the doctor's voice.

"Orders, Commander?"

Shilling told her how he had just received the new transfer orders and was packing his desk. "Commander, I am not working with Agent Litton," Laura said. Shilling stopped clearing his desk and looked at the speaker phone in a panic.

"Would you repeat that, please?" he said.

"I said I am not working with Litton on this," Laura said. Shilling collapsed into the chair near his desk. He wondered how he could be so stupid. He had worked so hard for so long. "Hello?" Laura's voice said over the speaker.

Shilling just looked at the phone, wondering if he should answer or not. He looked at his watch, only a few hours before the flight out to the North Atlantic. A plane, known as a COD, was on it's way to Jacksonville right then to pick him up and fly him out to an aircraft carrier a thousand miles away.

"Hello?"

He hadn't even told his wife yet. How could he? She had almost left him during his last sea tour. He had worked hard for this, his last duty. It was supposed to be on shore, with his wife, and his kids. She was to finally have a husband who would be there!

"Hello?" Laura asked again. She heard Shilling choke up as he saw his future fall apart in front of him. A future that had been guaranteed by a Senator's boy with a bad heart.

"Hello? Is anyone there?"

"Uh, yes, I'm still here," the doctor said trying to compose himself. Maybe she didn't know what he had said. "What can I do for you, Agent Wilson?"

"I assume you know who Airman Robert Lee is, if Agent Litton has already spoken with you?"

"I know who he is," Shilling said. No. She knew. But as long as he kept his mouth shut, he might still be able to stop the transfer from going through, he thought.

"Dr. Shilling," Laura said. "I need your help. As you are aware, the young airman is dead. What you may not know is that you may hold the key to another man's life as well..." Laura talked for a few minutes, telling the doctor what they had found out regarding Lee's medical condition and how the flight surgeon from Glenview had already examined Lee and he had failed. "Doctor," Laura said. "You were the first doctor that said Lee was healthy, and I am wondering how you came to that conclusion, and do you have copies of that physical in your files?"

"I have copies, but I need to catch a flight in twenty minutes thanks to that kid."

"Sir, what you know could save a man's career," Laura said. "Doctor, have you watched the news?"

"Yes," Shelling said. "I know what this is about. Do you think I would have signed off that young man if I knew he was going to Aircrew School? I knew this was gonna bite me in the ass. I was told he was going to work in intelligence. In fact I saw the orders."

"Orders? From where?"

"Admiral Tract himself signed off on them," he said. "I was asked to give him a flight physical because his father was a senator, and the admiral said the kid wanted to learn how to fly like his old man or something. I forget. But it certainly was NOT for him to attend Aircrew training. That's for damn sure."

"Do you have copies of the order?"

"Hell, yes! I have copies of everything," Shilling said. "I'm not stupid."

"So you knew about his condition?"

"Yes, I knew," he replied. "But I signed off because when an Admiral calls you up and asks if I would like spend my last tour in Jacksonville at a shore command with my kids and wife, instead of sea duty on some carrier of the coast of Iraq, then I sign off."

"Fine doctor," Laura said. "I understand why you did it, but.."

"No buts,," he said. "I am on my way to the Middle East right now, with twenty-four-hour notice because of this kid! And I haven't done anything! What do you think would happen if I opened my mouth for the record?"

"What if I say what you've told me?"

"I'll deny it," he shot back. "Listen lady, I am not going to throw away a twenty year career or retirement, never mind losing my medical license over this. I'm sorry--but I can't help you."

"What if this was your kid?" she said. "You said you had kids- What if this were your son?"

"I'm sorry."

"Doctor, what if I can get immunity for you? No one is blaming you!"

"I'd still lose my license!"

"I need those files," Laura said. "I will get them with or without your help!"

"Good luck, I mean that."

"That kid never had a chance!"

"It wasn't my fault," Shilling said. "Look, I'm not the only one!"

"Well help us get the people who are doing this to you!"

"I can't," he said. "I am sorry, really, I'm sorry."

*

Laura and Rick watched the sunset through the tinted glass window. She took a sip of her drink as the last sparkling rays reflected off the serene waters of the Gulf and tried to think of something to say. It was summer, and the resort's restaurant was full of families on vacation. Because there were only the two of them, she and Rick had been seated quickly.

But that was half an hour ago and now she turned her attention to Rick who spun his fettucini on his fork, but had not taken a bite since it had been placed on the table. He had barely said a word since that damn doctor had refused to help them. It was all she could do to get him out of the room. Laura was angry about the set back, too, but it just made her more determined to find a way out of this problem. She reached for the wine bottle at the center of their table, but it was empty.

Her mind had been racing a mile a minute since talking with the doctor, but she was running out of time. She knew that even if she managed to get Rick out of the Captain's Mast in the next twenty-four hours, Litton and the others seemed to be a step ahead of them. There would be no defense left if the Navy decided to prosecute Rick for Lee's death. She knew it was a race she would have to win, not only for Rick, but for herself.

"I'm going back to the room," Rick said. He stood and threw some money down on the table. She hurriedly caught up and grabbed his hand. They walked back to the room without a word.

Once inside, he walked out to the screened in veranda that overlooked the Gulf. She went in the bedroom and unpacked the suitcase. Laura emerged, now wearing a pair of shorts and an extra large nightshirt. She turned on the radio on top of the television then walked out to where Rick sat.

She stood in front of the large cushioned porch swing. He moved over slightly; she took it as an invitation to sit down. He leaned back and closed his eyes. He could not believe that this was happening.

"It will be okay," she said. "We'll figure something out."

"Why do you care about what happens?" She just barely heard him. It was almost a whisper.

"I don't know, I just do." She said, and rubbed his arm with her finger. She didn't really know why she wanted, no not wanted, needed to help him. But she did. She pulled his head down to her chest and held him against her as she played with his hair.

"No one cares about what happens to me. No one," he said. "If you do, then something happens to you."

"What does that mean?"

"Exactly what it means." He turned his head and looked up at her. "You're pretty, you're smart. Why would you want to throw away your life on me?"

"Why did you jump into an ocean full of diesel fuel," she asked, "and rescue so many people that they had to send Giles to pull you out?" He looked at her puzzled, then sat up.

"What are you talking about?"

"I read your record," she replied. "That navy training sub accident- the one off of Jacksonville three years ago? I read about the fire, and about you."

"How did you..?"

"It was my job. I needed to know your background," she said. He still looked puzzled. "You just said how smart I was." He laid his head back down to her lap. "It was no big deal. Anyone would do it."

"Rick, believe me it is a big deal," she said. "You and I both know that not everyone would do that. I wouldn't do that."

"You're doing it right now," he said.

"All I'm doing is risking a career," she said. She paused and thought about that for a minute. It just occurred to her that she was no longer risking it. Her career at NIS was already over. "It wasn't much of one at that. At least as long as Litton was a part of it."

"The NIS is a good career," Rick said.

"It could have been. But still it's only a job," she leaned down and kissed his forehead. "You, on the other hand, you would throw your life down in a minute for people you don't know. People you've never met."

"Yeah, and look what I get for it," he replied. "No warning, just a piece of paper saying thank you, but the Navy does not want you anymore. No hard feelings, okay?"

His mind raced back to the pool, then to his brother, then to the two pilots. He was quiet for a long time before she looked down and saw his eyes were shut.

Yet, even with his eyes closed, she could see how swollen and red they'd become. The stains on his face showed what was left of his tears. But she had heard not a sound, not a single sob. Strong to the end. She lightly stroked his arm with her finger, and gently pushed on the ground with her leg. They slowly began to swing back and forth.

The soothing motion reminded Rick of the sea, and soon he fell asleep. For the next two hours Laura listened to the gulls, and the waves, and silently watched the colorful display of the sun and clouds as they met at the horizon. She saw the sky turn from aqua to yellow to fiery red then to purple and finally to the darkest of blue. Rick did not stir at all, but stayed perfectly still.

Laura gently moved him off her lap, went inside and found a light blanket in the closet. She came back to him, and covered Rick as he slept. She laid down on the swing in front of him, and wrapped his arm around her before closing her eyes. She felt safe with him, and she realized at that moment, regardless of what anyone else told her, she knew in her heart that there was no way this man was guilty of any crime.

*

A few hours later, thousands of miles away, Dr. Benjamin Craft was up with the sunrise and drove into town. He parked and walked down through the market square, past the Samaria Hotel, and down to brick and stone streets to the sparkling Mediterranean Sea. The brightly painted fishing boats were heading out, and the restraunts along the beach were filled with Europeans. The beach had a few sun-worshipers already on it, and the doctor enjoyed his breakfast while watching the tourists.

After his breakfast in the small seaside cafe, he drove back to the small contingent of buildings and sailors that the Navy stationed on the tiny island paradise. He found an old computer and typed out his statement, repeating what he had told Laura the previous night. It did not take long. He had the duty officer sign his name as a witness and the JOOD faxed it to Reilly's office. Although it was almost noon in the Med, it was still the middle of the night in Pensacola.

*

Laura awoke to her cell phone ringing. It took a few moments before she realized that she was in her own bed. Rick must have woke up and carried her in. She answered the phone that was on the desk in the bedroom. "Laura Wilson."

"I left them in a locker. Do you have a pen?"

"Who's this?" She asked.

"You wanted the records, fine," Shilling said. "The locker number on it three forty-five. Jacksonville airport."

Laura quickly retrieved a pen from her bag and wrote down the number. "How do we get in without a key?"

"I left the key at lost and found under the kid's name. It's in a black Cannon camera bag. I hope you get the sons of bitches!" He slammed the phone down as he heard his flight called.

"Damn," Laura said. She looked at the clock. It was a little past two in the morning. She went out into the main room, and over to the little kitchenette. She turned the light on and opened the small refrigerator.

"What? Who was that?" Rick asked. He had been sleeping on the couch and sat up when the light went on.

"That doctor in Jacksonville," she said. "He is giving us the files!'

"Great!" Rick said.

"Not great!" Laura said. "How are we gonna get them when they are in Jacksonville?"

"We'll figure it out in the morning," he said.

"Why are you sleeping out here?" she asked walking over.

"There's sand in my bed. I forgot to take my shoes off before laying down," he said. "It itches."

"Well, you don't need to sleep out here," she said and grabbed his hand. "Come on and sleep in my bed."

"Where are you gonna sleep?"

"There's room for two," she replied. She helped him into her bed. They were both asleep in less than five minutes.

12

***

Saturday, June 20

Rick was up before the dawn and went for a swim in the Gulf. But this time his demons did not bother him, and for once the water seemed almost refreshing.

On the way back from the beach, he went to the resort's restaurant and ordered breakfast from room service. He returned to the bungalow and jumped in the shower. After toweling off, he checked on Laura. She was still sleeping, and he watched her for a few moments as she laid there. She seemed so peaceful. He wished he knew what it was like to be able to rest like that. He sighed, then went out to the patio. A few minutes later, there was a light knock on the door.

The food was brought in quietly, yet the commotion still managed to wake Laura. She came out into the living room and saw the food spread out on the table. "What's this?"

"Breakfast," Rick said. She smiled and walked over, smelling the different culinary delights that made her stomach rumble. "Someone sounds hungry."

"I'm starved," she said. She smiled at him as she sat down.

*

"Thank God some people remember how to write without a computer," Giles said to himself. He sat at the table in the mess hall eating breakfast with Daley. Rolo and Nick were there also, but most of the other tables were empty.

"Yeah, do you believe that shit?" Nick said to the instructor. Giles continued to read through the book as Daley and Nick pointed out entries they had read the night before. He shook his head in disbelief.

"I think I need a favor," Giles said. "Are you guys positive that you haven't said anything about this to anyone?" They all swore that only the three of them knew. "What about Lorner?"

"He was asleep when Daley read it," Nick said. "We didn't wake him up."

"But we thought you should know," Daley added. Giles put the book down and pulled out his wallet and car keys. "I need a favor from you guys."

"Shoot," Daley said.

"I need one of you guys to take this to Petty Officer Cox and Agent Wilson," Giles said. He told them to use his car and he'd give them money. "It will take all day."

"Where are they?" Daley asked. Giles told them where Rick was. Daley said he couldn't do it because they'd never get back by that night. He had been cleared to hop a flight with one of the reserve helicopters Sunday afternoon and couldn't risk missing it. It was hard for students to get any flight time, and Giles understood. These guys weren't getting any training as is, so anything they could do on their own was great.

"I'll do it," Nick said. Rolo said he'd go as well. "Make it a road trip, as long as we can stay over."

"I'm sure that would be no problem," Giles said. He was sure that Rick wouldn't mind once he saw what they brought him. "I just have to run a few errands this morning, then I'll meet you guys. Say nine o'clock at the BEQ? That gives me about two hours." He said he'd give them his credit card just in case there was a problem.

*

"Where's Agent Wilson?"Litton asked when he arrived at the office. All he received for answers were blank stares, before the other agents went back to work. Another Saturday morning, another day of solving problems between sailors and the locals. Litton went over to the receptionist to get his messages. "Agent Litton, Laura called in and said she was leaving the area for the weekend."

"When did she call in?"

"Yesterday," she replied. "But you told me you didn't want to be disturbed."

"Did she say where she was going?"

"No, but probably her parent's house in Georgia," the

receptionist replied. "She goes there a lot."

"Oh," Litton said. At least that was one less problem that he would need to worry about.He went over to the in-basket that contained the mail. He saw it was empty."Any envelopes from Washington come for me?"

"Not that I know of."

*

"I'm glad to see you're so relaxed," Laura said as they finished eating. "But you need to realize that the only people who know about any of this are in this room. We still can't prove any of it."

"But we will," Rick replied. "All I need to do is explain to Harding what we found out.."

"You can't do that," she interrupted. "You can't make accusations about Litton, about Hunt, Tract or any of them without proof. At the very least it would be heresy, and at the worst, you could be court-martialed."

"Why?"

"Because you can't make false accusations!"

"But they aren't false," Rick said. "Everything I would say is true. They are lying about me right now, why can't they go to prison?'

"Let's not worry about them right now, lets worry about you and make sure you aren't locked up and figure out how to get those documents," Laura told him. "The problem is we don't have the time to drive over there and be back here."

"I'll go by myself."

"No," she said. "What if something happens? It's too late to drive there tonight, and we can't chance a drive like that in one day. No, this is as far as I want you to be from the base."

"Maybe Giles could take a hop over to Jacksonville and get the notes for us?" he said. "It's a weekend. I'm sure there are some reserve flights leaving."

"Call him and see." Rick dialed the pager, and left a message. He then called Giles' apartment and left a message for him to find a flight across the state.

*

Litton drove by Laura's house again and looked to see if her car was in the driveway. It wasn't. The NIS agent's gut feeling told him there was something going on. She could have left for the weekend and driven back home to Macon. But with Cox missing too, it worried him. Everything was much too convenient. Hunt said, "It doesn't sound right, are you sure that's where she went?"

"No," Litton replied. "Why? Should we be worried?"

"Probably not."

"Because if you think there is something wrong here..."

"No."

"Are you sure?" Litton asked. Now he was concerned. "You don't think she found Craft or anything?"

"Hell no!"

"Because if that is where she went..."

"Calm down, Jack!" Hunt said. "You worry to much. There is no way she found him."

"I hope not!"

"Do you want to call him yourself?" Hunt said. "You're more than welcome to."

"Yeah, I think I will!"

"Fine!" Litton said and hung up. He grabbed the overseas phone directory and looked up the number. He paused, and thought better of using an official outside line that could be monitored. He pulled his cell phone from his desk and dialed. The duty officer in Crete answered the phone. Litton identified himself and asked to speak with the doctor.

"He's a popular guy," the duty officer commented.

"What do you mean?"

"You're the second call he's had since I came on last night."

"Who else called for him?"

"I don't know, the JOOD spoke with him."

"So it was a man?"

"I think so," the duty officer said. "Let me see if he's in." The phone went dead for a few minutes before the officer returned. "I'm sorry, sir. He's out."

"Do you know where?"

"No, sir," the officer replied. "It's Saturday night over here. He could be anywhere."

*

Nick and Rolo followed Giles directions and arrived at the resort around four. They went to the front desk and asked for Rick's room. The clerk called, but there was no answer.

"If you would like, you can leave a message with the concierge," the clerk said. "We have a bar out at the pool, if you would like to wait."

"Sounds like a plan," Rolo said. "Is there a place we could change?"

"There are restrooms at the pool, but swimming is for guests only," the clerk warned. Nick told her that they would be staying over in the room. She gave them directions to the pool. and the two headed there to wait for their instructor to return.

*

"I would like to meet with one of your students in the morning," Litton told Jackson over the phone. "I have some follow-up questions"

"Tomorrow is Sunday, Agent Litton."

"I realize that, Lieutenant," he replied. "But it is very important. The student's name is Simms, Airman Recruit William Simms."

"If this is really necessary, I will try to have someone notify him," Jackson said. "But it is a weekend. I don't know if he is on base or not."

"I'll meet him at the RSS school parking lot around noon," Litton said. "I'm sure you will be able to find him."

"I'll try."

Litton hung up the phone and turned to the others in the room. "He'll be here a little after noon."

"Thank you, Jack," Hunt replied. "I am sure the Senator will appreciate it."

Jackson was already on the phone making plans of his own.

*

Laura and Rick had taken a break and walked down along the beach for a few hours. The water relaxed Rick, and the sun and surf allowed Laura to clear her mind as well. For the first time in a week, she hadn't felt rushed or pressured. They acted like tourists, visiting the small amusement park, and shopped. But it was now time to get back to work, and they had returned to their room to find the message from Nick and Rolo.

"I'm gonna call Captain Reilly and tell him to expect that fax from Dr. Craft," Laura said. "If you want to go and find your student's."

Rick went out to the pool, where he found the two of them laying on the lounge chairs with two new bikini-clad friends. Only after the two college co-eds promised to go out later with them was Rick able to get Nick and Rolo back to the room.

Once there, Nick pulled Lee's diary and letters from a small book bag that also held his change of clothes. He explained where it came from, and told them Giles thought they would be interested in it.

"It starts around the same time Lee left for the University of Central Florida," Nick told them as he handed the book to Laura. "And ends a few weeks ago."

"Anything about me in there?" Rick asked. Nick said no. "But it talks a lot about his dad!" Laura started reading through the pages. Many were marked by Giles and the others, but she wanted to read the whole thing to make sure the context was correct.

"This is great," Laura said. "He has names of two doctors in college that he spoke to. One was a Navy doc with the NROTC unit there."

"What kind of doctor ?"

"Flight surgeon," she said. "It seems as though he was taking flight lessons and failed his flight physical while in Orlando."

*

"Okay, Willy," Jackson said. "You understand what to do?'

"Yes, sir," he answered. "What time do I meet with you?'

"Ten o'clock at RSS."

"Right," the Lieutenant said. He walked out of the student's room and down to his car. He just had one more stop to pick up batteries before he went home.

*

"Are Nick and his friends coming back?" Laura asked. The two girls had stopped by the room around an hour ago, and talked non-stop the whole time they were there. But it didn't seem to bother the two young sailors and Rick had offered to buy them dinner at the resort's restaurant just to get some peace and quiet.

He had just come back from the dining room. The waiter would not let Nick sign for the meal, and Rick had to go over and approve the charge.

"They went out," Rick said. "They said they'd be late."

Laura sat back in the sofa and gave a sigh of relief. She rubbed her neck. "What I wouldn't give for a nice massage."

"Come here," he told her. She walked over and sat on the floor in front of him and he rubbed her neck as they watched a movie on television. She leaned back and closed her eyes as she felt his strong fingers rub deep into the tense muscles in her shoulder. "I have a better idea," she said, and led him by the hand into the bedroom. She flopped on the bed face down and exhausted. "Can I have a back-rub?"

"It's the least I could do," Rick said.

"Okay, but no non-back areas." She said with a smile. He agreed. She closed her eyes and relaxed. She felt his hands push and kneed. He moved to her spine and back up to the base of her head, the tension drained from her with each circle. His hands traveled along her outstretched arms, and went to the base of her spine.

Each circle became wider and wider taking in more of her body. Rick didn't say a word, or make a sound. He just rubbed and squeezed. Laura had not felt so relaxed in a long time. But there was another feeling there too that she had not felt in a long time. Without warning she suddenly turned over onto her back. Rick looked down and pulled his hands back.

"Did I do something wrong?" he asked. She shook her head no. Then she took his hands and placed them in a distinctively non-back area.

13

***

Sunday, June 21

Litton woke up early and called Laura's house again. *Where the hell was she*? he wondered. Things were not at all going as he had planned. He needed an ace in the hole. The agent dressed and quickly looked through his camera bag before going out.

*

Giles woke up and looked at the clock. He would have plenty of time to get on base, he thought. He casually ate breakfast and jumped in the shower. He reached for the shampoo, but it was empty. "Damn!" he said out loud. He would need to stop by the store and pick some up. It was then that the thought hit him: *His car was in Panama City!* He had totally forgot about that. He ran out of the shower and started calling everyone and anyone he knew to get a ride before the helo left.

*

At the same time, but a few miles away, Litton had just parked in front of the Seaside Apartments on Pensacola Beach. The tropical painted buildings stood out from the white-washed apartments surrounding the complex. He walked around and up some stairs near the pool. The sun was up, and the heat would have felt like a blast furnace had it not been for the breeze coming off the water. Litton could taste the salt in the air as he stopped in front of apartment 2663.

The NIS agent knocked on the door and heard someone inside unlock the dead-bolt The door cracked open, still chained, and half of a man's face appeared. It was not a face Litton recognized, but that didn't matter.

"Where is Ensign Davis?"

"Who are you?"

Litton held up his NIS identification. "Your worst nightmare, sweetheart."

The door closed momentarily, while the man undid the lock before he let Litton in. The agent walked in as the man called for Davis. He heard some voices in the back room, and watched as the guy disappeared. Litton did not sit down, but gingerly searched through the room, picking up items of interest, not caring too much about getting caught. Davis appeared with his friend from the back room. Both men were now fully dressed, and his friend left without another word to Litton. Davis stood in the middle of the living room, arms crossed.

"How dare you come to my home. I want you to leave."

"Mr. Davis, I understand you are representing Petty Officer Cox."

"Did you hear me?" Davis repeated stepping closer to the agent. Litton thought he was much more defiant than normal, but figured it was because he was in the officer's home. Davis had never acted this way in public.

"You want me to stop following you," Litton said. "But I need something from you."

"I have nothing to say to you. Now get out!"

Litton opened his camera bag and dumped hundreds of photographs on the floor. The young lawyer looked down at them. He was in every one. And in every single one he was not alone. "Oh, I think you and I need to talk," Litton said. "But if you don't want the negatives, I am sure the Navy would like to see them."

"What do you want?"

*

Willy met Lt. Jackson at the RSS school a few hours before noon, as ordered. The Airman Recruit was not in uniform, nor was he expected to be. He had not told anyone about the morning's meeting, or any of the previous ones, also as ordered.

Inside the Lieutenant's office, the young sailor was given a list of questions, but no answers. That, someone else would supply. Jackson asked him about his hobbies, and about growing up. Willy was candid, and because Jackson was not in uniform either, he felt much more at ease talking to him.

Around eleven o'clock, there was a knock on the door, and another young officer walked in carrying lunch from McDonald's. The officer was also in civilian clothes, and was introduced to Willy. After they ate, the young Ensign sat down with Willy and went over what was expected of him.

It was close to noon, and Willy sat nervously out in the instructor's office. "I think it's time," Jackson said.

"Yes, sir."

"Have fun," Jackson told him and the two men walked out into the parking lot. It was not long before Litton pulled up. He opened the passenger door from inside, and Willy got in. His nervousness was gone. They quickly pulled away.

"I don't feel like doing this," Willy said.

"Too late to change your mind now," Litton said."So just shut the hell up you little snot-nosed bastard."

"Hey, you don't have to be an asshole"

"You want to go to jail for assault?" Litton asked. "Just remember, you attacked me. It was just your stupid ass luck that I am an NIS agent."

"I could go to jail for lying just as easy!"

"Well, then," Litton said. "I guess you'd better work with me then since I know that you did both!"

"Yeah," Willy said. "But you and Hunt are making me lie this time. You are making me break the law so that you can nail Cox."

"So?" Litton said. "I never saw that you had a problem lying before. What's different now?"

"The difference is that you're ordering me to do it!" Willy replied. "You are blackmailing me."

"The term is extorsion. Not blackmail, kid," Litton said. "If you are going to accuse me, then do it right."

Willy turned around and stared out the window. He had nothing more to say. *That wasn't exactly true*, he thought. It was just that he had no more rehearsed questions to ask.

Litton drove off base and through downtown. He followed the concrete and blacktop ribbon over the bridge and down to Pensacola Beach for the second time in as many hours. Willy just sat there looking out the window. They rode in silence past the rows of hotels and condos until Litton turned the car into a parking lot at one of the smaller complexes of condominiums.

"We're here," Litton said. "Get out."

Willy looked around. "What are you, some kind of pervert? I hope you ain't getting any ideas!"

"Shut up and come with me," the agent said. They walked in through the front doors and past the guard who did not stop them. After a quick elevator ride, they went down the hall, stopping in front of the last door. Litton knocked. It was opened by Hunt, who invited them in.

Willy saw that Hunt was not the only person waiting. He recognized the other man in there.

"We got that SOB Cox, Senator." Litton said. "And this is the man that made it possible.'

"Pleased to meet you, sir," Willy said. "I was a good friend of your son's. I hate what Petty Officer Cox did."

*

Daley felt the engines start and saw the shadow of the blades begin to spin on the concrete tarmac out the opening of the helicopter's door. He was strapped in, and felt the aircraft's crewman tap him on the shoulder. Daley gave him a thumbs up. The helicopters dry-crewman took a black cord and connected it to the student's helmet. Suddenly Daley could hear the radio traffic in his ears. The intercom, or ICS, wasn't very loud compared to the engine and rotor noise, but it was better than nothing. He heard the pilot tell the crew that they were on hold, a passenger was coming out to them.

Giles jumped into the SH-3 Sea King helicopter and slid the door shut. He went over and thanked the pilot for waiting then settled back in near where Daley was sitting. The dull, gray painted helicopter rolled down along the tarmac past the other aircraft on the line. At the end of the taxiway, Daley felt the vibrations increase dramatically and felt them roll forward just a little before the earth dropped away from view. A few minutes later, he and Giles were leaning out the window watching the north Florida landscape whisk by below.

*

Willy was met by Jackson when Litton dropped him back off at the Student BEQ. Willy pulled his shirt up and ripped the white surgical tape of his chest. "He took me to meet with Commander Hunt, and Lee's dad."

"And?" Lt. Davis asked.

"And it went just like I told you, sir." Willy replied. "Now when do I leave?'

"Start packing, sailor," Davis told him "You are out of here tonight." Lt. Davis looked over at Jackson and then at Willy, and the two officer's grinned.

*

Nick and Rolo packed the car and thanked Rick and Laura for lunch. They were going to head back early because both had spent all their money the night before.

"Do you need any cash for the trip back?" Laura asked.

"No," Nick said. "We have Petty Officer Giles' credit card."

"When are you guys leaving?" Rolo asked. Rick looked over at Laura, then said they were going to relax at the beach for a few hours before driving home. They had done all they could and it was now up to others to get the information to them. Besides, neither of them had gotten much sleep the night before. Rick could nap on the beach for a while. It might be the last time he would have the opportunity for a long time if none of this worked out.

*

The helicopter landed at NAS Jacksonville and taxied over to the transient line where other visiting aircraft were tied down. Giles and Daley thanked the helo's crew and offered to help put the aircraft "to sleep", putting on engine covers, tie downs, etc. But the crew said they would only be on the ground for about twenty minutes.

"We're doing some exercises off the coast," the pilot said. "Should take about an hour--two tops."

"Yes, sir."

"You two are riding back to Pensacola with us, right?"

"Yes sir," Giles said. "That's the plan."

"Be here by..." he looked at his watch. "Six o'clock. That's two hours, we will be back by then."

"Yes, sir," Giles said. "Please don't leave us, we really need to be back tonight."

"So do I," the pilot said. Not only was he a US Naval Reserve Commander, but a civilian financial planner as well. "I need to be at work in the morning."

"Six o'clock, sir," Giles repeated as he and Daley walked

toward the hanger. The instructor turned to his student. "That's plenty of time."

"Good," Daley said. "Now how do we get to the airport?" Giles told him they would just take a cab. Inside the hanger, they used the phone. The two went outside and waited for the taxi. It was only about a ten minute wait before it showed up. They jumped inside, still wearing their flight suits, and told the driver to take them to the airport.

"Looks like the Navy getting pretty cheap if they don't even let you fly your own plane," he said and laughed at his own joke. Daley had never been to Jax, and as they rode along, Giles gave him the grand tour. He and Rick had spent many years stationed here, he told the young sailor. "You'll be stationed at NAS or Mayport Naval Station which is not too far from here after you graduate." All of the RSS graduates who were assigned to squadrons stationed on the east coast went through advanced training in Jacksonville, Giles explained. Daley just looked out the window exploring what he could with his eyes as the instructor talked.

*

Nick and Rolo walked in the door to their room. Lorner was sitting on the couch watching a movie on television. He told them that Willy had been looking for them earlier. They went out and down the walkway to Willy's room. The door was wide open. Inside, they found him packing his duffel-bag. Two more bags sat on the floor already packed. "Where were you guys?" Willy asked when the two walked in.

"We went to Panama City for the weekend," Nick replied. "What's going on?"

"I'm leaving."

"Why?" Rolo asked. "Did they kick you out or something?"

"No," Willy replied as he continued packing. "I talked with Lt. Jackson. I'm not made for this stuff. But it's cool."

"Where're they sending you?"

"I'm gonna be a photographer's mate," Willy told them. "It's right down the street so I get to stay on base. But I get three weeks convalescent leave between now and when school starts so I leave in the morning to go home for a few weeks."

Nick slapped him on the back, "That's's cool. At least they didn't screw ya too much, huh?"

"I didn't know you're a photographer?" Rolo said. "Do you get to keep your aircrew status?"

"Probably not," Willy said. "I need to go to a counseling course before they decide."

"Do you need any help moving?"

"Sure," Willy said. "Thanks."

*

Litton drove home happy with himself. Davis would be no problem. Willy would be there, too, as a witness. At least it meant that he wouldn't need to approach Harding, even if Hunt had suggested it. With Davis and Willy both at the Mast, Rick did not have a chance of beating this thing. Then it would be a full blown court-martial and who knows? A senator would owe him big time, and the possibilities were endless!

*

Once at the airport, it did not take long before Giles and Daley located the lost and found office. They asked about a Cannon camera bag. After filling out some paperwork, and with key in hand, they set out in search of the locker.

*

Ensign Davis knocked on the door of his Commanding Officer's home. Captain Reilly answered and invited him in. It was not the first time he had been there. The Reilly's had many dinners for the lawyers in the small command. But this was different, and the captain could tell the Junior officer had something important to talk with him about.

The two went out to the boat dock that overlooked the inlet behind the house. Reilly was both a veteran lawyer and a Captain, and the house was what one would expect for someone who lived in both those worlds. It was meant to impress those that visited, and it had that effect on Davis every time.

They sat down across from each other on the two wooden benches built into the railing. Davis could not bring himself to look at his boss; instead, he pulled a folded and typed letter from his pocket and handed it to Reilly. Without a word, the letter was read, refolded and returned to Davis.

"Is that true?"

"Yes, sir," Davis said. "All true."

"Then I guess that's the best way to deal with it."

"Yes, sir," Davis said. They both sat there for a few minutes watching the water before Reilly invited the young lawyer in for a drink. They both knew it would be the last time, but there were no hard feelings. Rules were rules, and Reilly had suspected but never asked. Regardless, he knew Davis would do okay. He was a good lawyer.

*

"Do you have a tail number of the helo or pilot's name?" The Chief Petty Officer from NAS Jacksonville's base operations asked the distraught instructor.

"No, Chief," Giles said. He had told him everything he knew about the flight that had brought them there that morning: squadron, time they had arrived that day, the type of helicopter. But he had been running too late to remember the rest or notice names. Giles was told by the sailor to wait there and someone would get back to them.

*

Reilly picked up the phone and dialed. He heard the old man answer, and asked him how things were going. The man told his old friend that everything would be fine, he would see him in the morning.

"Thanks," Reilly said. "I owe you."

"Not for this you don't," the man said. "I owe you for allowing me to do this for you."

*

Giles and Daley sat in the transient coffee mess for over an hour, waiting for the helo to return. Giles was especially nervous and looked at his watch every few minutes after the clock on the wall passed six that evening. At six-thirty, he went back to the operations office and asked to use the phone. He called the helicopters squadron operations in Pensacola.

"Do you have any information about the flight?" Giles asked. "It was due back about thirty minutes ago."

Daley watched as Giles spoke, but could not really hear anything. It wasn't long before his instructor came back over looking very upset. "It seems that the helo was diverted during training to help locate some civilian boaters and landed at Mayport instead of here. They took on fuel there, and headed back to Pensacola twenty minutes ago."

"But they were supposed to pick us up?" Daley replied. "They said they would!"

"That's the pitfalls of jumping a ride, kid."

"How do we get home?"

"We can either get a plane ticket," Giles answered. "Or rent a car."

"Will Petty Officer Cox pay us back?"

"I'm sure he will," Giles said. He then went to call a taxi to take them back to Jacksonville's airport. He also called the Hotel in Panama City, but was told that Laura and Rick had already checked out. Nothing was going right.

*

"I guess you could stay with me," Laura said as they pulled onto the exit ramp from Interstate 10. "Either that or on base?"

"I'll stay with you, if that's okay," Rick replied. "You don't mind getting up early to give me a ride in?"

"Nah," she said. She would be coming with him anyway, if for no other reason than moral support.

"What about Litton?"

"Don't worry about him," she said. "I'm not."

He didn't feel like arguing, and he wanted her there anyway. Besides, both of them were tired, and they still had to stop at Rick's apartment to pick up his dress uniform. They stopped and ate on the way to her place, and it was almost nine by the time they pulled in her driveway.

Once inside she checked her machine. Captain Reilly had called saying he had something for her, and to meet her at his office at seven the next morning. Her father had also left a message wishing them both good luck for the following day. Litton left three messages for her to call him. He could wait till morning. She went outside and checked the mail. The next-day-air package was on the porch near the door. She opened it up and smiled. "I got you now," she said to herself.

Rick was inside using the phone. He called Giles, but there was no answer. He then called the duty office, but Watson said he hadn't seen or heard from him. As a last resort, Rick called base operations.

They said that the helo had been back for a couple hours and that the crew were gone until the following month's drill. "I guess they are back?" Rick said to Laura. "They would have called if there was a problem."

"I'm sure everything's fine."

*

Back in Jacksonville everything was not fine. Giles and Daley arrived at the airport and looked up at the board showing scheduled outbound flights. There were none going anywhere near Pensacola until the following day, and that would be too late.

"I guess we're driving," Giles said, then told Daley to wait as he arranged for alternate transportation. He went over to the row of rental car agencies, and checked for available cars. Only two would allow one-way rentals. They both required credit cards. Giles opened his wallet and realized that his credit card was with Nick and Rolo. "Shit!"

"What?" Daley asked when he walked over. He had watched the instructor search through his pockets and knew something was wrong.

"I need a damn credit card!"

Daley opened his wallet and pulled out a VISA gold. He handed it to the woman behind the counter. "I bet you're glad I came now, huh?"

"Okay, take a bow, and let's get going," Giles said. They finished the paperwork and went out to the terminal. It wasn't long before they were on their way back to Pensacola. "Only seven hours," Giles said. "We should be back in plenty of time."

"I hope so," Daley said.

14

***

Monday, June 22

Laura heard the phone ringing, but it was still dark outside when she opened her eyes. She picked up the receiver, and heard the unfamiliar voice of Petty Officer Giles.

"Is Rick there?'

"Who's this?" Laura asked, trying to wake up.

"Adam...Adam Giles. I assume that Rick is there," Giles said. "He didn't answer his phone when I called."

"He's here," she replied. She looked at the clock. "It's one-thirty in the morning."

"We know," Giles said. "We've been on the road all night."

"Where are you now?"

"We stopped for coffee," Giles said over the sounds of passing tractor-trailers a few hundred yards away. "We're right at the I-75, I -10 crossover near Lake City."

"Did you get the letter?"

"Oh yeah!," Giles said. "And this guy spelled out everything. He even included two sets of notes, the ones he placed in Lee's record and the ones he kept himself with the real test results."

"That's good, because I don't know where this guy's head is. He might have changed his mind again," Laura said. "If he got cold feet, we would have been out of luck."

"It doesn't matter now cause we've got them."

"How long until you guys are back?"

"A few hours," Giles said and explained how they missed a flight back. She asked them to hurry. Giles said he would and hung up the phone as Daley came out of the Waffle House restaurant with some coffee.

"Did you get a hold of them?"

"Yeah," Giles said. "Let's get back on the road. Do you want me to drive?"

"No," Daley said, "I don't mind. I haven't driven a car since before boot camp except the duty van. I might just keep this an few extra days. The rental charge ain't that bad."

The two men climbed back into the car and headed back onto Interstate-10 West.

Rick rolled over when he heard her put down the phone. "Who was that?" he asked, trying not to wake up. Laura told him, then turned on the light. "What time is it?" She told him.

"Okay," he said and rolled back over. She leaned across him, and gently kissed him. "See ya in a few hours."

*

Giles and Daley had been on the highway almost an hour. Giles was asleep against the passenger window when they hit it. The car suddenly lurched up then back down with a loud thump immediately waking the instructor. Giles held on as Daley tried to keep the car under control. "What the hell was that?!"

"I don't know," Daley said, as he slowed and pulled off onto the shoulder. The check engine light pooped on. They rolled to a stop. "I think I hit an armadillo or something."

"Is everything okay?"

"I don't know?" Daley replied as one of the hundreds of trucks who had taken over the late night roads went roaring past them at speeds way above the 70 mph speed limit. The shoulder was narrow, and it was too dangerous for either of the two men to get out and check damage.

"I passed a sign back there saying a rest stop was a few miles ahead."

"Fine," Giles said. "Let's go. There should be a phone, too."

Daley started the car and put on the emergency blinkers as he pulled out onto the far right lane. Trucks whipped past them for the terrifying five minutes it took before they pulled off onto the ramp leading to the rest area.

A sign told them the rest area closed at dusk. Daley slowed

down the car as they approached the gate that blocked the road. "What are you doing?" Giles asked.

"It's closed."

"Just go around, would you?!"

"It's closed!"

"We don't have a choice," Giles said. "I need to get to a phone."

Daley followed Giles instructions and drove around the gate and down the ramp over to where some small concrete block buildings sat in the dark. There were no lights except from the bank of vending machines lined in a shelter. Daley pulled up near the buildings and stepped out. He couldn't see any damage except for some scratches on the lower valance panel in the front of the car. He popped the hood, but it was too dark for him to see. Giles went to the back seat where their flight gear was piled, and took his flashlight from his survival vest. He walked around to the front of the car and shined the light under the hood.

"What's wrong?" Daley asked.

"I don't know," Giles said as he pulled on some hose fittings. He yanked on a wire that hung loose near the top of the engine.

"What's that?" Daley asked. Giles shrugged his shoulders"I don't know," he said fingering the wire. "I don't know anything about cars."

Daley grabbed the wire away from his instructor. "Then why are you playing with this stuff then. Just leave it alone before you screw something up!"

"Okay," Giles said backing off. "Then you tell me what's wrong!"

"I don't know! I'm stupid when it comes to anything about cars!" Daley said. "But you don't see me pulling out any goddamn wires!"

"Then why the hell did you pull off the road?" Giles asked.

Daley put his hands up in the air out of frustration. "I don't know- I just freaked out I guess! Shit! You didn't see that size of that damn animal, and the trucks flying by- Christ I thought we were dead, okay!"

"All right, all right!," Giles said. "Just go start the car, and I'll go call Rick again and tell him we're gonna be late."

Giles walked over to the phone near the building. He picked up the receiver and dialed as he watched Daley get in the car. He heard the line connect and ring.

"Hello?" Laura answered finally.

"Laura, this is Giles, is Rick there?"

"Hello? Is someone there?"

Giles spoke louder, "Its me! Adam. I need to speak to Rick!"

"This isn't funny whoever this is," Laura said. "People are trying to sleep!"

"I know- Laura! Don't hang up! Don't hang...," He heard the click. "Shit!" He said. "Shit! Shit! Shit!" he yelled and banged the receiver on the side of the phone booth. He looked down at the receiver and popped the cover off. The inside was empty. "Shit! Who the hell does this!"

"Does what?" Daley asked. He had walked over after trying to start the car- which wouldn't. "I think we need to call a tow truck."

"We can't."

"What do you mean, 'we can't.' Of course we can. We need one."

"Fine," Giles said. "Here, knock yourself out." He handed the phone to Daley, who looked at the broken mouthpiece. "How am I supposed to call anyone--this is broken."

"No shit!" Giles said letting the sarcasm flow as he walked over to the coffee machines. He reached in his packet, but remembered he had used the last of his change at the airport getting a coke. "Do you have any ones or change?"

Daley came over and handed him a dollar bill. "Last one," he said. Giles put the dollar in the machine. It came to life with the most hideous sounds; he took a step back just in case.

After a few moments he saw the lights come on for his selection and he chose the sweetener and cream, then watched through a small plexiglass door as the coffee, sugar, and whitener poured out of the machine and right down the drain before the cup dropped down into the space. "Son of a bitch!"

*

Giles was laying on the hood of the car when the spotlight hit him. The Florida Highway patrol cruiser pulled up to where the two sailors were parked.

"You boys can't sleep here, you need to move along," a voice boomed from a loudspeaker, waking Daley, who sprang up from the back seat inside the car. "This rest area is closed at dark!"

Giles was so startled he almost slid off the car. As the FHP officer slowed his car to a stop, Giles placed his hand up in front of his face to shield his eyes from the light.

*

"A flatbed is on the way, and one of our mechanics is bringing you a replacement car," the customer service rep said. It was leaving Tallahassee as she spoke, but would take about forty-five minutes to get to them. Giles thanked her and hung up. The state trooper poured Giles a cup of coffee from his thermos.

"Thanks."

"You boys should be on your way soon," he said. "Hell, you might be out of here before the sun comes up." The three men looked over to the east. The sky was still black as oil, but the summer sun would be turning the horizon to a dark crimson within the hour.

"Thanks for stopping." Daley said.

"I always check this place out," the officer said. "To see if anyone's here."

"Why do they close the place at night?"

"This is where some German tourists were shot and killed some years back," he said. "The Governor shut this site down himself on television."

"Did you find them?" Daley asked. The Trooper raised his eyebrows in surprise. "Do I look that old? No, I was still in high school. But I don't want the same type thing happening on my watch."

*

Rick woke up at six and quietly slipped out of bed, so as to not wake Laura. He went into the bathroom and pulled a large towel from the closet before heading to the living room. He placed the towel on the dining room table and laid his dress uniform on top of the towel. He went to the closet and searched the shelves.

"Looking for this?"

Rick turned and saw Laura standing in the hall holding her clothes iron. She looked radiant in the warm red glow of the summer sunrise that filled the room. He walked over without a word and held her close.

"Thanks," he said.

"It's only an iron," she replied in a whisper. Her words were playful, but hid the fears she hoped would not materialize later in the day. After a few minutes, he let her go and she plugged the iron in.

"I need a shower," she said.

"So do I," Rick replied. "Why don't you go first. I need to get my uniform ready." He picked up the iron and started to press his Dress Blues. She took the iron from his hand, and turned it off before placing down on the counter. She could see the tension in his face. Rick was worried, too.

"I have a better idea," she said. "I think a little water conservation would help you right now." Her sly smile provoked a laugh. This may be the last moment she had him to herself Laura thought as she led him back to the bathroom. They turned the shower on full blast as Rick embraced her.

Fifteen minutes later, they could not hear the phone ringing. But even if they had, neither would have left the other to answer it.

Giles listened as the familiar sound continued from the receiver of the pay phone. No one was answering. He looked at his watch--they would not have left yet. "Damn!" he said out loud and slammed the phone down. He went back out to the car and jumped in behind the wheel. Daley was still sleeping. The two men had switched seats about a half-hour earlier. They still had eighty miles to go until they reached Pensacola. Then they had to go through town, in Monday morning rush-hour traffic into Warrington where the Naval Air Station was located. No way he was going to make it in time. But, he decided, it wouldn't be for a lack of trying. He gunned the engine and headed west.

*

At about the same time, but a lot closer to Giles destination, Captain Reilly was opening the door to his office. He found the fax from Craft, and turned on the coffee maker. Unlike the other officers in his office, this was the time he normally started his work day.

He turned on the copy machine to let it warm up. He would be busy the next few hours.

"What time is it?" Reilly asked his secretary. He was told it was a little after seven. He told her he was expecting a visitor anytime, and just to send him straight back. "Also, I left a list of records I want on my desk before nine."

"Yes, sir."

"And bring me all the files that Ensign Davis has reviewed in the last two days."

*

Litton left his house early. He had barely slept and managed to not only shower and shave, but gave himself enough time to stop at the local Denny's to order breakfast.

It was going to be a good day, he decided. He got to bust the balls of one of those hot shot instructors and at the same time get himself a promotion. He went to the pay phone and called the BEQ. When the duty desk answered, he told the Petty Officer he need to speak with Airman Willy Simms, just to make sure the kid was awake. Who knew what the hell Willy did last night.

The sailor on duty came back and told Litton that Airman Simms was not in his room. "His roommate thinks he might be at the chow hall, sir."

"Thank you!" Litton replied. The kid must be on his way over. He looked at his watch. It was time for him to head over, too.

*

"Shit!" Giles said.

"What's up?"Daley said, trying to wake-up and stretch out in the small car.

"I don't have any fucking idea!"

The traffic flow on the interstate increased dramatically as people on their way to work headed into Pensacola. And of course some idiot had hit another idiot, closing two lanes of traffic.

*

"Rick, I'll just drop you off then come back ," Laura said. "That way I can meet Captain Reilly over at Legal."

"You're still coming to the mast, right?"Rick asked. She said she would be there and for him not to worry. She just wanted him to make sure he was there on time. "And don't argue with anyone, okay?"

"I'll try."

"Rick," she said. "I mean it. You can not have a temper today. Promise me."

"Okay, I promise."

*

Litton stood outside smoking a cigar and enjoying the moment. The sun was coming up, and the morning light never looked better to the NIS agent. He saw a familiar car pull up, and the naval officer casually got out and walked over. "Good morning, Jack."

"That it is."

"I saw your boss and the Senator come in a few minutes ago."

"We'll all be in the Admiral's office," Hunt said. "Come join us for a drink when this is all over, Jack."

"No problem," Litton said. "This is gonna be short and sweet!"

"Did you talk with Harding, like I asked?"

"No," the agent replied."I did one better."

"What's that?"

"You'll need to wait and see!"

*

"Right here's fine." Laura dropped Rick off in front of the Schools Command Building. He walked along the sidewalk to the entrance where Litton was standing. He hesitated for a moment, but continued to the steps. When he approached, he saw the agent exhale cigar smoke to form a little cloud. Rick stopped, waiting for it to dissipate.

"Where's your lawyer?" Litton asked. "Davis, isn't it?'

Rick did not answer. He was keeping his promise. Of course after the look he gave the NIS Agent, he did not need to say anything. Litton left him alone as the instructor went up the stairs and down the hall. Master Chief Russo was waiting near Harding's office and stopped Rick. He instructed him on what to do. The instructor was to wait until called, then walk to the front of the desk, stand at attention, and answer questions when asked. He went through the rest with Rick, making sure he understood what was going on, as well as the consequences that could come from the day's events to come.

"I did want to tell you," the Master Chief added, "I do think you're a hell of a good instructor. I'm sorry about this."

"Thanks, Master Chief."

*

Litton looked at his watch and stamped his cigar out on the step.

It was time. He walked down the hall and past Rick who was standing in the hall against the wall. The agent did not say a word to him, he just walked past the instructor and into Harding's office.

"Mr. Litton," Harding said. "I don't think your presence is necessary here."

"I don't mind," Litton said. "I have a witness coming."

"No," Harding said, "you don't. Airman Simms will not be joining us today."

"What!?"

"He withdrew his statement yesterday," Harding told him. He did not elaborate. Let's get this show going, Master Chief." He told the Master Chief to call Rick into the room before Litton had time to say a word.

*

Laura met Captain Reilly and another man in the Reilly's office. They were not there long, just enough for introductions and a quick review of some documents in both their possession.

"Is Davis ready?"Laura asked.

"Davis resigned yesterday," Reilly replied. "I'm handling this myself."

"Why?"

"Don't worry about it, Laura," he said. They walked out of his office. He stopped and gave some unrelated messages to his secretary. "Oh, yeah," he told her. "Call Base Security. I want a detail to meet me over at the Schools Command Building, and make sure they send an officer with them."

"What's that for?" Laura asked.

"I'll tell you in the car."

It was only a short ride to Schools Command, and a three-man security detail was waiting when Laura and Reilly pulled in. All five of them entered the building and quickly walked down toward Harding's office. Captain Reilly told the three military policeman to wait in the outer office. "I'll call you in, just relax for now."

The Captain's Mast had already started when Reilly walked in with Laura. Everyone looked up.

"What the hell are you doing here?" Litton said, interrupting the proceedings. Reilly walked over and placed a manila envelope on Harding's desk. "Pardon the intrusion, Commander."

"No problem, sir." Harding said relieved. He picked up the folder and saw that it contained all kinds of medical data. "What's this?"

"Proof, Commander," Laura said shooting a smile to Rick who still stood at attention. "Evidence that there is no way the sample you have based this charge came from Petty Officer Cox.'

"We have the proof we need," Litton replied. "It came from NAMI."

"This supersedes the earlier results," Reilly said. "This report is signed by Captain Michael Woodburn, and there's a letter attached by Ritter over at NAMI saying he agrees with the finding, and an investigation is now being conducted as to where the other sample came from."

"This is bullshit," Litton said. Harding looked over at the NIS agent. "Mr Litton," he said. "Do you mind if I run my own goddamn Mast?!"

"This is bullshit," Litton replied. "I'm going to go get the admiral and we'll see about this." He headed to the door, and the Master Chief opened it for him. The agent turned around before leaving, "Don't anyone leave this room."

He marched through the outer office, and was startled for a moment when he saw the three military policeman standing there. "Nobody leaves that fucking room!" Litton said and kept walking.

"Who was that?" one of them asked. The others shrugged.

*

Giles and Daley were waived through the main gate without slowing down. They passed the rows of white crosses that lined the right side of the main road through the base. The cemetery only bolstered both men's resolve to get to Laura in time. Rick was one hell of an instructor, but there would soon be a time when he would go back to the fleet, and maybe then he would save one more aviator from the depth of the sea. Maybe he would keep one more white cross from the rolling hills on their right.

*

Hunt was sitting at his desk when Litton burst through the door,

"Where's the Admiral?" he asked as he walked by, and, without waiting for an answer, barged into the Admiral's office before Hunt could say a word. Tract and the Senator were sitting there when the agent came into the room. They both stood, alarmed.

"What the hell is this!?" Tract demanded and looked at Hunt. His aide was speechless.

"Admiral," Litton said out of breath. "I think you need to come down here! Captain Reilly is about to have Cox go free, and Harding is gonna let him!"

"What!?" the Senator said. "We'll see about that!"

The four men, led by Senator Lee, walked past the three military policeman on their way to Harding's office. The security detail jumped to attention, but no one noticed. The door slammed shut behind the Admiral and the others. This was getting interesting, the security officer thought.

"Attention on deck," the Master Chief ordered as the brass walked in the room. Everyone but Laura snapped to attention as the Admiral entered. Tract walked right over to Harding's desk, "What the hell is going on here?!"

"The Commander is about to release Petty Officer Cox, Admiral," Laura said.

"You!" Hunt looked at Cox, then at Laura. "What are you doing here with him?!"

"She's about to be arrested," Litton replied.

"No, she's not, Admiral," Reilly replied. "I think Mr. Litton should worry more about where he is going than what Miss Wilson has been doing."

"Why is that?" the Admiral said.

"Because your little friend there is about to say goodbye to his career!" Reilly said and threw a small mini-cassette tape at Litton. It hit the agent in the chest and dropped to the floor. "That's from yesterday with Airman Simms." Reilly said as Litton picked the tape up from the floor.

"What the hell are you talking about?" Litton said. "This is about a sailor who took some drugs and got caught, not about some conversation I had with some kid!"

"Not hardly," Laura said. "This is about a crooked federal

investigator who thinks he can control everyone he meets!"

"What the hell are you talking about?"

"Mr. Litton," Reilly said. "Your life, as you know it, is now over."

"You don't know shit, Reilly! I'll tell you who's life is over!" Litton said. "Hers."

"How's that?" Reilly asked with amusement. The little guy is a fighter, he thought, but Litton doesn't know when to quit.

"I am charging Agent Wilson with obstruction of a government investigation and there is nothing you can do about," he replied. "I specifically told her she was off this case, and she was not to talk to that man again! And this will stick!"

"How can a defense attorney be charged with obstruction for simply talking with her client," Reilly said.

"What's that?" Litton said caught off-guard. Reilly opened his briefcase and pulled out a letter, handing it to the NIS agent. He only had time to glance at it before Reilly pulled it back then handed it to the Admiral.

"I'm sorry that you are so uniformed, Agent Litton," he said. "Laura Wilson no longer is employed by your agency." The Captain addressed the others in the room. "As you just read, she resigned two days ago. She notified my office of this on Friday, with that letter."

"How do I know that?"

"It has a received date stamped on it, you idiot," Hunt said reading it over his boss's shoulder.

"She also mailed a copy to NIS in Washington who verified that they received it this morning," The Captain continued. "It was accepted immediately, and I am sure that you, Mr. Litton, have a message to that effect waiting for you in your office as we speak."

"But she never notified me!" Litton protested.

"I did not need to," Laura replied in her own defense. "Regulations stated that I should notify you as a courtesy, not a requirement. I only needed to address my resignation to the Director of the Naval Investigative Service. I did that."

"Besides," Reilly said, "Ensign Davis did attempt to contact you a few days ago, when we were made aware of this development. He left a message with Mr. Hunt over there."

"The only message I got was that Davis called," Litton replied and looked at Hunt.

"You should have returned the call," Reilly said. "But that is neither here nor there. You have more serious problems than returning phone calls."

"I have more problems?!" Litton said smugly directing his words at Laura. "I think you, missy, have more problems. I don't give a shit if you resigned or not. You impeded a federal investigation. You harbored a sailor who was UA- Unauthorized Absence, babe. I will see your ass after I nail your boyfriend over there."

"You won't be nailing anyone," she replied. "Except some guy named Bubba in federal prison you asshole. I'm a member of the firm that represents Petty Officer Cox!"

"On Friday afternoon," Reilly interjected. "I contacted Commander Harding and informed him of such, and then we contacted Colonel Mahan who agreed to allow Miss Wilson to take responsibility and custody for Petty Officer Cox."

"Who's Colonel Mahan?" Hunt asked.

"I'm sure Litton knows Colonel Mahan, the local military magistrate," Reilly said. "Don't you?" Litton looked away and did not answer. "He's a Marine," Reilly continued. "A very *by the book* United States Marine Corps Judge. Even though Commander Harding offered to drop the restriction placed on Petty Officer Cox, I thought it best we get an outside opinion. So I contacted my boss at JAG in Washington, and he put us in touch with the Colonel."

"You have nothing," Hunt said. "Because there is nothing strange about this case. It's open and shut."

Reilly laughed out loud, but Litton did not. "That's not entirely accurate, Mr. Hunt," Reilly replied. He pulled another document from his briefcase. "I have copies of orders from Admiral Tract, transferring Dr. Benjamin Craft, Flight Surgeon, Medical Corps, to various places around the globe just to keep him quiet. I have another set of orders cut by your office, Admiral, transferring another doctor as recently as yesterday. I have depositions saying that you engaged in falsifying medical reports, that Mr. Hunt illegally used threats, and your authority, Admiral, to blackmail and bully Naval personnel to change records and assignments. Unauthorized use of U.S. Naval aircraft to transport personnel. I have signed letters from people at various commands who said you pressured them to overlook Airman Lee's background."

"That's a bunch of nonsense, Captain," Admiral Tract angrily shot back. "You don't accuse a Flag Officer or his Aide unless you can back it up, Captain. And these are lies."

"These are good people making these statements, Admiral. Take a look for yourself," Reilly said and handed the papers to the Admiral. Hunt reached out to grab them first, but Tract's look alone convinced him to withdraw his hands. Reilly continued. "Most of those people had spotless records. They now have put their careers in jeopardy by admitting their part in this scheme. Why would they all say the same thing?"

"Maybe they can't stand not taking a shot at a Flag Officer instead of taking responsibility of their actions," Senator Lee said while Tract read. The elder Lee was not interested in the documents at all.

"Senator," Laura replied. "Why are you angry at the Captain? I thought that if anyone would be upset by this, it would be you!"

"Why? Because you are attacking my friend? Someone who said he would look out for my son but who was failed by the men in his charge!"

"You're right. He was failed by the men in his charge," Reilly said. "But it wasn't Cox, was it, Mr. Hunt?"

Hunt stood silent. "The information that was changed would not only have prevented your son from entering the Aircrew and Rescue Swimmer programs, but more likely than not would have kept him out of the Navy all together. But of course you knew this, Admiral."

"Captain, don't you dare insinuate that I had anything to do with any of this," Tract said and handed the documents back to Reilly. "I assure you that I was unaware of any of this."

"Maybe you were, sir. Maybe you weren't," the Captain said. "Those facts will straighten themselves out over time." Reilly went over and stood looking into Hunt's face.

"Admiral, there are really only two possibilities here. Either it was you, or it was someone who had access to your signature, your stationery, your personal information. Someone who others assumed was speaking for you, or who others thought had the authority that was recognized as yours Admiral...Care to speculate on who that could be Lieutenant Commander Hunt?"

Hunt stayed quiet, shook his head slightly, and shifted his eyes away from the legal officer. "I figured as much," Reilly said. He moved over to Litton. "How about you, Jack? Any guesses?"

"None come to mind, Captain."

"Uh-huh," Reilly replied. " Well, whoever it was, they thought that they were pretty smooth. And I have to admit they were somewhat smarter than I gave them credit for." The Captain went over and pulled out a personnel file from his briefcase. He went to hand it to the Admiral.

"Give me that!" Hunt said and lunged at the Naval Officer. He caught Reilly off guard and he fell back off balance. Rick turned to lend a hand, but the Master Chief and Laura held him back. "No!" they both said. Master Chief Russo yelled, and the three military policemen entered the room.

The young Navy Lieutenant in charge of the security detail pulled out his side-arm, and yelled for everyone to freeze. Hunt saw the nine-millimeter drawn and pointed at his direction and stopped reaching for the manilla envelope. The two men under his command forcefully pulled the Admiral's Aide off Reilly and threw him face first against a wall. One kept his gun pointed at Hunt, while the other helped the Captain to his feet. "Captain? Are you okay?" the Security Officer asked.

Reilly looked around the room. It was totally quiet except for the hum of the air conditioner. All eyes were on the Lieutenant's weapon, which was still drawn. "I'm fine," Reilly answered, and slowly placed his hand on the officer's weapon. The man took the hint and placed the sidearm back in his holster. Reilly took a moment to straighten out his uniform. "Thanks for coming in like that. I'm just a little ruffled."

The Lieutenant asked if Hunt was to be taken into custody. "I think that would be a good idea," Reilly said. "And you may want to take Mr. Litton outside as well."

"Lieutenant Commander Hunt is not going anywhere," The Admiral replied, the authority coming back in his voice.. The Security Officer looked over at Reilly, who nodded at Litton. "Mr. Litton, please come with us."

"I'm not going ," he said looking at Tract. "Admiral, get these goons off me!" Tract said not a word, and the NIS agent looked around, then took a step back and placed his arms at his side. The two military policemen rushed him and spun him around; they forced his hands behind his back. For Litton's part, he fought them all the way. But he was no match.

Tract and Hunt seemed embarrassed about the Agent's reaction, but Laura was not the only person who enjoyed watching Litton being led out in cuffs.

Giles and Daley passed Litton as the security officers practically dragged the soon-to-be former NIS Agent down the hall. They stared down at his handcuffs, and when Litton saw who they were, he stood up and stopped fighting, trying to gain some kind of dignity, but the two sailors had seen enough, and just shook their heads in disgust as they continued on.

Giles told Daley to wait outside in the hall as he ducked into Harding's office, where the door was already wide open. He felt the eyes of everyone in the room fall upon him as he entered, and, looking around himself, all he noticed were the gold bars on the sleeves of the other uniforms. He saw Hunt up against the wall, with a security officer next to him. It was too much for the Petty Officer Second Class to be around. "Excuse me," Giles said sheepishly, with a nervous smile, "I just had to drop this off to Agent Wilson." He quickly walked over to Laura and whispered "The calvary's here!"

"If I were you," she whispered back, "I'd take the horses and wait out in the hall." He had already planned that course of action. Giles turned and quick stepped out of there, but not before giving a wink to Rick, who ever so slightly nodded back in thanks.

"What's going on?" Daley asked when Giles returned.

"I have no idea," the instructor responded.

"What's that?" Hunt asked as Laura opened the envelope. She ignored his question and quickly scanned the documents. "Here, Admiral," she said a moment later, still holding up pages to read as she passed the files over to Tract, one sheet at a time. "I think this will explain our accusations." Meanwhile, Reilly bent over and picked up the personnel record from where it had landed on the floor. He looked over at Hunt, almost daring him to try something as he handed Tract the manila folder containing the record.

"I don't know what to say, Captain," Tract replied as he read through the pages. "I can't explain my actions here. I have a lot of responsibilities, and I can't attempt to remember every document I have signed. I can honestly say that many of the events listed here I have no recollection of. I'm a smart man Captain, but I suppose my memory is not what it once was."

"I'm smart too, Admiral," Reilly said. "And I figured that anyone who would behave like this would not have stopped at some kid he could care less about. No, he would probably get something for himself too. But since the Navy isn't a business, it wasn't like he could embezzle company funds or anything. So what's the next best thing besides money?"

Tract stopped looking at the records, and looked up at Reilly. "What then?"

"Power, of course," Reilly said. He took the file from the Admiral's hands, flipped through some of its pages, then handed it back to Tract. "Perfect Fitness Reports, the path to promotions. A few awards and letters of commendation that happened to find their way in. The fast track to command. Power."

Tract read through the file. "I didn't write any of these," he said. He closed the folder and handed it back to captain Reilly. "And I certainly didn't sign them."

The Admiral looked over at his aide. Hunt defiantly looked at his boss before turning away. "Why?" Tract asked. Hunt said nothing.

"You will not be here forever, Admiral," Reilly said. "Admiral, bad judgement is not a crime, most of the time. But if I were you I would seriously consider retirement. And I would ask the Senator to get you one of his cushy jobs he offered you as soon as possible. Because I don't think he will be in any position to help anyone a few weeks from now."

"What's that supposed to mean?" the Senator said. But Reilly's attention was drawn to the security detail who returned to the room. "In a moment, Senator....Admiral?"

Tract gave the security officer a nod, and they handcuffed Hunt without incident. He said not a word, nor did he look at anyone as he was lead out to a second security unit that had pulled up outside.

"Don't worry about this, Donald," the Senator said as he watched his aide leave the room under guard.

"I'd worry, Admiral," Laura said. "You too, Senator."

"I had nothing to do with any of this," Lee said. He headed toward the door, but stopped next to face Rick. "You killed my son, you son of a bitch! It may look like you got away with it right now; but we both know the truth, don't we!"

"Yes, sir, we do," Rick said. "I can sleep at night, how about you?"

Senator Lee reached around and punched Rick in the mouth. The instructor fell to the ground as the Master Chief grabbed the Senator. "Let him go," Rick said. The Master Chief looked at Reilly who nodded.

Senator Lee composed himself as Laura bent down to help Rick. The Senator looked down at them and turned to the others in the room. "This was supposed to be justice. But you all sicken me. I will get justice for my son. I will make sure that you, Petty Officer Cox, that you pay for my son's death. The pain you have caused me and my family, you will pay for that. I promise." He turned toward the door.

"How dare you!" Laura yelled as she helped Rick stand up. The Senator stopped walking, but did not turn around. "How dare you accuse this man of deliberately hurting your son, let alone murder him! Senator if anyone is to blame, it is you!"

Senator Lee turned around slowly. "Excuse me," he said. "But I know where the blame belongs."

"No, Senator, you don't!" She told him. "It's bad enough that you abused your position by lying, bullying, and threats. That seems to be your way of doing things, or maybe that's what works in Washington. No wonder Litton wanted to go there. Maybe you throw your weight around and destroy people who you don't like or who you don't agree with. And that's fine up there. But the rules of real life aren't like that! Maybe in Washington people expect that and they accept what you do, but here it hurts real people. It affects real people's lives!"

"Don't you lecture me..."

"Maybe its about time someone did!" Laura said cutting him off. "Your son is dead because of you- and some peoples lives are ruined." She looked up at him, trying to find something in the man that acknowledged what she was saying. "Good people's lives will be ruined, careers destroyed. And for what?"

Everyone turned to the Senator, expecting some kind of reaction. But he showed nothing.

"Don't you dare stand there, you cold hearted bastard," Laura's eyes welled up, and tears started flowing from her eyes. Tears of frustration, tears for a boy who died and the realization that the only one in the room who didn't care was the one person who should have cared the most. But she ignored them. And the sadness burst out in anger. "Don't you dare try to lay the blame for your son's death on anyone but yourself!" She turned away.

"You hold it right there..." the Senator began.

"No, sir!" Laura said. "You, Senator, killed your son! No one else but you! You killed him the moment you bullied that first doctor into lying! He died at the moment you hung up the phone and that doctor in Jacksonville signed his name."

"There was nothing wrong with my son!" The Senator replied and pointed at Rick. "That bastard over there held my son under water and drowned him!"

"You just don't get it, do you?" she said and looked at the man. He really believed that he had nothing to do with any of it. But now it was clear. "You couldn't stand the fact that someone of your flesh and blood wouldn't be good enough for the military, that he couldn't pass the physical."

"That is preposterous!"

"Somehow it made you less of a man if your son could not get into the flight program," she said. She walked over to the table and pulled young Lee's diary from the briefcase. "Now I understand some of what he was writing about in here. You hated him for his weak heart, and you made damn sure he knew it."

"What kind of psycho bullshit is this?"

"It's not bullshit, Senator," Laura continued. "That's why you thought his mother cheated on you. That's why you cheated on her. You destroyed your family because you blamed her for your son's weak heart."

"Nonsense," he said.

"But you know that sad thing," she said. "Lee didn't have a weak heart. His heart was so strong that he gave it up for you. He loved you so much, even after everything you had done, that he was willing to go along with all of your bullshit, just to make you happy. Just to see if he could once make you proud of him. That's heart."

The Senator did not like hearing any of this. "No, no!" He repeated, and once again pointed at Rick. "It wasn't my fault! It was his!" He looked around for someone else to agree with him, but it was fruitless search. "This is bullshit! None of you know how I feel."

"You're right, Senator," Laura said. "We don't."

"This was a murder!"

"Yes, it was," Laura said. "But what you obviously don't understand is that you are the murderer. You had reckless disregard for human life. Tragically it was your son's life. That's a crime. But the bigger crime is how many others you destroyed on the way."

"Who the hell do you think you are?" Senator Lee said. "I didn't do this!" he yelled as ran around the room looking at each of them, trying to convince just one. But even the Admiral just shook his head and looked down at the floor. His friend was losing it right there. "I didn't do this, I swear I loved him! I did."

Then he got mad. The Senator ran over to Laura. "You have no right to make accusations like that! What gives you the right to say things?! I'm a Goddamn Senator! Who...who the hell are you? I don't need to take this from someone like you! These lies. You have no authority over me!"

The Senator started heading out the door. Reilly whispered something to the Security Officer who took hold of the Senator's arm as he walked past. "What are you doing?"

"Senator," Reilly said. "Miss Wilson doesn't have the authority to make accusations like that, you are correct. But the two U.S. Marshals and Justice Department Investigators that are flying down to speak with you do."

"What investigators? What are you talking about?"

"I have been asked to have you detained until they arrive," Reilly said. Two very large security officers walked in. "Now, we can do this the hard way, or the easy way. Your choice. Personally, I don't care one way or the other."

The Senator was stunned, and the two men each took an arm as Reilly winked at Laura. He followed the men as they walked out of the office. Admiral Tract looked over at Harding and the others.

"I'm sorry," the Admiral said. The man seemed to have aged ten years. He told them not to get up, and slipped out of the office. They could hear his footsteps echo on the tile floor as the man walked back to his office, alone.

"Cox," Harding said, watching Laura dab the blood from the instructor's lip. "I am so sorry about this. Why don't you have Miss Wilson take you to sick call and have someone take a look at that? Classes will be resuming soon, and you need to be ready to teach."

"Yes, sir."

15

***

Every new beginning is some new beginning's end.

Rick downshifted and followed Laura's BMW off the exit ramp where Interstate 16 and I-75 meet. He felt the U-haul trailer bounce around as they turned, then looped around and along Gray Highway. Her parent's house was only a few miles away now, past the cemetery where Greg Allman was buried, and past the Georgia Music Hall of Fame where she once worked part-time one summer.

Rick kept up the best he could, though his truck was on its last leg. But then, it had always been on its last leg. They climbed a hill, then went down and around a bend until she saw the familiar red brick home.

Laura pulled in front and parked. Rick pulled into the church parking lot across the street and stopped. She walked over to where he was standing.

"Are you sure it's okay?"

"They know you're coming," she said tugging at his arm. "It will be fine. You're the first guy I've brought home since high school."

"Your dad doesn't mind that I'm in the Navy?"

"No," she replied. "He's so happy I'm leaving for the FBI that I don't think he would even care."

"Did you tell him about my acceptance to Officer Candidate School?"

"Yes, I did," she said as they crossed the street. "And about the endorsement from Captain Reilly, and Harding, and he was especially impressed that you managed to get one from Admiral Tract before he retired."

They walked up to the door, and were met by Laura's father. "I've heard a lot about you," he said and they shook hands. "I've been looking forward to meeting you."

They went inside and there were two tall glasses of sweet tea already iced and waiting. The three of them sat down in the living room and spoke of the events of the last few weeks. The Senator's arrest and quick conviction had made all the papers. Litton and Hunt had been convicted too, but it wasn't as newsworthy, except for those who were there. Admiral Tract had retired, quietly, and had taken one of those corporate jobs, as he was promised. The rest of them stayed where they were, with the exception of Rick.

"I'm proud of you, son," Laura's father said. "And of this little girl of mine." He gave her a hug as the phone rang.

Laura's father excused himself, and went into the back room that doubled for an office. Laura stood up and motioned for Rick to follow her out back. Near the pool, a large porch swing hung. She went and sat down, and patted the cushion until he sat beside her.

"Thanks for coming back home with me," Laura said.

"Thank you," Rick replied as he kissed her. "For giving me a home to come back to."

The End

Laura and Rick return in BLIND PASS

An Island Paradise.
A twenty-year-old unsolved case. An abusive husband and ambitious District Attorney who won't let anyone, including his wife, stand in his way for a seat in the Congress of the United States.
But when the wife of a friend of District Attorney David Ranson turns up dead, fingers start pointing, and secrets start to be revealed. And it's up to soon-to-retire police detective Brian Doyle and FBI Special Agent Laura Wilson to unravel a mystery that leads them to a world of secret love affairs, drug smuggling, political corruption, and murder.

Sean Michael Dever flew in the US Navy as an Air Anti-Submarine Warfare Operator. After receiving an honorable discharge, he attended film school and graduated from Florida State University. He wrote The Movie Buff, a weekly entertainment opinion column, and has worked in feature films, television, radio, and the music industry. His first book BLIND PASS was #7 in trade paperbacks in Southwest Florida. Sean currently lives along the Gulf of Mexico in Southwest Florida.

Look for Rick Cox, Laura Wilson, and others to return in

Blind Pass

and

Dishonorable Men

To order additional copies of So Others May Live, or any other Fox Books title, call toll free :1.888.274.5371; or complete the information below.

Ship to: (please print)
Name ______________________________
Address ______________________________
City, State, Zip______________________________
Day Phone (optional)______________________________

____ copies of So Others May Live @ $8 99 each $_____
Postage and Handling @ $1.50/book $ _____
Florida Residents add 6% sales tax $_____
Total Amount enclosed $_____
____ place x if you would like a Fox Books catalog.

Make checks payable to : So Others May Live
Fox Books, Inc
PO Box 150053
Cape Coral, FL 33915-0053

Orders can be made on the internet at the following sites:

www.amazon.com or **www.barnesandnoble.com**

Laura and Rick return in BLIND PASS

An Island Paradise.
A twenty-year-old unsolved case. An abusive husband and ambitious District Attorney who won't let anyone, including his wife, stand in his way for a seat in the Congress of the United States.
But when the wife of a friend of District Attorney David Ranson turns up dead, fingers start pointing, and secrets start to be revealed. And it's up to soon-to-retire police detective Brian Doyle and FBI Special Agent Laura Wilson to unravel a mystery that leads them to a world of secret love affairs, drug smuggling, political corruption, and murder.

BLIND PASS

a novel by

Sean Michael Dever

 # 1 - TOP 10 BOOKS ON THE ISLANDS

-Island Sun 6/13/97